Year *of the* Firefly

MALCOLM IVEY

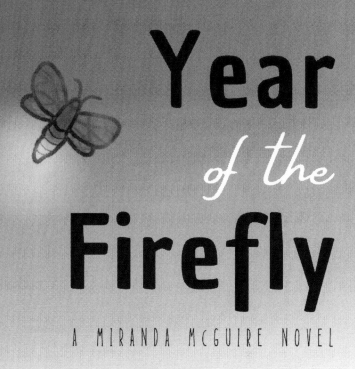

Year
of the
Firefly

A MIRANDA McGUIRE NOVEL

Miranda Rights
-BOOK ONE-

tempus fugit ☾ *amor manet*
ASTRAL PIPELINE BOOKS | ORLANDO ★ PENSACOLA ★ SAN DIEGO

First Astral Pipeline Books Edition, December 2020

Astral Pipeline Books LLC
1317 Edgewater Dr., Ste 2023
Orlando, Florida 32804
astralpipelinebooks.com

ISBN: 978-1-953519-02-3 (paperback)
ISBN: 978-1-953519-03-0 (ebook)
Library of Congress Control Number: 2020949384

Cover design by Rob Williams
Cover firefly art by Steve-O
Interior firefly art by Leah Dorris

ALSO BY MALCOLM IVEY

Consider the Dragonfly

With Arms Unbound

On the Shoulders of Giants

Sticks & Stones

www.MalcolmIvey.com

For my incarcerated sisters

"All of God's children are not beautiful. Most of God's children are, in fact, barely presentable . . ."

—FRAN LEIBOWITZ

PART ONE
Eight Weeks

1

Miranda had never seen a Gucci eye patch before. Funny how that was the focal point of her attention. The patch. Not the ginormous pile of cash on the table. Not the musclebound tattooed man who was counting it. Not the naked woman snuggling with the pitbull on the leather sofa. Not the oblivious little boy tapping furiously on the Xbox controller. All these storylines were riveting, but it was the designer patch that the monocle of her consciousness was fixed upon. She wondered if it was a fashion accessory or a medical device or both. The aspiring author and English Lit major in her needed to know.

Still tingly and warm from the blunt on the ride across the bridge, she followed with hooded eyes as its wearer rummaged through kitchen cabinets in search of a scale. He caught her staring and paused. The sculptured mustache and goatee that framed his mouth pulled back into a diamond- and platinum-encrusted scowl. "Yo Nick, you sure this bitch ain't troll?"

Uncertain which was more offensive, being called a *bitch* or a *troll*, she felt her face redden with indignation as she sputtered to assemble a lethal riposte . . . something Katherine from *Taming of the Shrew* might serve up in her icy Shakespearean tone. *Nice eyepatch . . . are you wearing matching Gucci panties?*

Two things stopped her: the small arsenal of urban warfare weapons stacked on the coffee table and Nick's firm hand on the small of her back.

"I'm positive," he said, in that deep, confident voice that made her forget her outrage, forget she was standing in a trap house, forget the world, forget herself.

"Well she looks like troll." Eyepatch found his scale and set it on the counter. "Like one of them redheaded CSI bitches. I don't trust no redheads . . ."

Nick removed his hand from her back and ran his fingers through his dark unruly hair. His palm left an impression, hot against her skin. A thermonuclear handprint. "Come on, Gucci," he said. "You know I don't fuck with twelve."

Miranda stifled a giggle. *His name was Gucci? Was Gucci, the company, like, secretly sponsoring drug dealers or something?* She thought of her sociology professor, Dr. Bonilla, and his fiery disquisitions on consumer culture and materialism. He would choke on his own mustache if he ever crossed paths with this walking designer brand billboard.

"She ain't gotta be twelve," said Gucci. "She could be an informant. How do you know she ain't wearing a wire?"

Nick glanced down at her. His eyes were dark chocolate caged in black lashes. A secret smile played at the corners of his mouth. "Because I watched her get dressed."

His words seemed to hang in the air. She blushed, suddenly as exposed as the naked woman snoring on the couch. Gucci appraised her from over his scale. Fitting, because she felt like she was being weighed. His one eye moved up and down her body. Apparently the *MeToo* movement had not yet reached the criminal underworld. She wished Nick would put his arm around her.

"Don't bring nobody else over here," Gucci muttered as he pulled apart the Ziploc and began heaping Boi onto the didgies with a silver spoon.

Boi and didgies.

The arrival of Nick Archiletta on the timeline of her life had brought a strange new lexicon of colloquialisms and street slang. Words that did not appear in the pages of her beloved Random House College Dictionary or even the online Urban Dictionary. Sometimes it was as if he was speaking an entirely different language.

Miranda loved words. She grew up doing *New York Times* crossword puzzles with her dad and was a self-proclaimed etymologist by the time she reached middle school. Her plan was to write a novel after the fall semester and midterms, maybe a gritty romance she could self-pub and market herself. The bad boy patois of Nick's urban ecosystem would make for snappy, realistic dialogue. This was perhaps the sexiest thing about him. True, he was lean and handsome with just the right number of tattoos. True, the danger was thrilling, the passion was electric, the money was fast, and the drugs were convenient. But take all that away and his vernacular alone was worth the price of admission. Especially to a word-nerd like herself.

The dope was the color of Gulf of Mexico sand, a growing anthill atop the matte black digital scale. Gucci added a little, then more, then grunted, shook his head, and sliced off the tip of the mountain, transforming it into a mesa. Satisfied, he spun the scale.

Miranda read the display. *28.7.*

"Can I put some cut on it?" said Nick.

"You better." Gucci shook a Newport from his pack and fired it up. His teeth dazzled beyond the flame. "You know how we rock, bruh. This is that good Frank white shit. Pure as your bitch."

She winced. He pronounced *pure* like *purr.* Calling her rude names was one thing. But lazy mispronunciations she could not tolerate. They circumvented her filter, triggering a response that was almost reflexive.

"I believe the word you're looking for is pure. *P-U-R-E.* All you do is take the possessive *your* and stick a *P* in front of it. *Pyour . . . Pure.*" She enunciated with the exaggerated patience of a kindergarten teacher. "You try it."

He stared at her for a solid ten seconds. He even pursed his lips. Then he looked at Nick. "What is this crazy-ass bitch jaw-jackin' about?"

Nick shrugged. "She takes off like that sometimes. I think it's a college thing . . . here." He reached in his jeans pocket, grabbed a roll of bills and tossed them across the kitchen.

Gucci caught the money, removed the rubber band and began to count.

"Everything good?" said Nick, when he reached the last hundred.

"Better than good." The one-eyed dope dealer looked up and smiled for the first time that day. "Everything's Gucci."

2

For a car manufactured at the turn of the century and on the wrong side of 200,000 miles, the Avalon was in pristine condition. *"Can't beat these Japanese cars and their timing chains,"* said her dad when he handed over the keys for her sixteenth birthday. *"Damn things run forever."* And he was right. He usually was when it came to cars. Almost three years later the old Toyota was still gliding along.

She hit *unlock* on the key fob and settled behind the wheel, pouting as Nick swaggered around to the passenger side. "What's up, bae?" He folded his long body into the leather bucket seat and slammed the door. "You feeling some type of way?"

For all of her gushing about his street slang, a few of the more nonsensical phrases grated on her; *feeling some type of way,* for example. Typical vague noncommittal male statement. *What type of way?*

She started the car and backed slowly down the steep driveway. "If by some type of way you mean livid, then, yes. I am. I'm feeling some type of way about your complete lack of chivalry."

Impossibly long lashes blinked in her periphery. "What are you talking about?"

"I'm talking about you not objecting when Captain Hook in there insulted me."

"Gucci?" He frowned. "How did he insult you?"

"Um, he called me *your bitch* for starters."

Perplexity. "Wait . . . you're not?"

She shot him a withering look. "I'm nobody's bitch. That's an offensive, derogatory, misogynistic word."

"I don't think he meant it like that, bae."

"No?" she smirked, "And what about when he called me a troll? Was that intended to be a compliment? I've never been so humiliated in my life."

A stray dog loped across her rearview. She braked to let it pass before pulling out onto Sixth Avenue. When she shifted from reverse to drive, she noticed that Nick was grinning. "It's not funny asshole."

Laughter spilled through his smile. "You're trippin' bae. Not troll as in some ugly monster. Troll as in *pa*-trol . . . as in police. Feel me?"

The dog looked up from the sidewalk as they passed. Defeated bloodshot eyes touched hers. She stopped the car.

"Miranda? What the . . . ? We're ridin' dirty. You can't just stop in the middle of the street."

She fumbled through her purse and found a trail mix bar, her go-to snack between classes. "This will just take a sec."

The musclebound money counter stepped out on Gucci's front porch and glared a question at them. *What the fuck?* Nick responded by raising his index finger. *One moment please.*

Miranda unwrapped the breakfast bar, broke it into pieces and opened the door. The dog bounded over to her outstretched hand and devoured the food, licking her palm clean as she scratched its dirty head. "That's a good boy."

"Bae? Can we flex already? This neighborhood is crawlin' with troll and I've got a zip of Boi and my fire on me."

"Okay, okay." The dog clearly wanted to come home with her. She gently pushed it away and pulled the door shut. For a moment it trotted along next to the car, but by the time she reached the light at Cervantes it was barely a speck in her mirror.

She reached for the stereo. NPR's Acoustic Interlude came jangling through the speakers. Gillian Welch was singing "The Way It Goes" over Appalachian strings. She adjusted the volume.

He grabbed her hand. "Look at me." Deep, soulful, almond-shaped eyes narrowed with intensity. "I wouldn't let nobody disrespect you. If anything, I'd go to war about you."

His grip morphed into a caress. She melted beneath his touch. The light turned green. "Which way?"

He released her hand and flipped down the sun visor, removing a rolled blunt. "To your crib? You know the way. Bust a left."

She hesitated before tapping the blinker. "I thought you said you were getting some pills." Her voice was weak with need. She hated the sound of it.

After an anti-Trump rally turned violent outside the Civic Center, she tripped over a rain-slicked curb on Gregory Street while running to her car, skinning her knees and injuring her back. Dr. Metzer prescribed Percocet for the pain. By the time her prescription ran out, the pain had subsided, but a new ache bloomed within her. She had fallen in love with the muted warmth of opiates. After a second script was quickly gobbled up, she was on her own, forced to overpay and scrounge and trade her Adderall for Lortab. Until Cassy Myers, her lab partner in Anatomy and Physiology, introduced her to Nick at a frat party a month earlier.

He pushed in the cigarette lighter and shook his head. "It don't make sense to pay a dollar a milligram for pills when I've got some of the most fire dope in the city right here in my pocket. You heard Gucci say how pure it is."

"Actually, he said it was purr."

"This shit'll *make* you purr." He reached across the console and squeezed her thigh. "Just like a little kitten. Want me to fix you up a bump?"

She shook her head. It wasn't that she was snobby and only wanted pharmaceutical grade opiates. She just didn't want to cross that line. It was bad enough that she had graduated from popping pills to snorting them. But heroin was a Pandora's box with an escalator inside leading straight down to the bathroom floor with a needle in her arm. No way. She had a GPA to maintain, novels to write, dreams to chase.

He puffed the blunt to life. The familiar aroma of Girl Scout cookies filled her car. *Such a strange name for designer weed,* she thought, *Girl Scout cookies.* She was a Brownie and a Scout all through elementary school, had probably moved more crates of cookies than Gucci had dope, but she had never run across any that smelled like Nick's stash.

There was a certain sensuality in the way he smoked, a level of intimacy and attention to detail that reminded her of his lovemaking. He took a deep pull followed by small sips, frequently turning the blunt sideways to inspect it, licking his finger and dabbing out runs as seductive tendrils of smoke drifted from his mouth up into his nose, inhaling and exhaling almost simultaneously.

He extended it toward her with one hand while reaching for his phone with the other.

She was never a big fan of weed. It made her too self-conscious. Her inner narrator was chatty enough as it was. No need to pump up the volume. But lately she found herself doing all kinds of things she didn't normally do.

She accepted the blunt and took a tentative drag. It was moist from his lips. She wasn't sure about any Girl Scout cookies, but she could definitely taste *him*. On the radio, Gillian Welch faded into a digital hiss of dead air. For a moment, the only sounds were the road noise and Nick tapping away on his phone. Then a swarm of banjoes burst forth through the speakers, jolting her upright. A yodeler began to yodel.

Nick stopped texting and looked up. "What the fuck are we listening to?" He jabbed an insistent finger at each radio preset until he found the rap station. An autotuned emcee was crooning about kidnapping someone's bitch if they played with his money. He began to bob his head hypnotically and settled back into his seat. She passed him the blunt.

The familiar businesses and street signs that lined Cervantes flew by in a fluorescent blur. She was stoned by Twelfth Avenue. As they neared Seventeenth, she eased into the turning lane. Maybe she would try a little bump of heroin when they got home. Just a taste.

"Don't turn on your street," said Nick. "Keep straight."

She glanced over at him. He was texting again.

"I'ma get you some pills, bae."

Her heart rate accelerated with the Avalon. The thrill of hope alone was intoxicating. She cut off a pickup as she swerved back into the middle lane. Brakes shrieked. She winced and sucked air through her teeth. "Sorry," she mouthed into the rearview, but the truck was already surging along the right side of her car.

Through the passenger door mirror she could see a Rebel Flag license plate bolted to the chrome front bumper. Muddy axles and Super Swamper tires quickly pulled even. Snarling faces, purple with rage, shook fists and shot middle fingers. She could hear them through the glass despite the rap music pumping through her speakers. "Pull over you stupid bitch!"

Still bobbing his head, Nick looked up from his phone, took another hit from the blunt and passed it to her. "Hold this." Then he reached down the front of his jeans and produced a pistol. He didn't wave it or even aim it at them. He just set it in his lap and clicked off the safety. With a barely perceptible raise of his dimpled chin, he asked a question, simple yet deadly. *What's up?*

The truck roared off, belching exhaust as its taillights vanished over the Bayou Texar bridge. Nick stared after it, his jaw tensing and relaxing. The gun lay heavy in his lap. Though her eyes were locked on the road ahead, she could still sense it, a dark and ominous shape, seething on the perimeter of her vision. She ventured a quick glance. There it was. She absently raised the blunt to her lips for another hit.

Nick lowered the volume on the radio. "Everything good, bae?"

"Better than good." She exhaled a torrent of smoke, her voice an octave higher than normal. "Everything's Gucci."

He smiled and retrieved the blunt from her trembling fingers. "There's some apartments coming up on the right. *Village on the Bluffs*. Take the second entrance."

Cervantes bent into Scenic Highway. Glimpses of Escambia Bay flickered through the oaks and pines. The sun was still high enough to sprinkle diamonds over the water. It occurred to her that Florida was shaped like an inverted pistol.

Her phone chirped. Dad was texting. She glanced at the message as she pulled into the apartment complex. *Biloxi?* She rolled her eyes. Her last trip to the casinos with her father cost her every dime in her purse and almost a thousand in student loans. No thanks. A speed bump rose from the asphalt unannounced. Tired shocks creaked and groaned in the immediate aftermath. The gun bounced from Nick's lap and tumbled to the floorboard.

"What the heck?" She objected, increasingly more stoned as her adrenaline ebbed. "I thought they had to paint those yellow. It's like a law or something."

He reached between his Jordans for the pistol. "Pull up on that curb by the dumpster."

She scrunched her nose and surveyed the parking lot. There was an open space between a Yukon and an Alero. "How about over there?"

He was tapping on his phone again. "Yeah. Good. Whatever."

She pulled in, shut off the car and began checking her makeup in the mirror.

"You can't go in with me this time, bae."

"Oh," she frowned. "Okay.'

He stuck the phone in his pocket. "Misty's got a script for Roxy 30s. But she won't even open the door if I've got somebody with me. Her son weighs 500 pounds. Rarely ever gets out of bed. Her apartment's a mess . . ."

"Say no more," said Miranda. *You had me at Roxy 30s.*

"There's a cop that lives across from her. Fucks with me every time he sees me. Frisks me, threatens me with jail. Petty shit." He thumbed the gun back on safety and held it out, handle first. "Hold this down for me. Just in case he's snooping round."

She hesitated. "But . . . what if he follows you back here? What if he searches my car?"

"He won't. He's probably on duty anyway. I just can't get caught slippin'. With my record, I'd never see daylight again."

The internal floodwaters of anxiety were already up to her throat. She regretted smoking the weed. Her inner narrator wasn't helping. *A gun!?! Don't you dare Miranda. What kind of a hypocrite are you? I cannot believe you are even considering it. How many anti-gun rallies have you attended? Didn't you just post a Gabby Giffords quote on Facebook last month? What would she think about this? What would Nancy Pelosi think about this? WHAT WOULD MICHELLE OBAMA THINK ABOUT THIS?*

Why did her inner narrator sound so much like her mother? She wished she had a Xanax.

"I'm just doing this shit for you, bae. You know how I feel about pills. Want me to hit her up right now and let her know I ain't coming? She won't stress it. Hard as it is to get pills these days, they'll be gone in an hour."

"No!" She grabbed the gun and looked for a place to put it, finally settling on her purse. "Just . . . just please hurry up."

"You sure?" he said. "I'm supposed to be getting some lean soon. Maybe tonight. If you can hold out."

Lean. Sizurp. Codeine promethazine. Medicated cough syrup. Favored beverage of rap stars and drug dealers. Nick mixed his with Sprite. She had guzzled her share over the last month. It definitely took the edge off. But compared to snorting Roxys, it was baby aspirin.

She shook her head. "It's fine. Really. I was just having a moment. You know I get weird when I smoke."

"Just chill bae. You with me now. I got you." He reached for the door handle, paused and pulled the Ziploc of heroin from his jeans. "Damn. Slippin'. Almost forgot this."

He dropped it in her purse himself.

3

She sank into her seat and stared over the steering wheel as Nick sauntered down a narrow walkway between two buildings. His gait was confidence personified;

loose-hipped, head high, shoulders alternating at 45-degree angles as he strode past the squat green air-conditioning units and bubble-faced electricity meters that were staggered along the beige vinyl-sided walls of the alley. She wished he would forego the coolness and step it up.

She watched him swagger past a rusty barbecue grill, sidestep a ten-speed and duck beneath a distant stairwell before disappearing altogether into the byzantine apartment complex. She exhaled and glanced up at the rearview. Her own eyes were there waiting . . . judging.

"What?" Her voice split the silence.

An elderly man labored past the front of her car, hand in hand with a ponytailed girl in a purple tutu, four years old at most. With breathless enthusiasm and energy to burn, the child hopped down the sidewalk, tugging her grandfather along, babbling happily about the spectacular world she was discovering, a world of magic and music and colors and bugs and birds. He noticed Miranda and nodded hello.

She managed a tight smile despite her anxiety. It wasn't so long ago when she was a little ponytailed girl in a tutu herself. Now she was almost 19 with an opioid habit and a loaded pistol in her purse.

And an ounce of heroin, her inner narrator pointed out. *Let's not forget that.*

She glanced down at it. Talc-like powder glazed the inside of the bag. What color was that? Not quite white but lighter than beige. Biscuit, oatmeal, eggshell? *Taupe.* It came to her. *Rhymes with dope.*

The plastic brushed her hand seductively as she reached for her phone. She answered her father's text first. "Sorry. Can't go." She typed with her thumbs. "Midterms." His response was instantaneous. "Can I borrow 100 bucks?" She rolled her eyes but didn't respond. Next, she checked her Twitter feed. Some troll was making lude remarks about her Michelle Obama retweet from the 2016 DNC. "When they go low, we go high." Probably a bot. Possibly a Russian. She lamented for a moment how a country that gave the world Tolstoy and Dostoyevsky could be synonymous with human rights abuse and election meddling . . . then she blocked his ass. Next up, Facebook, or, as her dad called it, *Myface.* The last post on her timeline was a Molly Ivins quote. "Freedom fighters don't always win, but they're always right." *Right on,* she thought. Even though she didn't remember putting it up. The days and nights had been running together since Nick started crashing in her apartment. Eighteen likes, eight loves, no shares, and a single comment. Lauren Talbot gushed her customary, "Love you bunches!" Again.

She glanced at the time. It was almost 4 o'clock. The little girl and her grandfather were all the way to the end of the sidewalk where the bluffs descended into the bay. Straight ahead, the alley yawned, unspooling into shadows. She squinted through the windshield, willing a swaggering shape to materialize.

She slid the phone back inside her purse, careful to avoid the black handle of the pistol that protruded from the open zipper like a rubber phallus. She wondered if it had ever killed anyone. *Guns don't kill people,* her inner narrator piped up, *people kill people.* A half-moon auburn eyebrow rose in the rearview. *A famous NRA slogan? Where on earth did that come from?* But she already knew the answer. The voice in her head was not bound by loyalty to any specific set of principles. It hopscotched shamelessly across the ideological aisle, sometimes contradicting itself in sequential sentences. If it was loyal to anything, it was the sound of its own incessant chatter.

Fine, she clarified. *I wonder if Nick has ever killed anyone.*

The heavy question sank in her mind like a brick in the bay, falling through the murky depths before thudding to the floor in a soundless *poof.* Even her inner narrator went quiet. But the silence was soon filled with the relentless palpitations of her pounding heart.

Serenity whispered from the glassine baggie in her purse, beckoning like a forbidden lover. A quick sniff would slow the speedbag that was hammering against the cell bars of her ribcage, muffle the running soliloquy in her head and massage the anxiety from her nerve endings with warm opiated balm.

Almost in a trance, she pulled her keys from the ignition and reached for the dope. It wasn't that big of a deal. Poppy derivatives were poppy derivatives—Roxys, Percs, Tabs, Dilaudid, Boi . . . Same family. A tiny bump meant nothing in the great scheme of things. She just needed a little tide-me-over. Something to take the edge off. Something to turn the sound down.

She looked long down the worn and narrow trail that snaked between the apartment buildings for a final time before pulling apart the Ziploc.

The pungent smell of vinegar wafted up from the bag and filled the car as she submerged the key and scooped a miniscule amount onto the tip, jiggling off the excess granules, fully aware that any one of which could be a lethal crystal of Fentanyl despite Gucci's boasts of purity.

Fentanyl is the least of your worries, her inner narrator snipped. *It's Carfentanyl you should be concerned about. The equivalent of a single salt grain is enough to tranquilize an elephant. That's what guys like Gucci are using to stretch their beloved product. And do you think he'll lose a minute of sleep when you overdose? Do you think anyone will? Please. You'll just be another dead face in the obituaries. I cannot believe how reckless you've become. What's next? Meth? Crack?*

The answer was something far more sinister. There was no next. Heroin was the final stop.

With a trembling hand she carefully raised the dope encrusted key, eyeballing it all the way. The distance between the bag and her itchy nose felt like Everest. Home stretch. She used the rearview to guide key to nostril. Blue eyes stared back at her from the mirror, consciousness aware of itself. Then, like a foreboding black storm cloud moving over the sun, a police cruiser crept slowly across her back window.

4

She dropped the key. It clattered against the emergency brake and slid down the side of her seat. A flurry of dope drizzled over the console.

"Shit!" She forced the Ziploc and the pistol to the bottom of her purse, burying them beneath the moisturizers, sunglasses, lip gloss, writing journal, trail mix bars, packs of gum and miscellaneous receipts. Then she grabbed her eyeliner and returned to the rearview.

The trunk and back bumper of the cruiser disappeared behind the Yukon in the neighboring parking space. She exhaled. Relief washed over her.

You see? What if he would've seen what you were doing? What if he would've walked over to your window and saw that gun? What could you have said? "It's not mine officer. It belongs to my drug dealer boyfriend. I'm just holding it while he goes to score me some Roxys . . ." You know what your problem is? You never— Oh shit. Here he comes again!

The cruiser slowly reversed back into view and stopped behind her, its passenger door directly between her taillights, hemming her in.

A lanky deputy with thinning hair stepped out and casually unlatched the protective strap on his sidearm. Gravel crunched as he approached her window. Big sunny panhandle smile. The skin around his eyes rippled outward. Like someone dropped a pebble in the center of his face.

She held up the eyeliner pencil for a beat longer, belaboring her message. Subliminal subterfuge. *No sir, that was absolutely not a key you saw me holding to my nose but rather a harmless eyeliner pencil. See? Common mistake.*

His smile dimmed a few volts as he motioned for her to roll down the window.

Problem was she needed her car key for that, and her car key was somewhere beneath her seat, possibly still covered in suspicious white powder.

It's not white, said her inner narrator, *it's taupe.*

This was a perfect example of why she hated smoking weed, this paralysis by analysis. Should she reach under her seat for the key? And if so, via what route? Down the side or between her legs? She knew there was an acceptable thing to do, a way to act so as not to draw suspicion, but she was damned if she could figure it out. In the end she just opened the door.

He took a step back. His hand brushed the butt of his service weapon. "Easy darlin'. The window would have been sufficient. This your car?"

She nodded. "Do you wanna see my registration? I think it's in the glove—"

"In due time." He was staring at her breasts, smiling at them. "You don't live here, do you?"

"Um, no. I'm just waiting on a friend."

"Thought as much." He continued to ogle her. "What's your shirt say? Astronauts?"

"Close." She attempted a coquettish smile. "Argonauts. It's like adventurers." She wished she was adept at the subtle art of flirty manipulation, like some busty, sharp-tongued getaway driver in an Elmore Leonard novel. But she was far too awkward for that. Sober, maybe; stoned, no chance.

"And who is this friend?"

"I'm sorry?"

"This resident you're waiting on. What's her name?"

"Oh, um, Nick . . . Nikki. Nicole." Floundering. Not good.

His smile diminished further. He towered over her, stepping inside the open car door, one hand on the roof. "Nicole what?"

"Um . . . Nicole, *sir?*" *Gosh what a jerk.*

He shook his head and spoke with exaggerated slowness, enunciating each word as if she were a lost foreign tourist. "What is this Nicole's last name?"

"Ohhh." It dawned on her. "It's, um, Gucci . . . onni!" she added quickly. "Nicole Guccionni."

"Italian, huh?" He tapped his fingers on the roof, surveying the interior of her car. "My wife's family is from Naples. Well, her mother's side. Her dad was just stationed over there. Navy. Her grandmother still lives in the house she was born in. 106 years old, can you believe it? Her *Nona* she calls her. Lives right near that volcano, Mount Etna."

"Vesuvius is the volcano closest to Naples," she heard herself saying. *Shut up Miranda! Just let him be right!* "Etna is in eastern Sicily."

He frowned and sucked something between his teeth. "Same difference. You a college student or something?"

She nodded. Even though Italy's volcanos were covered in her tenth-grade geography class. "I'm a freshman at West Florida." She tried to redirect his attention back to her breasts. "Argonauts."

"Interesting." He looked behind her into the back seat. "I wonder if that's a lie too."

"Excuse me?"

He continued to tap on her roof. Apparently, her breasts had been weighed and found wanting because now he was staring straight at her face. Tapping and staring. Until finally he spoke. "I've been living in this apartment complex for going on ten years. I know every resident. By face and by name. There's no Guccionnis here. There's no Italians here. Except my wife. Trust me, if there were, she'd be on their balcony right now drinking wine and complaining about what a *strunze* she has for a husband . . ."

"Oh, she doesn't live here," Miranda scrambled to explain, willing the storytelling gears in her brain to crank out something believable. "I think she left her purse at a bible study last night. One of her friends from Scenic Baptist. I just drove her here to get it."

"Scenic Baptist, huh? Who's the friend?"

"Um, Monica something? She said her name, but I can't remember."

Movement in the alley caused her to doubletake. Her heart leapt. *Nick!* He paused in the middle of the trail, rising on the toes of his sneakers, craning his neck for a better look. Then, just as quickly, he vanished into the shadows. Gone.

"Monica something," he repeated, following her eyes. "It's possible, I guess."

Nothing in his demeanor suggested relief. *Think Miranda! There has to be a way out of this. It's a puzzle. You love puzzles . . .*

He slapped the roof. A metallic twang went through her, jolting her upright. About to say something, he paused and raised a sandy eyebrow. "You all right darlin'?"

She nodded. There was heroin on her kneecap.

"Well, here's what we're gonna do," he said. "My instincts are telling me you're up to something. I should just run you off. But I'm curious about this Italian Baptist friend of yours. Maybe we'll wait for her together."

The little girl and her grandfather returned from the bluffs. He waved at them. The child smiled and waved back then pointed at Miranda through the windshield and said, "Bad!"

A burst of static erupted from his radio. He adjusted it without looking. "Listen, I already know you're getting high. This car smells like a Colorado dope dispensary. I'm just trying to figure out why you're doing it in my apartment complex."

She swallowed what little saliva remained in her mouth and tried not to look at the incriminating tumor that bulged from the side of her purse.

He held out his palm. "Let me see your identification."

Now she had to look. Luckily her wallet had somehow risen to the top. She grabbed it and plucked her driver's license from between her library and debit cards.

"Miranda McGuire," he said. "Nice Irish name. And only 18 years old. Just a baby." He shook his head. "So tell me, Miranda, what are you really doing here? Buying dope? Selling dope? Maybe you're driving around the little thugs who've been breaking into apartments over the last few weeks?"

"No!" she sputtered.

He eyed her coolly. "Step out of the car, ma'am."

"W-w-why?" Her hands were trembling.

"So I can search your vehicle."

A cliché formed in her brain. The residue of every *Cops* rerun she had ever watched with her dad. Before she had time to weigh its wisdom, her mouth was pried open like a second-story window and the words leaped into the air between them. "Do you have a warrant?"

"I don't need a warrant, darlin'," he smirked, "I've got probable cause."

Defeated, she reached for her purse and moved to exit the car.

"Leave it," he commanded.

Writer brain. Hers switched on at the strangest times: while Leah Oglethorpe from English Lit was sobbing to her about her girlfriend ditching her for a grad assistant on the swim team, when faking an orgasm with Nick because she was high on K-4s and couldn't get off, when Brady Vaughn overdosed in the admissions parking lot on the first day of school. It was during those tense situations—no matter how humiliating, how crushing, how nerve wracking—that the aspiring novelist in her would switch on a lamp in some dusty office in the right hemisphere of her brain and begin mining for literary gold.

Imagine if there was this girl maybe she had a minor opiate problem definitely not a criminal though but her boyfriend sells drugs and one day they go to buy pills and he leaves a pistol and dope in her car and this really mean police officer shows up . . .

She leaned against the back bumper of her car, forearms flat on the trunk, staring through the rear window as he dug beneath the seats, lifted the floor mats, checked the door panels, the console, the glove compartment, the visors, all while whistling some arrogant little tune. Whistling. As her life was circling the drain.

"Found your key," he called from the floorboard.

She considered running. But to where? And how far would she get? Even her writerly imagination could not concoct a scenario where she fled on foot and disappeared into the Pensacola underworld. She didn't even know where the Pensacola underworld was located. And anyway, her money and credit cards were in her purse.

He stood and clapped the dust from his hands. "Everything appears to be in order . . . less you got a body in the trunk."

A glimmer of hope. "I can open it for you!" Anything to get him out of her car.

"Hang on darlin'." He raised his palm. "I think I know how to pop a trunk." He glanced back inside the car and shook his head. "I hate going through a woman's purse. Anything in there I should know about? Knives, needles, pipes?"

She swallowed and forced a smile. "Just tampons and makeup and, um, my hairbrush."

He stared at it for a moment, chewing his lip, as if on the fence about such an invasion of her privacy. Then he ducked back inside the door, grabbed it from the console and dumped its contents onto the driver seat. Although she couldn't see, she could hear it. A waterfall of frivolities and trinkets culminating in a distinct successive *th-thunk.*

Then silence followed by a low whistle.

She closed her eyes and clung to the stable steel of the Avalon as if her trembling legs were dangling from the side of a cliff.

While she had yet to begin her first novel, she did take copious notes in Professor Duncan's creative writing class. Enough to grasp the mechanics of storytelling at a fundamental level. And enough to recognize that in the three-act structure of her life, she had just arrived at what the professor referred to as *the first doorway of no return.* The moment where everything changes.

Her hands were pulled behind her back with humiliating gentleness. Steel teeth nibbled at her wrists. When he spoke, his voice was solemn. His words floated over her shoulder in a gust of breath mints and aftershave.

"You have the right to remain silent . . ."

6

The holding tank of the Escambia County jail is a medieval dungeon of leaky ceilings, poor lighting, and appalling smells. Located on the ground floor of a crumbling monument to the war on drugs, it groaned beneath the weight of six stories of concrete and reinforced steel. Its damp walls and iron bars seemed to bear the blood and fear and prayers of the thousands upon thousands of others before her that were dumped in its unforgiving cages.

She finally stopped crying, but she could not stop shivering. She pulled her knees to her chest and stretched her t-shirt over them, slipping her arms inside and hugging herself. She noticed mascara on her collar. Though there was no mirror to confirm it, she could guess how she looked: like the cover of one of her dad's old KISS albums.

"Hey Red!" One of the men in the tank next door called. "Come to the bars. Fuck with me!"

A couple of the women looked over at her. A black woman with copper-colored hair smiled and shook her head. More tears threatened; she shook them off.

Her feet were freezing. She saw herself getting dressed that morning, an eternity ago, with Nick shirtless in her bed, arms crossed over his chest, leaning back against the headboard, watching, smiling. She almost went with boots. She had a closet full of them. But it was Fall in the Florida panhandle and her rhinestone sandals were comfy. She was regretting that decision now. She was regretting a lot of things.

"Hey yo! Next door! Y'all bitches deaf?"

"We wish we was deaf," the woman who smiled at her snapped. "That way we wouldn't have to listen to your beggin' ass!"

"Send that snowbunny to the bars," he persisted. "Hey Red! Check me out!"

She rolled her eyes and moved closer to Miranda. "You cold baby?" She had the high cheekbones and long elegant neck of a runway model. Silver polished nails tapped the hard iron bench as she awaited an answer.

Thoughts, fears, and questions raced through Miranda's head. *Why is this woman talking to me? Potential ally? Angel of mercy? Lesbian predator? Don't I get a phone call? What's a snowbunny?*

"Of course you're cold," the woman smiled again. "This your first time in jail?"

"Yes ma'am," said Miranda through chattering teeth.

A door slammed. Radio static. Keys. Voices. Two police officers in tight uniforms and gelled hair half-escorted, half-dragged a ranting leather-faced prostitute to the front of the holding cell. ". . . *murderers, carjackers, kidnappers, armed robbers, rapists! And you two cocksuckers wanna haul in a damn lady of the night!?! What else am I gonna do? Where else am I gonna work? Y'all gonna give Rhonda a job? You should. Much time as I spend in this god-forsaken Castle Grayskull shithole of a third world jail! I wanna be a fuckin' receptionist! Hello? HELLO!!!"*

The men in the next cell cheered as the officers threw open the tank door and pushed her roughly inside. "Give 'em hell baby!" one called out.

"I shoulda kicked their asses is what I shoulda did." She smiled through her hair. Jaundiced eyes glowed yellow with madness and hepatitis. "Shoulda kicked 'em right in the stimulus package."

"Hey yo Red!" Mr. Indefatigable doubled down on the volume. "Come holla at me Red! Red!"

The prostitute stumbled to the filthy stainless-steel toilet in the back of the cell and without preamble snatched her sagging spandex to her bony knees and took a seat, mumbling to herself. "Red Rover, Red Rover, send Rhonda right over."

Miranda knew it was rude to gawk at someone who was obviously mentally ill and beaten down by life, but she couldn't look away. Especially when the woman pulled a syringe from her vagina.

"Hey Snowbunny! I know you hear me. Get your fine ass to the door!"

"Hang on a goddamned minute," Rhonda the prostitute rasped. "I'm doing something."

"Not you, you AIDS infested gut bucket!"

The men next door erupted in laughter. Rhonda shrugged and hunted a vein. A tendril of need awakened in Miranda and began to whisper in its secret language of craving. The woman beside her on the bench was unmoved, expressionless, as if all of it were some movie she had seen a hundred times. "What did they get you for?"

"Drugs," said Miranda. "An ounce of heroin and a gun."

The woman's eyes narrowed. Her head cocked back on her regal neck as she searched Miranda's face for evidence of duplicity. "Armed trafficking? You? Lemme guess. You're taking a charge for your man?"

Miranda didn't answer.

"Don't do it baby. He ain't gonna ride. They never do."

Like she had a choice in the matter. The contraband wasn't just in her car, it was in her purse. She stared across the holding cell at Rhonda, jabbing her skinny thigh on the toilet. She wondered if she had anything else on her.

"Here," the woman said, pulling off her tennis shoes and removing her socks. They were thick and soft, the kind with gray on the heels and toes. "You gonna need these."

"No thank you," said Miranda.

"Girl, you better quit being polite and put these damn socks on! Look at your toes. They blue! It's gonna be even colder when you get upstairs." She laid them on the bench between them. "Go ahead. Take 'em."

Miranda couldn't remember ever wearing even a friend's socks. Wearing a stranger's in the county jail felt almost promiscuous. "What about you? Won't your feet be cold?"

She was already slipping back on her red bottom Nikes. "I'm about to be outta here. My sister's probably out front with the bail bondsman right now."

"Hey yo Snowbunny Red! Why you running from me?"

Miranda pulled the luxurious cotton socks over the manicured blocks of ice that were once her feet. "What's a snowbunny?"

The woman chuckled. "You serious?" A few of the other ladies were laughing too. Even Rhonda, still struggling to find a vein on the toilet, began to cackle.

Miranda looked around. "What's so funny?"

"We ain't laughing at you baby." She hooked a loose strand of copper-colored hair with her fingernail and dragged it across the slope of her forehead. "It's just . . . you asking what a snowbunny is would be like me asking you what a black bitch is."

Miranda flinched, unaccustomed to such harsh political incorrectness. Then, slowly, it dawned on her. "Me?"

The woman smiled. Perfect ivory teeth lit the gloom. "You got it . . . Snowbunny Red."

A matron appeared at the door. Her slate gray hair was pulled back into a ponytail and tied off with a purple ribbon that matched the loose bags under her eyes. "Applewhite, what are you doing back there?"

"I'm taking a shit," Rhonda snapped, cuffing her rig. "Wassit look like I'm doing?"

The deputy wrinkled her nose and scanned her clipboard. "McGuire?"

Miranda pushed her arms back through her shirt sleeves and raised her hand as if it was roll call in English Comp. "Present."

Rhonda scoffed from over the toilet. "*Present?* You gotta be kidding me."

"Front and center," ordered the deputy, pulling a flat brass key from her belt and opening the door.

Miranda stepped out into the hallway. The bars clanged shut. An unladylike eruption of flatulence detonated behind her, accompanied by what sounded like a watermelon being tossed in a pool.

"There's your damn present." Rhonda's scratchy voice followed them down the hallway. "Merry Fucking Christmas."

Arms sprang like vines from the crowded men's holding tanks, spilling out into the corridor. Hairy arms, skinny arms, muscled arms, tattooed arms. The deputy steered her closer to the safety of the wall as they passed.

"Oh shit! There she go y'all! Snowbunny Red."

"Hey baby, why you ain't answer me when I was calling you?"

"Damn, she got a fat pussy!"

"Don't talk about my old lady like that."

Miranda hugged herself as she hurried down the hall, burning with humiliation. *Animals!* And to think she marched outside this very jail with the local chapter of the ACLU for their humane treatment.

"This way." The woman led her down a wider corridor with waxed linoleum floors. An elderly black man in a county jumpsuit was mopping and singing church hymns while a white kid around her age was on his hands and knees wiping down the baseboards. He paused to wring his dirty rag in the bucket. She read the tattoos on his knuckles as they passed. *METH* on one hand, *COOK* on the other.

There was a mirror-tinted window the size of a chalkboard at the end of the hall. She studied her own approach. If it wasn't for the red hair, she would not have recognized the girl in the reflection. Blinding white socks and rhinestone sandals, shoulders hunched forward in defeat, face smeared black like some culturally insensitive Halloween yearbook photo from the eighties.

The matron waved at an unseen person behind the glass. A door unlocked and she held it open. Tremulously, Miranda stepped into the harsh fluorescent light of central booking.

7

In the summer of the fifth grade, right after her mother ran off to the other side of the continent to start her new family with Chase Echelhardt of *Echelhardt Honda and Acura*, her dad went a little crazy. He had always been quirky—concocting wild schemes to "beat the house" in the Gulf Coast casinos, scribbling down probabilities and equations while shuffling eight decks of cards, arguing vehemently with the commentators on *Monday Night Football* as if they could hear him—but when her mother left, he added paranoia and insomnia to his growing list of symptoms. Sleep deprivation only accelerated his unraveling. By the time school started she could hear his teeth grinding from her upstairs bedroom. Most mornings she would awaken to find him tapping away on his calculator, still wearing his rumpled clothing from the night before, bloodshot, unshaven, pausing every few seconds to peep through the blinds, an overflowing ashtray on the windowsill next to him.

He began running errands at odd hours, claiming to prefer the blinking caution lights and deserted streets of late-night Pensacola to the bustle of daytime traffic. Sometimes he would take her with him on 2 a.m. grocery runs to the Walmart on the west side of town. It was like the walking dead in that place after midnight. Nothing but crackheads, cops, shoplifters and streetwalkers. But in her young mind she saw zombies and vampires lurking on every aisle. This is what she thought about as she was escorted into the booking area of the Escambia County Jail: Westside Walmart with Dad.

"Have a seat on one of those benches," said the matron, probably a westsider herself. "I'll pull you for prints in a few minutes."

Miranda scanned the room. A long incurvated counter of blond ash with ornate molding served as a demarcation line between captor and captive. Behind it, uniformed deputies and county employees in khaki and green sipped coffee, tapped keyboards, and engaged in friendly office banter, apathetic to the subhuman dreck that shivered and sobbed on the opposite benches.

A pale man with shifty tweaker eyes and ears like the tuning pegs on her ukulele motioned her over with a jerk of his head. He scooted to the left to make room between himself and a plus-sized woman who kept sneezing into her meaty palms and inspecting the post-nasal damage.

Miranda turned and found the matron fiddling with a large machine with a plastic encased monitor that flashed fingerprints on its screen. "Don't I get a phone call?"

"Over there on the wall." The woman glanced over her shoulder. "Hang on and I'll tell you your bond amount . . . McGuire, McGuire . . ." She flipped through a stack of papers. "Here we are. Miranda McGuire. Armed trafficking of a controlled substance." She looked up. "My goodness. $150,000 dollars."

The room began to tilt. "How much?"

"Your family will need to pay ten percent so it's really $15,000. *If* they have the collateral."

"Collateral," she repeated numbly.

"You know. Insurance in case you decide to skip out. Hey, it happens. You'd be amazed at how many felons leave their poor mothers homeless and saddled with debt these days. Sign of the times, I guess. Damned opi*odd* crisis."

Opioid, she silently corrected as she turned and headed for the phone. *How is Dad going to come up with—* Her toe caught on the curled lip of a loose piece of linoleum and she stumbled forward, ripping the leather thong from the sole. The rhinestone vee of her sandal flopped back against her ankle. Conversation behind the counter went silent, shifty tweaker eyes bulged in alarm, another sneeze. She went down on a knee. She almost gave up, almost just curled up in the fetal position on the booking floor and remained there until they scooped her up with some industrial-sized dustpan and dumped her wherever they discarded women with fractured minds. But instead she gathered herself, took a deep breath, and slinked over to the phone, dragging her broken sandal with her.

The receiver reeked of halitosis and homelessness. Her fingers dialed on autopilot. Muscle memory. The first phone number she had ever learned. Each ring felt like a countdown, a countdown to her own execution. He picked up on number nine. "Hello?"

The sound of his voice brought a fresh wave of tears to the window ledges of her eyes. "Dad?"

"Jeez, Andy. I thought you were a bill collector. You're having second thoughts about Biloxi, aren't you? I knew it! Tell you what, we'll split whatever we—"

"Dad. I'm in jail."

"In jail? For what? Underage drinking, I bet. You college kids . . ."

The tears spilled over, streaming down her cheeks and pooling against the lip of the receiver. "Listen to me, okay? I'm in jail for drugs and a gun—"

"A gun!?!"

"They weren't mine, Dad. But I'm in trouble and I need your help. I need fifteen thousand—"

"Fifteen thousand what? Dollars?"

She closed her eyes. "—so that I can bond out of here and find an attorney who will represent me and hopefully continue going to school while I fight this."

The sound of his ragged breathing on the other end of the line came through in waves.

"Hello."

"I wish I could help you, Andy. But the credit cards are maxed out and the bank is talking about foreclosing on the house again. If I was still working at the dealership, I'm sure Vinnie would float me a few grand . . . Wait a minute!"

She gripped the phone tighter.

"There's a poker tournament at Treasure Bay this weekend. Thousand dollar buy in. Winner gets a hundred thou. I could pawn my tools and—"

"Oh my God. Are you off your medication again?" Her reflection was distorted in the steel casing of the phone. Still, the blurred image staring back at her looked closer to fifty than twenty. "You are, aren't you?"

His silence said it all.

"I should have had you Baker-Acted when I was twelve."

"Don't say that Miranda."

"I used to think Victoria was such a selfish bitch for leaving you. Now I understand why she did what she did. She was just escaping a sinking ship."

"Maybe you can call her," he said. "I know they've got the money. I have the number around here somewhere."

"I know the fucking number!" She slammed the phone down.

"Hey! Strawberry Shortcake!" A swarthy deputy leveled a hairy finger in her direction. "You break that thing and you're gonna have way bigger problems than bond money. We understood?"

She nodded without making eye contact and turned back to the phone. *"See? That's the problem with this generation,"* he was saying as she punched the numbers into the keypad. *"No respect whatsoever."*

She glanced up at the clock as the phone rang. It was a little after 4:00 a.m. That meant it was 2:00 in Escondido.

Click. "Hello."

"Victoria?"

There was a brief pause. Then, "Miranda? What in the world are you doing calling this number this late?" Her voice was as icy and terse as ever. "And why on earth does it say you're calling from the Escambia County jail?"

Miranda stared up at the water-stained ceiling tiles. "Because that's where I'm calling you from. I'm in trouble."

"Are you asking for money? Is that why you're calling?"

Tweaker Eyes was watching her. She curled her top lip in her best snobby mean girl sneer and turned her back to the zombies on the benches. It was humiliating to be unloved. Even in front of the westside undead. "I've never asked you for anything in my life."

"Very thoughtful of you," her mother spat. "No reason to start now."

She shook her head incredulously. "What kind of a mother are you?"

"Oh, I'm a very good mother," she hissed. "A den mother, a PTA mother, a soccer mother. I'm just not your mother. You're your father's daughter. And evidently his freeloader DNA is already rearing its ugly head."

Miranda did not cry. Just the opposite. Whatever moisture lingered in her tear ducts quickly evaporated in the cold wind of her words.

"You call Dad a freeloader? Dad's not the one who abandoned his family and ran off to California with some rich car salesman."

"Chase *owns* a car dealership, Miranda. You're a smart girl. I'm sure you can appreciate the difference. But even so, if you're calling to ask for a handout, the answer is no.

I'm sorry you're in trouble. But honestly, I'm not at all surprised. Please do not call this number again."

The line went dead.

"Are you almost finished over there?" The deputy called. "I need to get your prints."

"One second," she said, staring at the keypad as the reality of her mother's words sank in.

Tentatively, she dialed Nick's number. She knew it was a longshot. Nick didn't even own a car, much less $150,000 of collateral. But he did have a shoebox full of cash in her apartment closet. Twenties, fifties and hundreds rolled into thousand-dollar cylinders and tied off with rubber bands. There was at least $15,000 there, or *15 bands,* as he would say. Maybe he knew a bail bondsman. The more she thought about it, the more she became convinced that he would help her.

Of course he'll get me out. Not only because it's the right thing to do since I'm stuck in this nightmare for his stuff, but also because he truly cares for me.

His phone went to voicemail. "We're sorry. The subscriber's mailbox is full at this time."

Her inner narrator snorted.

With a sinking feeling, she replaced the foul-smelling receiver. Across the room, the deputy was waiting. It was difficult to tell whether her smile was sympathetic or sarcastic. "Any luck, Sugar?"

Miranda stared down at her broken sandal.

"Okay," she smacked her gum. "Well let's get you fingerprinted, photographed and dressed out. There's someone who wants to speak with you before you go upstairs."

Hope flared. "Who?"

"Detective Sandifer," she said. "Narcotics."

8

The interrogation room was nothing like the ones she remembered from *Law & Order* or *LA Law* or any of the other police procedural reruns that her dad liked to watch. There was no two-way mirror, no dangling light bulb, no craggy-faced detective attempting to soften her up with a cigarette. Just a small office with a table and chairs and a plexiglass view of the main hallway of the jail.

Detective Sandifer was an attractive man in his thirties with Adam Levine hair and a blue pastel tie that matched his eyes. He laced his fingers together and rested his stubbled chin on the apex as he stared at her from across the table.

"Nice t-shirt. Are you a student at the university?"

She nodded.

"My little sister just transferred there. From Pensacola State. It feels weird calling it that, doesn't it? It's been PJC my entire life. You probably don't remember that. You can't be older than twenty. Sophomore?"

"Freshman," she said. "I'll be nineteen next month."

"Jamie's a junior. Communications. I've never quite understood what that means, a degree in communications. I'm not entirely convinced that she does either." He removed a box of gum from his pocket and shook a piece into his palm. "Want one?"

She eyed the box with suspicion. She absolutely wanted one. *Needed* one. It had been close to 24 hours since she'd brushed her teeth and her breath tasted like Nick's Girl Scout weed and gingival jail phones. But in the end, she declined. She may have been naïve, but she knew what he was up to. And she refused to sell her soul for a piece of gum.

The door opened and a tall, blond, hatchet-faced woman strode in. She wore faded jeans, boots, and an unbuttoned oxford shirt over a white tank top. A detective shield hung on a beaded chain inside her collar. "Sorry about that," she said to Sandifer. "This our armed trafficker?"

He leaned back in his chair and nodded. "This is her."

"Not exactly from central casting, is she?" The woman sat down. "What are you, an aspiring junkie? Some dealer's side piece?"

"She's a college student," said Detective Sandifer.

"Nice." The woman crossed her arms and smiled coldly. "You introducing all your little sorority sisters to the wonderful world of the needle?"

"No!" Miranda blurted.

"Go easy on her, Beth." Sandifer's eyes softened with sympathy. "She's just a kid."

"Yeah?" The woman smirked. "How old are you?"

Miranda stared down at her chipped fingernail polish. How old was she? She felt as if she had aged exponentially over the past 24 hours.

"She's eighteen," said Sandifer.

"That's old enough to die in a war, old enough to work in a Las Vegas brothel, old enough to vote." She leaned forward and glared at Miranda. "And it's old enough to know better than to be driving around with an ounce of heroin and a loaded nine-millimeter. You're in deep shit sister."

"Beth . . ." He touched her shoulder.

"No." She shook it off. "I'm so sick of these scumbags contaminating our communities, enslaving our citizens. How many overdosed nonresponsives did we see last month? How many neglected children? How many funerals? Nonviolent victimless crime, my ass. These drug-dealing ass-wipes are the worst kind of criminal."

"I don't think it was hers." He cocked his head at Miranda, his eyes now imploring. *Help me out here. I'm on your team.* "You said it yourself Beth, she doesn't fit the mold. Look at her. I could see if it was trespassing, retail theft, maybe simple possession, but armed trafficking? No way."

"I wouldn't be so sure about that." Detective Beth smirked. "Have you listened to the radio lately? Everybody's a drug dealer nowadays. It's the new fad."

Her look was pure disgust. Miranda wanted to slide under the table. A tear dove down her cheek, cliffhung from her chin and freefell onto her folded hands, where it exploded on a trembling knuckle. She wiped her face with the back of her wrist. It came away smeared with mascara. "I'm not a drug dealer."

"See there," said Sandifer.

"Oh yeah, that settles it," she sneered. "Interesting that we're giving her the benefit of the doubt. Where was your *let's not rush to judgment* attitude last night when we were interrogating the kid from Truman Arms?"

"All's I'm saying is that maybe it wasn't hers."

"Of course, it wasn't hers!" She slapped the table.

Miranda flinched.

"And you know what?" She smiled sweetly. "I don't give a damn. These little bimbos who ride around in their wannabe-Scarface boyfriends' Corvettes and Escalades, with their fake boobs and their dyed red hair and their designer handbags bought with blood money . . . They're just as guilty as the pushers they spread their legs for."

Miranda was mortified. This woman was the single most horrible person she had ever met in her life. It was like being interrogated by Ann Coulter and Cruella Deville all in one.

Detective Sandifer's face reddened. "You're out of line, Beth."

"Yeah? So file a report with Internal Affairs." Her words were acid. "Probably won't be the first time you've ever done it."

"I resent that," he said, staring at her for a moment before speaking again. "Look, I know you're angry right now and I understand why, but I just don't see it."

"See what? A conviction? You're insane. With the physical evidence we have, there's not a jury in the panhandle that wouldn't find her guilty."

He shook his head. "I don't see the logic in settling for a minnow when Jaws is swimming around out there. Sure, we could nail her and have her put away for, what? Ten years? Fifteen?"

"Try 25 . . . and that's without the firearm enhancement. Trafficking over 28 grams of heroin carries a minimum mandatory of 25 years in prison." She paused, flashing that cruel smile once again. "The amount of heroin seized from her vehicle was 28.4 grams. It was in her *purse*, Sandy, and regardless of how cute and innocent you think she is, possession is still nine-tenths of the law."

"Fine, 25 years. Whatever. All's I'm saying is that I don't see any reason to put her away for that long while whoever's dope and pistol she was holding remains free to, as you say, *contaminate the community and enslave our citizens.*"

Miranda had to swallow to keep from vomiting in her lap. *25 years?* She hadn't even lived 25 years yet.

"Oh, we'll get him too." She flicked a mote of dust from her detective shield. "Eventually . . . We always do. And if not us, some desperate junkie or rival drug dealer will."

"Yeah? And how many Scarlett McGhees will we run across between now and then?"

She froze. Then quietly, "That was a low blow."

He shrugged. "And you think your Internal Affairs comment was above the belt?"

"Touché," she ceded after an ice age. Her jaw worked beneath the thin pale skin of her face. "What are you proposing?"

He glanced at Miranda. "Let me talk to her." His look was subtle. More blink than wink. But it spun out toward her and splashed amid the rising waves and circling sharks with all the promise of a life preserver.

Beth's eyes narrowed as her head swiveled back and forth between them, vibrating on a frequency of suspicion and contempt. Miranda gnawed a thumbnail behind her bangs as the tension mounted.

"Okay," she finally said, hands flat on the table as she rose from the chair. "I'm gonna get a Yoo-hoo from the machine and step outside for a smoke. If Molly Ringwald can't remember her boyfriend's name by the time I get back, I'll make sure Donna houses her with the meanest, ugliest dyke on the sixth floor."

She slammed the door behind her.

Miranda slouched in her chair. Gratitude washed over her with every fading footstep. Even a five-minute break from Kellyanne Conway was a relief.

"You'll have to forgive my partner," Sandifer smiled. "She's a little jaded but she means well."

"She's horrible," said Miranda.

"Nah, she just hates heroin is all. Can't really fault her for that, can we?"

Miranda shook her head slowly. Nobody hated heroin more than she did at that moment.

"But I do think she's wrong in wanting to lock you up and throw away the key. You don't belong in prison. You belong in school."

"I know," she began to cry again. "Oh . . . God."

He leaned in. "So real quick before she gets back, help me out here. Who did the dope and pistol belong to? Where did he get it? Do you know his suppliers? Any info you can come up with will look good. Especially in Beth's eyes. Names, addresses, phone numbers. Help me help you."

Her inner narrator, who had gone radio silent since the holding cell, finally stirred. Her tone was even more condescending than usual. *Seriously? You turn down his gum on grounds of suspicion and then you fall hook, line and sinker for this Hollywood cliché?*

She chewed on her bottom lip and contemplated the detective with new eyes. This was the part in every *Law & Order* where the suspect breaks down and sings like Selena Gomez. Those pivotal few hours between the time her rights were read and the moment an attorney was appointed. This was the sweet spot where confessions were secured, codefendants were named, and Oscar caliber good cop/bad cop routines were performed.

Nick's words from the parking lot came back to her. *"I just can't get caught slippin'. With my record, I'd probably never see daylight again . . ."*

Detective Sandifer glanced at the plexiglass window. "I don't mean to rush you, but time really is of the essence here. Gimme something. Anything."

Fear. Nausea. Exhaustion. Turmoil. All these things churned within her as she stared down at the socks that the nice woman in the holding cell gave her. Socks that were now filthy from the jail floor. In a small voice she uttered the words she was pretty sure would put an end to this meeting. "I want to speak to my attorney."

A hush fell over the interrogation room. Even the roaring AC vent went silent. "That's unfortunate," said Sandifer.

She didn't bother looking up.

"Well here," he pushed a business card across the table. "In case you change your mind."

9

She sleepwalked her way through first appearance, vaguely aware of the austere, robe-clad figure on the video screen who upheld her bond, appointed a public defender, and kept the line moving.

A few of the male inmates hissed and catcalled as the deputy escorted her back down the aisle with a group of women, but she looked through them with dead eyes, too embarrassed to be offended, too numb to care. She staggered forward in a daze, swallowed by the green and white striped county jumpsuit, occasionally jolted awake by shooting pain and cramping in her legs. Even in her addled state, she recognized this for what it was: a distant early warning. The first flashes of lightning in an approaching storm. Though she had no idea what time it was, her body was telling her that it had been too long since she snorted her last pill. The dreaded misery of withdrawals was looming.

Hopefully Nick was working on getting her out.

Her stomach lurched as the elevator rattled and whined its way up to the sixth floor. The white-bearded, rosy-cheeked deputy was humming a tune that sounded strangely similar to Blind Pilot's "Just One." She wondered, not for the first time, if she was trapped in some vivid opioid nightmare. How did this grandfather guard know Blind Pilot? He must have read her mind because he winked at her as the doors hissed open. "Good luck, ladies. Hopefully your stay is a short one."

There were three other women in the elevator, all black. A tall corn-rowed butch with her sleeves rolled up to accentuate her massive biceps, a bespectacled old woman with wiry gray chin hair, and a petite honey-skinned girl with wide-set green eyes and a jumpsuit that was three sizes too small. She followed them out into the hallway, a wedge-shaped corridor that dead-ended into a painted blue door with a scratched plexiglass window. They waited there a moment, each lost in her trauma, each no doubt processing the recent events that led to her standing in the sixth-floor lobby of the Escambia County jail. Miranda certainly was.

Until the musclebound woman stepped forward and slapped the plexiglass hard enough to make the building tremble.

The older lady screamed, "Jesus!" Miranda flinched. The door buzzed. They walked inside.

A stump of a woman with straw-colored hair and jagged brown teeth pulled her belt almost to her breasts and led with her crotch as she exited the officers' station. "My word. Are y'all that impatient to go sit in a cell? Just chomping at the bit ain't you?" She paused to scratch her nose and mumbled something into her hand that sounded a lot like *damn lezbos* before pointing a dirty fingernail at a cart in the corner. "Bed rolls are over there."

Miranda followed the other women to the cart and grabbed a cylinder of wool. Wrapped inside the blanket were a towel and washcloth, two sheets, a pillowcase, a roll of toilet paper, a thin bar of soap, a tiny toothbrush, and a small clear tube of *Maximum Security* toothpaste.

"All right," the guard clapped her hands, "any of y'all been on Blue Six before?"

No one spoke.

"Nobody?" She looked from face to face. "Well, well, well, a bunch of virgins."

Cornrows crossed her powerful arms. "I ain't no virgin. Facts."

"Figure of speech," she scratched her nose again. "Dang, y'all are about the least social bunch I've had this year. Where's your sense of humor?"

Sense of humor? thought Miranda, tired eyes surveying the lay of the land. *Was this woman serious?*

LED lights blinked from the control panel in the dark officers' station. Computer monitors divided into frames flashed black and white images of inmates playing cards, watching television, exercising. The booth itself was a capsule of concrete and glass in the center of the unit with a panoramic view of the four surrounding color-coded pods: Blue, Green, Orange and Red.

"Well, seeing that nobody's feeling social, I guess I'll give y'all the short version. My name is Officer Woodley and Blue Six is my floor . . ."

You can have it. Miranda stared through the thick glass of the nearest pod. Everything was painted Halloween orange. Women were gathered in groups on the second tier, leaning against the mesh railing. Others were standing inside their cell doors. A diminutive girl with big eyes and wild black curly hair shooting in every direction waved shyly. She waved back without thinking.

"Excuse me, Orphan Annie. Whenever you get done flirting, I'll continue."

Miranda dropped her hand.

"Good girl. Now, a couple of ground rules." She patted the canary rubber weapon holstered on her side. "This here taser is capable of sending thousands of volts of electricity into your body. It won't kill you, but it'll make you wish you was dead. I try my best not to shoot nobody in the face but," she shrugged and smiled, "my aim ain't all that great."

Another scratch of the nose. Miranda looked into her eyes. Pinpoint pupils. Definitely an opiate user. She wondered what she was on, wished she would share.

"I know some of y'all are pissed off because you got caught doing whatever you were doing out there. A lot of women come in with a chip on their shoulder. But I'm letting you know right now, I don't tolerate any fighting on my floor. If I catch you fighting, I ain't going in there trying to break it up. Damn near got my finger bit off doing that once." She glanced down at her hand as if to make sure the digit in question was still attached. "Won't happen again. If you fight, you're getting tased. Bank on it."

Miranda stifled a yawn. She had never been in a fight in her life and she had no inclination to turn over a new leaf on the sixth floor of the Escambia County jail. She just wanted to sleep.

"Second thing," shrunken narrowed eyes swept back and forth over the bedraggled group of women, "if I catch you in someone else's bunk, you're getting tased. No questions asked."

"Just for sitting on someone's bunk?" The green-eyed woman in the extra tight jumpsuit sucked her teeth; a petite, more voluptuous Rihanna whose only blemish was a scar across her cheekbone.

"Sitting is fine," Officer Woodley explained, "sitting is not an abomination in the sight of the Lord or a violation of the rules of this here facility. Sitting I have no problem with."

Sitting is the new smoking. Her inner narrator chimed in, apropos of nothing. The sleep deprivation was clearly taking its toll.

"But if I catch you doing unnatural things, fornicating for instance . . ." She drew her taser like a gunfighter, fired an imaginary dart, and blew on the barrel. "I'll zap you like a bug."

Though she said nothing, Miranda was incredulous. Appalled. This was the exact type of Draconian institutional abuse that her chapter of the Students Against Mass Incarceration had marched against.

"Last—and this is a pet peeve of mine—do not bang on my glass. Unless you're dying." She turned and glared up at the towering woman standing next to Miranda. "If I wanted to work around a bunch of zoo animals, I'd ask my shift commander to reassign me to the fourth floor."

Cornrows scowled but said nothing.

"Do we understand each other, ladies?" Instead of waiting for an answer, she leaned back into the officers' station and grabbed a printout. "Jones?"

"Yes ma'am," said the elderly woman.

"You're going to Red Three Low." She pointed to her left. "Right over there. The rest of y'all are going to the Orange side. Who's Bradshaw?"

Green Eyes stepped forward.

"You're moving to Five Upper." She frowned at her printout and looked up at the hulking figure standing next to Miranda. "Jackson?"

"Good guess," said the dyke.

She scratched her nose again. "Nebraska? Is that an alias?"

Her jaw worked. "Nah, it ain't no alias. It's what my momma named me. Why? You got a rule against that too? You gonna tase me cuz my name's Nebraska?"

"I might," she said, "especially if you keep on with that attitude."

The woman named Nebraska smirked. "Well, if you do, you make sure you give me all the electricity you've got in that little toy gun you so proud of. Zoo animals like me are a little harder to bring down than these domesticated bitches you've got up here. Facts."

Tension crackled in the ensuing standoff. Bad vibes washed over Miranda like a January wave in the Gulf. She had to say something. "Maybe we're all just tired and cranky—"

"Stay out of this!" snapped the guard. Her eyes locked on Nebraska. "What are you in here for? Robbery? Aggravated assault? Attempted murder?"

Nebraska's nostrils flared. "I don't do attempts."

Officer Woodley opened her mouth then closed it, then finally said, "Well, I'll just look your charges up on the computer."

"I'm sure you will."

"Orange Three Low," she icily read the bunk number from her printout. "But don't get too comfortable, I doubt you'll be there long."

Powerful shoulders shrugged.

The guard aimed her opiated pupils in Miranda's direction. "McGuire?"

"Yes ma'am."

"Hmmph . . . 'least somebody's got some manners." She slapped the paper against her palm. "Orange Nine Low."

Miranda looked over her shoulder through the thick wall of glass into what would be her home for the foreseeable future. At least until Nick figured out a way to get her out. The women of Blue Six Orange were congregating on the landing, smiling, scowling, watching, waiting. *Maybe it will be similar to a college dorm room,* she thought.

Officer Woodley walked back into the officers' station and leaned over the control panel. An orange painted steel door rumbled open. Miranda followed Nebraska and Rihanna into the holding cage. The door rumbled shut. As they waited for the bars to roll and release them into the pod, she felt the big woman glowering down at her. She ventured a glance. *Oh my gosh.* Such pain in those eyes. They held a lifetime of struggle, abuse, oppression, poverty, strife . . .

Instinctively, she reached up and touched her arm. "I don't think it was Ms. Woodley's intention to call you a zoo animal."

She frowned at Miranda's hand like it was a splat of bird shit on the sleeve of her jumpsuit. "Get your motherfuckin' hand off me, bitch."

10

Violent diarrhea surged through her bowels, jolting her awake. She sat straight up, her sweat-dampened hair compressed, sponge-like, against the overhead steel of the top bunk. Gripped by confusion and panic, her eyes darted around the alien landscape of the cell. A shaft of moonlight sliced through the mesh-plated window, illuminating the stainless toilet near the barred door.

She rolled out of the bunk and stumbled across the floor, hobbled by searing cramps. The blinding pain took her breath away. She tugged at the buttons of her jumpsuit, shedding it on the way, before crash landing on the frozen tundra of the toilet seat in the nick of time. The sloshing sound of water on water echoed from the walls and spilled through the bars out onto the catwalk.

Then came the vomit.

There was nothing she could do but open her trembling cramp-ridden legs and aim for the toilet. She puked all over herself. Luckily, it was mostly fluid and bile. It had been days since she had eaten.

Footsteps. Humming. The powerful scent of cologne washed through the cell bars. A flashlight beam fell over her. She covered herself with her hands. Another expulsion sluiced from her bowels.

"Well that's attractive," smirked the masculine silhouette on the other side of the flashlight.

Her humiliation was quickly strangled by her intestines. Her body tensed as another geyser of membranous bile rocketed up her esophagus and overflowed from her lips. She retched, coughed, spat, then wiped her mouth on the back of her hand. Mercifully, the flashlight moved on.

An army of chills burst forth from the sweaty pools of her collarbone, climbing over her shoulders and scampering down her back. She shivered as the storm subsided.

Silent darkness followed, broken only by the hollow drip of excreta that trickled from her body into the water below. She felt disgusting, she felt sticky, she felt weak, she felt . . .

Eyes on her.

She scanned the cell and found them hovering a few feet above her. Big owlish eyes in the face of a child. Toes curled over the side of the top bunk, skinny arms wrapped around skinny knees, hands clasped at the shins.

"Be careful you don't lose it," she cautioned. Her voice childlike and atmospheric, little more than a whisper.

Miranda frowned at the ethereal creature. "Excuse me?"

"You have to be careful," she repeated, "or you'll lose it."

"Lose what?"

"Your baby."

Miranda glanced at her concave stomach, slick with bile. "I'm not pregnant. Just a little dopesick."

The girl rocked herself on the edge of the bunk, entranced. "Your hair is red, like fire."

Just what we need, her inner narrator stirred, *a psycho cellmate.*

She covered her breasts and reached behind her for the toilet paper. "Would you mind giving me a few minutes of privacy?"

"It's okay," announced the girl, seeming to emerge from her mystic daze. "I'm not a lesbian. Officer Woodley hates lesbians. She says she likes to zap them with her stun gun. But I've never seen her do it."

"Good to know," said Miranda. "I just want to finish up down here. And it's a little awkward, wiping, with you . . . watching me."

"I wouldn't mind if you held my hand sometimes, though," the girl continued, unhearing, "like if it was thundering real hard outside."

Is this part of the nightmare? Miranda wondered as she cleaned herself.

"Are *you* a lesbian?" the girl asked.

Instead of answering, Miranda flushed the toilet. The powerful roar of institutional plumbing thundered beneath her. She could feel the centrifugal force pulling her against the cold seat. The thing could suck down a blanket. Rivulets of sweat and bile were vacuumed from her thighs. After a full thirty seconds, she glanced up at her cellmate, still babbling away. She reached behind her and hit the button a few more times. Then she struggled to her feet, dampened the toilet paper in the sink and cleaned the remaining vomit.

It was difficult to do in the dark, especially with her knees buckling from shooting pain and cramps. She gripped the stainless steel with one hand while dabbing at herself with the other. As the deafening roar of the toilet diminished, the girl's voice returned, fading in like a radio signal.

". . . she was gonna name me Sunset but then changed her mind at the last minute and named me Amity. Amity Davenport. It means friendship."

There was a sliver of soap in the sink, thin as a wafer of consecrated bread. She worked it between her hands and managed some weak suds which she then rubbed against her sickly sallow skin.

The girl hovered over her shoulder at the end of the top bunk, floating there like an apparition. "What's your name?"

"Miranda." She cupped sink water in her hands to rinse away the soap.

"Like Miranda Lambert?" said Amity.

She shook her head and squinted into a rusty reflectionless piece of metal that was bolted into the wall over the toilet. Even if the cell lights were on, she doubted she would be able to see herself. Probably for the best. "Miranda is one of five moons that orbit Uranus," she recited mechanically. The irony of spouting fun facts about moons and Uranus while naked and withdrawing over a county jail toilet had big scene potential. She made a mental note to remember it for the memoir. But then a round of cramps tore through her body like a power surge, overriding all mental activity with a white-hot explosion of pain. She gasped and gripped the sink as her knees buckled again. A fingernail splintered and chipped from the pressure.

"Are you okay?" The girl slid from the top bunk, landing nimbly on the balls of her feet. Unruly coils of frizzy black hair spiraled out in every direction, merging with the darkness. Her palm was cool against Miranda's shoulder blade. "You're sweating. Do you want me to wash your back?"

"No!" She spun around.

Amity's hand fell to her side. "I'm sorry."

Miranda grabbed her rumpled jumpsuit from the floor and hastily put it on, stealing glances at her cellmate as she fiddled with the buttons. She wore tattered thermal long johns bottoms and a sports bra. *Biracial or Latina?* It was difficult to tell. Her unblemished skin glowed like amber in the moonlight. Mocha-colored baby fat encircled her dimples. A full head shorter than Miranda's five feet six inches, Amity looked like she belonged in middle school, or summer camp . . . anywhere but the Escambia County jail.

The dreamlike image of her waving from the top tier on the day Miranda arrived pulled sharply into focus and held for a moment before fragmenting and finally disintegrating back into the murky depths of her subconscious. "How long have I been here?"

"Two days," said Amity. "But you haven't really been here. You've been asleep. That doesn't count. They can only hold us here when we're awake. Do you believe in astral projection? It's when the soul leaves the body . . ."

Instead of answering, Miranda staggered over to her bunk and sat down. *Two days. That meant it was—*

"So, what did they arrest you for?"

Miranda leaned back in her unmade bunk. "Heroin."

"Me too," said Amity.

"And a gun."

"Me too."

She closed her eyes. The four walls of the cell soon melted away. The nausea evaporated. The cramps diminished. The howling ache settled back into a whisper. Suddenly she was back in her car, staring down a narrow alley of adjacent apartment buildings, awaiting Nick's return. As she faded off to sleep, she wondered if she was astral projecting or merely dreaming.

11

"Wake up!" Amity tugged on her hand. "They're gonna leave if you don't hurry!"

She opened her eyes. A torrent of disturbed dust roiled up a shaft of sunlight.

"Come on," she implored, breathless with excitement. "If you don't come right now, you'll have to wait all the way till next week."

Her stomach churned with nausea. Her lips felt dry and cracked. "Come where?"

"Downstairs," she said, eyes shining. "Someone sent you a package!"

"Like . . . mail?"

A chaotic mass of black curls shook back and forth. "Uh uh. Shampoo, lotion . . . candy! A care package. Somebody loves you!"

Miranda stared blankly at the hyperventilating girl who was currently pulling her arm from the socket as the fuzzy details of the cell behind her sharpened into vaguely familiar landmarks: the mesh plated window slat, the steel desk bolted to the wall, the overhead fluorescent light, the toilet . . . *Somebody loves me?*

Her inner narrator scoffed. *I wouldn't bank on it.*

Amity released her hand and flew to the open cell door. "Yes ma'am. Miranda McGuire. She's coming right now." She looked over her shoulder and urged her to hurry with her eyes.

"Well if she ain't front and center in about thirty seconds," a voice shot back, "she can just get this shit on the next run. I ain't got all damn day."

Miranda swung her legs over the side of the bunk and stared down at her feet. *Somebody loves me? Like who?* She wiggled one foot into a shower scum-whitened croc, followed by the other. *My ice princess mother? My bipolar dad?*

The nice lady who gave me these socks? She stood up. The combination of lightheadedness and her rumbling stomach almost caused her to sit back down. But then a handsome smiling face cut through her thoughts like a blowtorch, stabilizing her unsteady legs, clearing her vision, filling her pounding heart with hope. *Nick!*

Amity was waiting on the tier. She clutched her wrist and led her past the open cell doors and down the stairs to the front of the pod where a humongous-boobed woman in a FloraBama t-shirt was frowning through the bars.

"McGuire?"

Miranda nodded.

"Took your sweet fucking time, didn't you?"

Everything about her was overpowering and boisterous. Her energy, her language, her boobs. "Sorry," said Miranda. "I'm sick."

"I'm sick, I'm sick," the woman mimicked. "You weren't sick when you were out there selling your ass for—" Her words were drowned out by a sudden bronchial explosion. Her face turned purple. Her unrestrained breasts convulsed beneath her t-shirt. Miranda took a step back from the bars. When the coughing died down, the woman finished her sentence, "—crack!" Then she turned to the trustee in the hall, a petite blonde with broom straw stuck through her eyebrow piercings and cobalt nautical stars tattooed on her elbows. "Baby, hand me that last bag."

She tore open the plastic and dumped the contents on her cart, separating the items. Then she snatched off a triplicate receipt that was stapled to the bag and began to read. "Okay. One Irish Spring soap . . ." she pushed the green box forward.

Amity elbowed her in the ribs and held out a dingy yellowed pillowcase.

"Well," the woman snarled, "are you gonna fucking admire it all morning or are you gonna drop it in the damn bag?"

"Oh." Miranda grabbed the soap. "Sorry."

She rolled her eyes and exchanged looks with her trustee. Then she checked the next items off the receipt. "One shampoo, one condish, one lotion."

Miranda dropped them in the pillowcase. Zip, zip, zip.

Look at you, her inner narrator piped up, *ever the little people pleaser. This bitch mocks your voice, insinuates that you prostitute yourself for crack, talks to you like you're an idiot, as if she's the honor student and you're the middle-aged jail employee. Yet here you are, raking it in as fast as she can count it. Maybe she'll give you a gold star or a pat on the head. Maybe one day you can take Broomstraw's place and she'll call you baby. Dream big, Miranda. Aim high.*

"Three Twix, three Mounds, three Almonds, three Milkys, three Butters . . ."

Amity elbowed her again. "Butterfingers," she mouthed without volume, eyes dancing.

"Three Reeses, ten cocoas, ten coffees," she pushed the last items forward and slapped the receipt on the cart with her pen. "Sign your name by the X."

Miranda scribbled her signature without thinking, the same signature she had been scrawling on essays and exams and love notes since elementary school.

"Aww, look Shyla . . ." She held up the receipt for her trustee. "She dots her i's with little hearts. How sweet."

She felt her face flush with humiliation. "Um, do you have any idea who sent this? I didn't see a name on the—"

"How the fuck should I know? Go check the kiosk like a normal inmate."

Miranda flinched but persevered. "Well, um, I was just wondering if you had the info there in your paperwork. I think it came from Nick Archiletta, but I'm not sure . . . Could you check?"

Amity tugged at the sleeve of her jumpsuit. "Come on, Miranda."

The woman detached the yellow copy of the receipt and leaned toward the bars. "You didn't see his name on this?"

Miranda shook her head. "That section was blank."

She leaned closer, massive breasts squished against the steel. "Is this Nick your boyfriend?"

Miranda shrugged and attempted a smile. "It's complicated."

"Hmm, complicated," she sighed. "Well I'm no expert on these types of things, but if I had to guess, I would say that right now . . . Nick is balls deep . . . in your sister."

Her neck fat gyrated as she threw back her head and cackled maniacally which quickly turned into violent hacking.

Miranda's fists clenched. Her jaw trembled. She didn't have a sister, but that was beside the point. "You. You're a horrible person."

The hacking died away. She cleared her throat and swallowed the remaining phlegm. "So says the criminal."

12

Amity led her down the last few steps into the dayroom where a number of hard-faced women sat watching *The View* on television. Meghan and Sunny were going back and forth about the Democratic primaries. Miranda paused at the mention of Bernie Sanders.

"Girl, if you don't get your little flat ass from in front of that TV!"

She turned and noticed Nebraska among the women on the bench. Her jumpsuit was tied around her waist and the sleeves of her t-shirt were rolled up to showcase her powerful biceps. She appeared to have picked up some muscle mass while Miranda was sleeping.

"Oh." She tiptoed out of the way. "Sorry."

"Stankin' skin ass cracker," Nebraska grumbled as she positioned herself for a set of pushups.

Miranda frowned and sniffed her arm. "Do I really smell that bad?"

"Don't worry," said Amity, leading her away from the television. "She says that to me, too."

She hefted the pillowcase over her shoulder and surveyed the pod with sober eyes for the first time. A total of twelve cells—six upstairs, six down—faced a wall of plexiglass across the unit. In the space in between, 24 women talked, watched TV, played cards, exercised, bathed, video visited with their children, talked on the phone, ate, paced, and waited.

The kiosk was on the back wall behind the shower, a bulky monstrosity encased in steel with a bulletproof monitor and a metal keyboard. She handed the pillowcase to Amity and typed in her name. After a series of questions, she was allowed access. There was a single message in her inbox.

Hey Andy. Dad here. I sent you a package off the jail website. Hope you received it. I'm guessing you're having a pretty rough go of it right now, coming off the pills and all. I read on the internet that people withdrawing from opioids crave chocolate. Hope the candy bars help. At any rate you won't be there long. Dad's got a plan. Hang in there.

"Oohhh, a plan!" a voice behind her whispered. "What kind of plan?"

Miranda glanced over her shoulder.

"Sorry," Amity quickly looked away from the message on the screen. "Do you wanna split a candy bar?"

Her stomach rumbled in response.

"I'll take that as a yes." She watched as her cellmate dug around in the pillowcase, found a Butterfinger and snapped it in half before peeling off the wrapper. "Here."

"Um . . . thanks?"

"No problem," Amity smiled, her teeth already covered in chocolate. "So your dad thinks you won't be here long. Awesomesauce! I doubt I'll be here long either."

Miranda nibbled on the candy bar. It hurt to chew. "My dad is bipolar."

"Me too."

"Well then you know all about the wild schemes and delusions of grandeur."

Nebraska swaggered over, dripping sweat and pumped from a morning of pushups, her ebony skin like polished ceramic. She reached inside the pillowcase and grabbed a Twix.

"Hey!" Amity protested.

"Shut your stank little half-breed ass up." She rose to her full height, towering over the tiny girl. "This shit ain't yours no way."

"It's fine," said Miranda. "You can have it. I don't have much of an appetite anyway."

"I know," Nebraska smiled. "I've been eating your trays since Monday. That was you throwing up the other night too. I heard you after lights out. Dog food got you like that, don't it?"

"I'm sorry. Did you say dog food?"

"That's what you was on out there, right? That good dog food? You sure act like it."

The image of a greasy pink mound of Alpo, heaped and quivering in a dish, invaded her mind. So vivid she could smell it. Her stomach lurched. "Gross! Is that, like, a thing? I would never even consider eating dog food."

Nebraska erupted in laughter. "For real? Girl, you is green as a pool table and twice as square! Facts."

"Actually," Miranda pointed out, "pool tables are rectangular."

"Shut up." She reached back into the pillowcase, fumbled around and came away with the lotion. "Hey baby! Bring your little ashy self out here."

Moments later, the woman with the tight jumpsuit and Rihanna eyes emerged from the corner cell.

Baby? Her inner narrator raised an eyebrow. *Hmm . . . apparently we were the only ones listening to Officer Woodley's orientation monologue.*

"Hold out your hand." Nebraska squirted a healthy amount in her palm before chucking the bottle back in the pillowcase. "Let me know if you need some help rubbing that in."

She smiled and rolled her eyes as she sauntered back to her cell. Nebraska watched her all the way then turned to Miranda. "In my hood, dog food is boi, heroin, dope."

"Oh." She made a mental note. "Well, I'm definitely not into that. Just pills."

"Same shit." Nebraska yawned and walked off.

"See?" Amity said when she was out of earshot. "She called me stinky too. She says that about everybody. Well, everybody except . . ." She motioned toward Rihanna's cell.

Miranda watched her stroll over to the television and change the channel, defiantly facing down the women on the bench, daring them to object.

"I can't stand her," said Amity.

"She's probably had a difficult life."

"That's no excuse. My life is difficult too and I don't act like that." Her top lip curled in disgust. "But at least you won't have to deal with her for very long. You'll be out of here soon. What do you think your dad's plan is?"

"Who knows?" Miranda took a final nibble of the candy bar and passed her the remainder. "It probably has something to do with Powerball or the World Series of Poker or Publishers Clearing House Sweepstakes."

13

Ancient gears and chains creaked and groaned as the cell doors on the sixth floor rolled shut and locked into place.

She sat on the desk, feet on the metal stool, knees and forehead pressed against the diamond-shaped mesh that covered the window. Six stories below, the streaking lights of Fairfield Drive pulsed in the night like some high-fidelity equalizer. Headlights, taillights, police lights, traffic lights, neon lights . . . yet it was all so surreal without the soundtrack. Like a movie on mute. No revving engines, no honking horns, no wailing sirens. Nothing could penetrate the thick plexiglass and sarcophagal concrete walls of the jail.

A homeless man in camo pants and a sleeveless hoodie pushed his empty grocery cart into the twitchy yellow circumference of a streetlight. He inched across the pool hall parking lot beside the jail and disappeared behind a dumpster. She tracked him with envy. Even homelessness looked appealing from the window of a cell.

As the last traces of opiates evaporated from her bloodstream and the withdrawals settled into a more tolerable nausea, her circadian rhythm also leveled out. She spent less time asleep and more time staring at the peeling paint on the wall that bordered her bunk, more time staring out the window, more time thinking.

How did this happen? Wasn't I just at Starbucks studying for Dr. Bonilla's sociology exam? Wasn't I just on my couch watching Netflix while Nick mumbled along with the rap song playing in his headphones? Nick . . . weren't we just making love in the back seat of my car? Now it's all slipping away. School, my Pell Grant, my apartment, my car, my dreams, my future, my freedom.

Tears slid down her face and crashed against her kneecaps, melting into the faded green material of her jumpsuit like rain on pavement. She scanned the night sky for a star but couldn't find one. *Come on Nick . . . where are you? I'm scared.*

The cell door rattled behind her. In the window's reflection she caught a glimpse of Officer Woodley making her 10 p.m. security check. The lights would be going out soon. It bothered her that she knew this. To acknowledge the schedule—the meals, the counts, the security checks, the television shows—was to surrender to the mechanical monotony of jail life and accept her new identity: inmate.

She glanced over at her bunk. At the head, beneath the mattress, was the Gideon King James Bible where she hid Detective Sandifer's business card. It was not too late. She chewed her bottom lip. *Yeah, but then what? It's not as simple as just giving his name. There will be taped statements, written statements, sworn statements, court hearings, testimonies, cross examinations, ". . . and is the man to whom the drugs and gun belonged sitting in this courtroom, Ms. McGuire?"*

Could she do that? Could she calmly raise her finger and point out Nick in a court of law? He said that with his record, they would put him away for life. Could she live with that on her conscience?

It was his shit, her inner narrator argued, *better him than you.*

"Are you talking to yourself?" Amity peeked out from under her blanket.

"It's called *thinking,*" she slid off the desk and climbed into her bunk. "Everyone does it. Don't make it weird. It's weird enough in this place as it is."

"Jail isn't weird," said Amity, "just cruel, and lonely, and cold. Trust me, I know all about weird. I grew up around palm readers, fortune tellers, carnival people. You should see my great-grandmother Tita's basement. She lives in Akron, Ohio. I once found a cobra head in a bottle of brine down there. Talk about weird. When I asked what it was, she said it helped old men get boners."

"Gross," said Miranda.

"Yeah. I guess the Roma don't trust Viagra. You know who Roma are, right? Gypsies like me. Well, at least my mother's side of the family. They're from Romania. Know where that is?"

"Eastern Europe," she said to the steel underside of the top bunk which looked more and more like a coffin lid as days passed. "One of the Balkan states. Capital, Bucharest."

"Wow." Amity's inverted face hung over the side. "You should go on *Jeopardy*. I can barely remember the capital of *Florida*. Jail blocks my brainwaves."

The cell lights clicked off.

Miranda smiled and rolled over. "Wake me up for breakfast, okay? Nebraska doesn't need any more extra trays. She's got enough muscles as it is."

"Kay," Amity giggled and settled back in her bunk.

She closed her eyes. "Goodnight, Amity."

"Night."

Toilets flushed, sink water ran, and conversations died down as the women of Blue Six prepared for bed. Someone was already snoring downstairs.

Her thoughts reverted to Nick. *I don't want to tell on him. And I definitely don't want him to be sent away for life. I just want him to hurry up and get me out of here so we can hire an attorney to right this. Together. Preferably before midterms.*

The words were still warm in her mind when her breathing leveled, and she began to drift down the river between sentience and sleep. Slowly, the walls disintegrated, the bars became columns of sand, and her apprehension burst into a colony of monarchs which fluttered away on a breeze.

"Gabriella?"

Her eyes snapped open. "Huh?"

The top bunk was squeaking. "I didn't mean to. It was an accident. Please don't . . ."

Muffled laughter trickled down the wing. "Mommy, help! It's cold in here."

"I'm sorry," Amity wailed, her voice drenched in agony.

"Momma," another voice wafted through the cell bars. "Get me out of here. Don't leave me."

"I can't," Amity sobbed. "I can't."

More squeaking from above. The bolts groaned in protest. Tentatively, Miranda stood, expecting cramps but feeling none. The cold concrete floor was like a hockey rink beneath her bare feet. When her eyes adjusted to the darkness, she found her cellmate hunched over and rocking her pillow in the corner.

"I can't," she kept repeating. "It's too late."

"Hey." Miranda reached for her. "It's okay. Do you hear me? It's not real. You're just having a moment. Look at me. It's okay."

"Mommy," the voice returned. "I can't feel my toes."

More laughter. She rocked the pillow harder, her eyes wide with fear, panic, desperation. "Gabriella," she whispered.

"Ignore that," Miranda patted her knee. "It's okay. Look at me. I'm right here."

"Mommy, I'm freezing—"

"Enough!" Miranda marched across the cell to the bars, rattling them for emphasis. "You don't have anything better to do? Get a life, you fucking losers!"

A few cells down, someone snorted. "Really? We're defending Amityville now? A baby killer?"

Amity whimpered behind her, low and mournful. The final shards of glass that fell from an already shattered heart.

Nebraska's voice boomed from the bottom tier. "Shut the fuck up and go to sleep! Or you gonna need somebody to defend *your* stank ass when they pop these doors in the morning and I break this size ten croc off in it. Facts!"

Miranda lingered a moment before turning back to Amity who had managed to wedge her tiny frame even further into the corner, eyes vacant, lip quivering, still rocking her pillow.

"Hey," she waved a hand in front of her face. "Can you hear me in there?"

"It's too late," Amity kept mumbling, miles away. "Too late."

Miranda stepped on the bottom bunk and vaulted herself up. She crawled over next to Amity, leaned against the wall and rubbed her arms. "Wow, it is cold up here. No wonder you're always wrapped in that blanket."

"Too cold," she echoed softly. "Too late."

Her inner narrator stirred. *Way to go, Ginger Zee. Keep on with the climate chat and she may never snap out of it.*

"I mean the vent," Miranda pointed at the metal grill above the cell door. A stubborn shred of toilet paper clung to a slat and danced in the jet stream. "I guess they pump in the arctic air to cut down on bacteria. Makes sense. Plus, they probably like us shivering in our beds. Less work for them, right?"

Her discarded blanket lay tangled between them. Miranda shook it out over the side of the bunk and gently wrapped it around her trembling shoulders.

"It was an accident," she said, her voice barely registering. "I would never . . ."

Miranda pulled her close and began to rock her as she rocked the pillow. "Shhh, I know. It's okay. They were just being cruel . . . and unconscious. It's over now."

Hot tears spilled on her hand. "It will never be over."

"Yes it will." Miranda rested her chin atop Amity's curls, brushing them back from her eyes. "I'm here now."

"You'll be gone soon. Your dad is gonna bond you out."

"IF I bond out," said Miranda, "it won't be because of my father."

And let's be honest, her inner narrator added, *Nick is starting to look like a longshot too.*

"Yeah, but he said . . ."

"I know what he said." Rocking her slower now, she stared into the dark. "My dad has always been a terrific promise-maker but a terrible promise-keeper."

"Well at least he was nice enough to send you some candy bars."

Miranda released her and leaned back against the wall, glad that she was communicating, grateful that she had emerged from the hellscape of her past. "Wanna hear a story about my dad?"

Amity responded by laying her head on her shoulder.

"Ten years ago, he was the best mechanic in Car City. No one could turn a wrench like Patrick McGuire and I'm not just saying that because he's my dad. It was common knowledge. He could fix any problem on any make or model before other mechanics could figure out what was wrong. He used to work on our neighbor's car for free. Just so he didn't have to drive me to school. He was even the crew chief for some racecar driver at the Snowball Derby for a couple of years . . . until he got fired for gambling."

Amity shifted beside her. "Why? Is it bad to gamble on racecars?"

"It is when you're gambling against your own driver." The memory of her parents arguing that night flickered in her mind. Larger than life shadows clashing on the living room wall as she peeked over the banister. "Victoria left a few months after that. She ran off with some Republican from California with a double chin and a combover."

"Who's Victoria?"

"My mother."

"Is your dad handsome?"

"I don't know. He's my dad." Another image, this one of her father grinning beneath the hood of her Avalon, his stubbled face streaked with grease, perpetual cigarette dangling from his mouth. "But compared to Chase Echelhardt, he's George Clooney."

"Your dad looks like George Clooney?"

"Sorta," said Miranda, "like a Southern, WD-40'd, chain-smoking version. More *O Brother, Where Are Thou?* than *Ocean's Eleven.*"

"I love that movie," Amity sighed, her recent trauma seemingly forgotten. "So why did your mom leave?"

"Money," she said. "My parents *worked* at a car dealership. Chase Echelhardt owned one. He was a millionaire. And when he strolled into the finance department of Enfinger Automotive and flirted with Victoria, he must've looked like one of those lifeboats on the *Titanic.* She jumped."

"Your mother is a millionaire?"

"She married one." Miranda shrugged. "But calling her a mother is like calling Donald Trump a president."

"Donald Trump *is* the president."

"Not to me," she yawned. "Anyway, after that my dad never totally recovered. He started staying up all night, missing work, bouncing from dealership to dealership. The gambling got out of control, too. By the time I was ten, he was taking off for Biloxi for days at a time. Sometimes he'd come home with hundred-dollar bills falling out of his pockets, but mostly he'd return grumpy and penniless."

"He was sad because she left him."

Miranda shook her head. "I used to think so. But looking back, I'm pretty sure he saw Victoria as a prison guard. And when she ran off, he just sorta . . . exploded. Things got consistently worse. The year I turned twelve, we had to skip Christmas. We were on the verge of losing everything when I googled his symptoms and discovered he was bipolar. I threatened to have him Baker-Acted and put myself into foster care if he didn't get on medication."

"Wow," said Amity. "You were bossy."

"That's a derogatory term for young girls with leadership traits," said Miranda. "But if by bossy you mean *taking charge*, then yes, I was. I had aspirations for student government, honor society, college. But we could barely even keep the power on. And my school clothes were embarrassing. So I gave him that ultimatum."

"And?"

"And the next morning we went to the walk-in clinic at Lakeview. It took all day, but he was eventually diagnosed and prescribed meds. Two weeks later he got a job at a mechanic shop in Cantonment."

Amity leaned into her. "That's awesome."

"Not really," said Miranda. "Things would be way more awesome if he stopped going off his medication, bouncing from job to job and disappearing on gambling binges every time his life settles into a normal, predictable routine. But he is doing much better. I'll give him that. I'm not being negative. You've just brought up his message a couple of times now, and I wanted you to understand why I'm not turning cartwheels over his big plan. He has a history of not coming through."

"I understand," Amity said.

"I, on the other hand, am a woman of my word." Miranda patted her bony, long john covered knee. "And when I tell you I'm here, that will be true whether I'm sleeping in the bunk below you . . . or at home in my own bed. We're friends now. No turning back."

A flashlight clanged against the bars. Its white beam swept over the cell before it found them huddling in the top bunk. Amity buried her face in the crook of Miranda's neck as she squinted into the light.

Officer Woodley's bun resembled a samurai topknot in the back glow. "What the hell is going on in here?"

Miranda braced for the bolt of electricity that would be coming any second. "We're having a rough night."

After a pause, she aimed the flashlight at the floor and sighed. "Yeah, I heard 'em on the intercom. Damned nest of vipers. Davenport, are you all right?"

"Yes ma'am," said Amity.

She scratched her nose.

Wow, Miranda thought. *Again?* A familiar ache welled within her as she guessed at Woodley's pill of choice. *Probably Lortab . . . lightweight.*

"My next security check is in an hour," she said. "Make sure you're in your own bunk when I come back through."

Her footsteps retreated down the catwalk.

Amity hugged her pillow and whispered. "See? She's not so bad."

"Not at all," Miranda agreed. *She'd be even better if she shared her hydrocodone.*

A hand found hers in the dark. Small clammy fingers wrapped around her knuckles and pressed into her palm. "Do you wanna hear about the man who raised me?"

14

"My mom's maiden name is Evans," said Amity. "Monica Evans. I know what you're thinking. Monica Evans is a blue-eyed blonde American name. Not some gypsy girl."

"Actually—"

"Evanovich." Amity squeezed her hand. "My great-grandparents were Bache and Tita Evanovich. They Americanized the family name when they arrived in New York after World War II. Do you know anything about gypsies?"

Miranda was embarrassed to admit she did not. Only because she prided herself on knowing at least a little something about everything. "Um . . . aren't they like wanderers?"

"We are," said Amity. "A thousand years ago we wandered all the way from India to Europe. Least that's what Tita says. But sometimes it's hard to know if she's stretching the truth. I'm not even sure if she knows. When you've been telling the same stories for over a hundred years, they kinda become true to you whether they happened or not."

"A hundred years?" Miranda glanced over at her. "How old is she?"

"Nobody knows. She gives different ages. 108 one year, an even 100 the next. The oldest she ever told me she was 117. I know she's still alive though. Gabriella would've told me if she died."

Gabriella. Miranda shivered. *Infant poltergeist clairvoyant.*

"One truth I know for a fact that she wasn't stretching was her time in Nazi concentration camps. She showed me the serial number tattoos and everything."

"Your great grandmother is Jewish? I thought you said she was a gypsy."

"She is. Jews may have suffered the most under Hitler, but they weren't the only ones who suffered. More than 100,000 Roma were slaughtered too, with thousands more thrown in camps. Mostly Sinti. Gypsy is a derogatory term by the way." A sad smile flickered in the dark. "Like bossy."

Miranda was enthralled by the history lesson. The aspiring novelist in her could almost hear the gnarled and ancient Tita as she spoke of life in the old country to her wide-eyed great-granddaughter. She imagined a golden hoop earring dangling from a headwrap, gleaming in the candlelight as heavily accented memories slipped through crooked yellow teeth and wrinkled lips, filling the Ohio basement like a scratched old phonograph.

"Tita had one son, George," said Amity, "my grandfather. In our culture the sons remain with their parents. Even after they marry. Wives move in, children are born, the sons stay and the daughters are married off. Usually for a fee. Most of our marriages are arranged."

"That sounds horrible," said Miranda. "Arranged marriages for a fee? That's almost like human trafficking."

Amity shrugged. "It's the way we've always done things. Believe me, my mom hated it too. But I'll get to that in a minute. So for years Grandfather George ran an oddities tent in a traveling carnival—"

"Oddities?"

"You know. Siamese twins, snakewomen, sword swallowers, fire eaters, stuff like that. That's how he met my grandmother. She was a palm reader."

Miranda felt like she was peeking beneath a canvas flap into a parallel universe. "I didn't know those were still around."

"Palm readers?" Amity shot her a skeptical look. "That's pretty much every aunt and cousin in my family. I was raised by fortune tellers."

"No, I meant the freakshows," said Miranda, immediately regretting the political incorrectness of her words.

"The oddities, I mean. I didn't realize that was still a thing."

"They're around." Her voice grew wistful and faraway. "Mostly on the small-town county fair circuit down here in the south. But you're right, they *are* dying out. A lot of that stuff is fake anyway. And bearded women and grossly obese men are way less fascinating since the internet. Anita—that's my grandmother—she talked Grandfather George into going into games and concessions a few years after my mother was born, so I missed that era. Although sometimes, when we visited Tita, I'd awake to some strange guests crashing on her couch. A tiny woman, a green-skinned man. Visitors from the sideshow days."

Miranda was captivated. Caught up in the cinematography of her own imagination. There was something literary about the world Amity described. A world rich in texture, dark and arcane, a world begging to be transcribed into prose. Carnival life, gypsy life, gothic Americana. She ached for her MacBook.

"You're not falling asleep, are you?"

"Uh uh." Miranda opened her eyes. "I was just picturing what you were saying."

"Well, see if you can picture my mom," said Amity. "She looks just like me, only beautiful. And stubborn. Everyone says she gets that from Tita. Gypsy women are not known for their disobedience."

"I thought you said the word *gypsy* is culturally insensitive."

"It is," said Amity. "Tita says that it comes from half-wits in the dark ages who just assumed our Indian ancestors were from Egypt because of their darker complexions. *Egypt* and *Gypsy*. They are kinda similar. She hates the word. I don't really care. It's what the whole world calls us. Anyway, I was just trying to get you back for *bossy*."

Miranda smiled and shook her head.

"So when my mom hit her teens, men started noticing her. You know how confusing that age can be." She paused; a heavy silence fell over the cell. When she spoke again, her words were monotone and flat. The playful tone from moments before iced over and withered like dead branches on a tree. Summer to winter in the space of a breath.

"Most of the attention came in quick glances from strangers buying cotton candy and elephant ears at Grandfather's concession stand. Perverts and weirdos staring at her legs and looking down her shirt. Carnival kids began to notice her too. All of a sudden, teenage boys were fighting each other to help my grandparents set up the tents. By her sixteenth birthday, Grandfather George was fielding some serious offers."

"Offers for his daughter?" Miranda's blood began to boil. "Like she was some bike on Craigslist?"

"Like I said, it's the way we've always done things."

"Um . . . so was slavery and child labor and oppression and tyranny and . . . and . . . bleeding people as a legitimate medical practice, until someone finally came along and said *enough!"*

"Yeah," Amity nodded to herself. "That would be my mom. Grandfather eventually settled on a man named Ghitsa, the nephew of one of his old business partners in Akron. Tita told me his family put up twenty thousand dollars, but she might've been stretching the truth again. Seems like a lot of money."

For a human life? thought Miranda. *For an only daughter? Twenty thousand dollars is a preowned car with low mileage, a down payment on a three-bedroom house, a couple of semesters at a state university. Not a sixteen-year-old girl.*

"When the carnival was passing through Ohio, Ghitsa and his father paid a visit. Mom hated them on sight. Her husband-to-be was a small man with cruel eyes who grunted and smacked while he ate. His father spent the evening ogling her like a piece of meat and pinching her every time she passed between the kitchen and the dining room table."

"What did her mother think about that?"

Amity shrugged. "I don't know. I wasn't even born yet. But the story goes that the next night, Mom put on her scarves and makeup and perfume and slipped into the fortune teller's booth. When a tall, handsome biker showed up reeking of liquor and wired on crystal, she traced a seductive black nail over his palm and told him his future. That he would be leaving the fairgrounds with a beautiful young gypsy on the back of his motorcycle."

"Good for her," said Miranda. "I think."

"The biker's name was Jaime Davenport. He was the leader of a small outfit from Detroit called Blackguard Motorcycle Club. You've probably never heard of them."

Miranda realized this was a question and shook her head. "Uh uh." She couldn't name a motorcycle gang if her bond money depended on it.

"Anyway, she took off with them and disappeared into the underworld. Grandfather was PISSED. By the following summer my grandmother, the most respected seer in the clan, was saying she no longer felt Mom's presence on this plane and pronounced her dead. But then one night three years later, Tita got a collect call from an unlisted number in Mission, Texas. Mom was in a battered women's shelter with a broken jaw, a fractured skull and cigarette burns all over her. She was also seven months pregnant . . . with me."

"Oh my God!" Miranda gasped. "What did they do to her?"

"My father, Jaime Davenport died in a motorcycle accident. After that happened, I think the remaining members may have taken her *Property of BMC* tattoo a little too literally." Amity rested her head against the cinderblock wall and took an audible breath. "The wounded animal who stepped off the Greyhound was nothing like the feisty girl who ran away. Maybe Grandmother's pronouncement of death was not so far off. She was just dead on the inside."

"Poor thing."

"Yeah. Grandfather sent word to Ghitsa Toth who was still unmarried and still very interested. Not interested enough to fork over twenty grand though. Not for a pregnant runaway with a wired jaw and a biker tattoo. He made a thousand dollar offer and Grandfather snapped it up. A week after I was born, we were shipped off to northeast Ohio."

Aside from a senior trip to Washington, D.C., Miranda had never been ten miles from the Gulf Coast. But she could see Akron in her mind. It felt . . . *brown*. She imagined skies thick with billowing factory smoke, dirty snow on empty streets lined with boarded windows. "Were these carnival people also?"

She shook her head. "Roofers. But it was just Ghitsa. By the time we moved in, his father had passed away and he was running the family business on his own. I . . ."

Her words fell still. Miranda knew better than to speak. The storyteller in her sensed a revelation gathering in the quiet.

"I think maybe it was because Mom was so cold. She just went into a shell. You know how people have vibrations? Hers was like white noise. Snow on an old television set. Basically nothing. Until you touched her. Then it was like . . . high voltage."

She thought of Victoria. What was her own mother's vibration? Something frigid and reptilian. Avarice, deceit, ruthlessness, selfishness.

Amity's voice pulled her back into the present. "But I'm pretty sure that's why he started sneaking into my room at night."

It took a second for the gravity of her words to register. *Sneaking into my . . .* Slowly, she turned toward her cellmate. "How old were you?"

"The first time? I don't know. Third grade?"

"Oh my God." She pulled her close, smoothing her unruly hair again as she rocked her like a little sister, rocked her like a third grader. She had once read that 90 percent of incarcerated women were victims of sexual abuse, usually by someone in the household. But statistics were just numbers. Soulless symbols on a printed page. Here was a fractured human being. Living proof of the devastating effects of abuse. Up until that moment she merely tolerated Amity. Half dismissing her as immature and flighty. Now, even in the yawning darkness of a cell, she could see the wide-eyed innocence for what it was: a coping mechanism. She was clinging to the childhood that was ripped away when she was eight years old. Her cellmate was a survivor.

She didn't know the half of it.

"I used to stay up late listening for his footsteps. Hoping he wouldn't come. Sometimes he didn't. Sometimes weeks would pass. That was almost worse. The waiting. The not knowing. Have you ever noticed that? Like with bad stuff? That the fear leading up to the moment can be more terrifying than the moment itself? It definitely lasts longer. For me it lasted all the way up until the day I was arrested."

Miranda thought about the *post* in post-traumatic stress disorder. How oftentimes the prefix was misleading. Especially in situations like Amity's where the trauma was ongoing.

"He was strong for his size. Not that it took much to overpower me. I wasn't even nine years old when it started. No match for a grown man."

"Of course not," said Miranda.

"His hands were always calloused from working on roofs. The dead skin was sharp and would sometimes leave scratches on my face and throat. It got so bad that my teacher called the house. Of course, he answered the phone and lied on the spot. He told her I had a pet kitty that hadn't been declawed yet. He even brought one home the next day to back up his story. Abigail, I named her. Crabby Abby. He threatened to crush her skull if I opened my mouth."

"What an asshole."

"Yeah. He also threatened to poison my mom, burn down Tita's house, and sell me to his cousin in Romania who wasn't nearly as gentle as he was. That was right before he clapped a hand over my mouth and put my front tooth through my top lip."

"My God." Miranda pulled her closer. "What did your mom say?"

"Same thing she always said. Nothing. She was lost in her own little world. Between her depression and the daily slog of household chores, she barely noticed I was there. It went on like that for years. All the way up until just before my sixteenth birthday . . . when he got me pregnant."

Sixteen couldn't have been too long ago. "How old are you now?"

"Twenty."

Older than I am, thought Miranda, *yet she could pass for twelve.* "How long have you been in here?"

"Two years."

She shook her head. She wasn't even at the two-*week* mark and it felt like an eternity.

"I had no idea. Even when I was late. Even when I was sick. Even when I was starting to show. I just thought I was getting fat. I *wanted* to get fat. Maybe that would keep him out of my room at night. I guess I had a block or something. Mom noticed though. Isn't that crazy? All those years of white noise then one night I was coming out of the bathroom and she was standing there in the hall. She reached out and put her hand on my stomach. First time I ever remember her touching me. I'll never forget the look on her face. You have to remember she was not an expressive person. But there was murder in her eyes that night.

"Later when my door pushed open, I thought it was him. But when I peeked from under my blanket, Mom was standing there. I could see the blood on the front of her shirt. She told me we were leaving and there was no time to pack. I wrapped the blanket around me, grabbed

Crabby Abby and followed her barefoot out into the snow. Just before I closed the door, I glanced into the kitchen and saw him dying . . . Flopping like a fish on the bloody floor. Slapping at the steak knife in his back, buried to the handle.

"We took his truck. I'm not sure if Mom had ever driven before that night. At first I didn't think we were gonna make it to the end of the street. But by the time the sun came up we were halfway through Kentucky. It took us three days to get here. She drove all the way to the Gulf then parked the truck and stared out at the waves like she wanted to keep going.

"We got jobs at a maid service, cleaning condos in Perdido Key. There was no way I was enrolling in school down here. It was too late for an abortion, and being the new girl with a baby was . . . too awful to even think about.

"We slept in the truck for two weeks, living off whatever food we could scrounge in the timeshares and washing our clothes on the job. First payday, we found a two-bedroom house in Navy Point. The landlord was a hairstylist named Ray. Gay Ray. Every time he came to collect the rent, he'd have this little snow-white French Bulldog in the crook of his arm. Jiles. When Gabriella was born, he knitted her a pink onesie with matching footsies.

"I didn't know how I was going to feel about my baby. I was worried she'd have his face. But all that fear and worry went away the very second the nurse placed her tiny body in my arms. I never felt love until that moment. She was the most beautiful little miracle I had ever seen. Six pounds, nine ounces of pure sweetness. She even made

Mom smile. If you knew my mother, you'd understand how impossible that is. Everybody loved Gabriella.

"I never went back to work. I kept planning to, but I couldn't tear myself from my daughter. Every day was a new breakthrough. Her first smile, her first crawl, her first word. I wished Tita could know her but any contact with our old life was too risky. The Roma are too tight knit for secrets. Mom had killed her husband. Killed him for what he did to me. At least that's what I believed at the time. All the way up till the morning I heard boots on the porch.

"Looking back, I think I just wanted to believe he was dead. Closed chapter, nightmare over, you know? But when I looked through the blinds and saw Ghitsa creeping around the side of the house, it all came rushing back. Gabriella picked up on my fear and started crying. I covered her mouth and rocked her. *Shhhhh.* She started screaming. I could hear the twigs snapping as he passed the kitchen window. I didn't know what to do. I couldn't let what happened to me happen to her. I panicked. The cabinets were too thin. He'd hear her crying. I ran to the refrigerator. There was no room. So I grabbed the rug from in front of the sink, wrapped it round her blanket and opened the freezer.

"It was supposed to be just for a second, just until he looked through the back door and saw that no one was home. I didn't know the door was unlocked. He found me hiding under the table."

Miranda had never felt so powerless. Powerless to help little Gabriella, powerless to help Amity, powerless to do anything other than listen as this horror story vaulted to its tragic ending.

"He pulled me out into the center of the floor by my hair, muttering in Romanian, calling me every name for whore in existence. *Slut, harlot, prostitute, hooker, tart, adulteress . . .*" Her tears dampened the collar of Miranda's jumpsuit. "Then he did to me, what he'd been doing my entire life . . . Did it to me while my baby was dying a few feet away."

"What happened to him?"

"He took off. My best guess is Romania, but I don't really know. I hope he is. I hope he's a million miles away. As soon as he got off me, I ran to the freezer. It was too late. She was blue. I was still rocking her on the floor when Ray came over to collect the rent. That's how he found us."

15

Violent clashes in Hong Kong, North Korean missile launches, trade wars, police shootings, migrant children sleeping in cages. The world as experienced through the lens of a news camera was a terrifying and depressing place.

Nebraska elbowed her in the arm, almost knocking her off the bench. "You got any more of them candy bars?"

Miranda shook her head.

Although oppressive and confrontational with the personality of a steamroller, Nebraska Jackson did have a few redeeming qualities. One was her unwavering insistence on watching the news. She had no qualms whatsoever about walking straight up to the television in the middle of a Lifetime movie and changing the channel. "Y'all watch this bullshit all day long," she'd say as women slunk back to their cells, muttering under their collective breath. "News time is my time, bitches. Y'all know the drill."

She meant it too. Local news, world news, 20/20, GMA. If they were discussing current events, Nebraska was all over it. Miranda was grateful for this unlikely ally. Up until Nick, her life was about resistance. If she wasn't studying, she was marching, protesting, picketing, organizing. All this despite her dirty little secret. No opiate could desensitize her to the atrocities of the Trump administration. If anything, the pills gave her stamina to fight. Luckily the elections were still a year away. Although she had much bigger problems in the interim, she looked forward to casting her first vote.

A commercial came on, some busty blonde seductively eating a hamburger. Nebraska gave a low whistle. "I don't like white hoes but that is one sexy bitch right there."

Miranda glanced over at the hulking figure sitting next to her on the bench. "You better not let Bianca hear you talking like that."

"Who? Bianca ain't running nothing but her mouth. I wear the pants in this relationship." She cracked her knuckles and risked a quick look back at her girlfriend's cell.

Oboes and cellos groaned from the television speaker as a pale grimacing man trudged through gloomy weather in a hemorrhoid medication commercial. City buses doused him with water as they passed, a woman saw him coming and crossed the street, even a stray dog refused to sniff his hand. Then came the product details. When we see our hero again, the sun is shining, he's walking hand in hand down the beach with the woman who gave him the cold shoulder in the rain, playing fetch with the stray.

"Damn, I wish I could get my hands on some of that," said Nebraska.

Miranda glanced over at her.

"What? Don't look at me like that." She rapped her knuckles on the bench. "I've been sittin' on this steel my whole life. Wait till you get my age. You're gonna have some flare-ups too, Ms. Prim and Proper."

World News came back on. Trump's bloated face filled the screen. He was standing on a tarmac addressing reporters.

"Speaking of hemorrhoids," said Miranda.

Nebraska shook her head. "They just ain't ever gonna leave him alone."

Miranda was staring at the neon white bags beneath his eyes as he spoke to the crowd. "Wait. What?"

"All they do is try to dig up dirt on him," she said. "And all he does is bob and weave. You gotta respect that."

"Respect? I can assure you I do not respect anything about Donald Trump. And there's no need for anyone to *try* to dig up dirt on him. He's covered in it. He wallows in it like a pig. I can't believe that after everything he's said about women, and people of color and the LGBTQ community, that you would see him as an innocent victim in all of this."

"Oh, I don't think he's a victim, and he damn sure ain't innocent. That's what I respect about him. He's a gangster. He's got mansions and bitches and billions of dollars on deck."

"He's not a billionaire."

"He ain't? Well, he will be. Watch. And I bet he pardons all his homeboys that they sent to prison for refusing to turn state on him. I'd do the same shit. Wouldn't you?"

Miranda changed the subject. "Who named you Nebraska?"

Her face hardened into a scowl. "My momma. Why? You got a problem with my name?"

"I just think it's interesting."

After a pause, she cleared her throat. "My daddy used to drag her, kick her ass, cheat on her, take her money.

You know the type of shit they pull. The place mats at the diner where Momma worked were maps of the USA. She used to close her eyes and point to the place where she would run away to when she got some money saved. Her finger always landed on Nebraska. Then she got pregnant with me."

"So you were like her escape?"

She shrugged. "I guess. Funny, I got named after the whitest state in America though."

"Hey, she could've pointed to Utah," said Miranda. "I like Nebraska. It sounds cool. Fits you."

"Everybody in my hood calls me Brass."

"Brass. That's even cooler. Sounds like a character in a book."

"Damn right." Nebraska popped her collar. "Brass Jackson. Hustler, lover, enforcer. You got a nickname?"

She thought back through high school and middle school. Nothing. *Snowbunny Red?* Her inner narrator quipped. "My dad calls me Andy, short for Miranda."

"Andy?" Nebraska shot her a look. "That's a white boy name. You a stud or something?"

"I'm sorry. A what?"

"Never mind. We gotta get you a better nickname. Can't have you going down the road as Andy."

"Down what road?"

This apparently was amusing to Nebraska because she laughed and clapped an enormous hand on Miranda's shoulder. "What's your last name?"

"McGuire," said Miranda.

"Let's see," she stroked her chin. "Miranda McGuire. How about Me-Me?"

"That's my grandmother's name. I'd feel weird calling myself that."

"You like M and M?"

She scrunched her nose. "I think it's already taken." *By a galloping misogynist,* her inner narrator added.

"Yeah, facts. Hmm . . . Miranda McGuire. Maggie? Nah . . . Mandy? Hell nah. Mira . . . Mac? Miramac. Miramax?" She glanced over at Miranda, eyebrows raised.

"Seriously? Miramax? As in Harvey Weinstein? Absolutely not."

"Harvey who?" Nebraska frowned.

"Just call me Red," Miranda grumbled. "That's what everyone in here does anyway."

"Red!" Nebraska slapped her leg, nearly dislocating her kneecap. "Why didn't I think of that?"

The world news segued into the local news. A few of the women trickled out of their cells as the anchorwoman previewed the top stories. Amity floated down the stairs and squeezed in next to her on the bench.

They led with the weather. A cold front was coming through. Just in time for the fair. The late October chill was almost a cliché on the panhandle, global warming or not. Amity hugged herself and shivered. "It's always winter in here."

After the weather came a story about a house explosion on the Westside. A Latina reporter in a blue windbreaker interviewed neighbors in front of a home reduced to a pile of matchsticks. Although the cause was unknown, preliminary reports suggested a natural gas explosion. "Natural gas, my ass," said Nebraska. "Them crackers were cooking meth!"

The third item was from a pawn shop on Pace Boulevard. The anchorwoman warned that it contained violence. A citizen had shot cell phone footage of a Chevy Suburban plowing through the entrance of Pensacola Gun and Pawn. The driver could be seen tossing weapons, power tools and musical instruments into the back of his truck through the crumbling brick and unsettled dust. The approaching wail of sirens picked up in the relentless slapping wind that battered the cell phone's mouthpiece. "Uh oh," said a voice off camera.

The clip fast-forwarded to the man diving back into his truck. The taillights flared, the engine roared, but the tires merely spun, churning rubble and glass back into the parking lot in a cloud of black smoke. He smashed the back window of the Suburban with a guitar and emerged wild eyed just as the police arrived.

The camera locked in on his face. Miranda gasped.

"Look at that silly-ass crackhead," said Nebraska as more women gathered around the television to watch.

"He's not a crackhead," she said quietly, her heart breaking as he fell to his knees in the parking lot, his hands high.

Nebraska glared at her. "How the fuck do you know?"

"Because," she swallowed. "He's my dad."

"Wow," said Amity as the news turned to sports. "He really does look like Clooney."

16

She sat cross-legged on the floor, numbly picking the lint from her jumpsuit. The thin metal frame of her bunk pressed hard and cold into her shoulder-blades. Hard and cold. Just like everything else in the jail. The toilet seat, the benches, the water, the people. Especially the people.

Amity's long john covered leg dangled beside her, swinging back and forth. "You have such pretty hair," she said as she braided. "This is fun."

Well, most of the people.

Miranda's head snapped back as she yanked on a strand, pulling it tight.

"Sorry."

A daddy longlegs hung in the corner, suspended in an empty web, shriveled and long dead in the absence of prey. She wondered what inspired it to set up shop on the sixth floor, where gnats and flies were as rare as Roxys.

Daddy longlegs is a chauvinist term, her inner narrator observed. *Do we even know it's a male?*

Daddy. She closed her eyes as the voice in her head prattled on and on. The running monologue was so constant, the stream of words so endless, that she some-times forgot it was there.

There needs to be a more gender-neutral name.

She imagined her dad, somewhere in the bowels of the jail; no one to call, bruised from police batons, pacing for lack of cigarettes. The last words she said to him before slamming the phone down replayed in her mind, words cold enough to freeze her inner narrator into silence, cold enough to make her shiver.

Amity stopped braiding. "Are you okay?"

"Huh?" she said. "Oh . . . yeah."

The braiding resumed. "Does your mom have red hair?"

"Blond," said Miranda. "The only thing I inherited from Victoria are my eyes."

Really? Her inner narrator thawed. *What about her cold reptilian heart?*

"Fuck off," she muttered.

"What?"

"Nothing."

"Gabriella's eyes were blue like yours," said Amity. "Mom told me they were my father's eyes. Jaime Davenport. I think that's why she loved her so much. And why she hates me . . ." Her words evaporated into a whisper. "Maybe that's why she won't write or visit."

Sensing the dark direction of the conversation, Miranda put away her own pain and seized control. "So blue-eyed redheads are rare. There are more than seven billion people on the planet but only 0.17 percent have red hair and blue eyes."

"Who told you that?"

"The internet. A girl in middle school called me ugly and I stayed up all night reading up on why I looked different than everyone else."

"I think you're beautiful."

"I have something called a MC1R gene variant. The melanocortin one receptor. Anyone who looks like me has it."

Little fingers pulled and twined her hair. "I wish I had it."

"I don't know," said Miranda. "I guess it's a blessing and a curse. It has its downfalls like sensitivity to cold and the sun . . . and mean girls. But it also comes with a high pain tolerance which can come in handy."

"I wish I had a pain tolerance."

"Knock knock," trilled a voice from out on the tier. Amity muttered something unintelligible. Miranda glanced toward the cell doorway. An emaciated blonde with black roots and hard eyes did her best impression of a smile. "Can I come in?"

Before either could answer, she stepped inside and took a seat on the toilet. Miranda recognized her from the night before. Long, pale, skinny legs in the next shower, skeletal ribs protruding as she washed her panties with state soap and sang Florida Georgia Line. "Hi Amity."

Nervous energy pulsed from her cellmate's fingertips. Tiny forks of electricity that crackled and zapped down into her hair follicles as she braided in spasmic jolts. "Devin," she acknowledged curtly.

"I heard about your dad." She leaned toward Miranda, elbows on knees, fingers interlaced. "That sucks."

A few of the women had said similar things since the news broke. Sympathy had always been awkward for her. She looked away. "Uh, thanks."

Thanks? Her inner narrator smirked. *What are you thanking her for?*

"My dad's been in and out of prison for as far back as I can remember," said Devin. "My earliest memories are of Mom stuffing my diaper with dope to go visit him in Central Florida. I've still got Polaroids of us in the visitation park."

"That's . . . that's horrible," said Miranda.

"It paid the bills," she shrugged. "But to this day I can't figure out how they get a *park* out of a room full of folding tables and chairs with a few shitty toys and coloring books in the corner. Guess I'll find out when I get there."

Miranda admired her nonchalance. "You think you might go to prison?"

"I know I will," said Devin. "I just copped out to three years. Possession. I'll be leaving on the next prison run. Whenever that is."

A drop of water dangled from the lip of the sink, swelling in the ensuing silence as each woman measured three years in her mind. Finally it released, bursting against the corroded steel drain and slipping down a hole. Miranda had barely outgrown Bieber three years ago. She was still a sophomore in high school, still snapchatting. The only pills in her life back then were the Lithium capsules in her dad's medicine cabinet, counted regularly to make sure he didn't miss any days.

"Anywhoozles," Devin glanced over her shoulder before lifting her pants leg, revealing a flash of calf. Dry powdery lines etched in pink skin, scratched raw. "This probably would've been more helpful when you first came in but . . . better late than never, right?" She dug in her sock, searching the ceiling with her eyes as her fingers traversed the elastic. Then she smiled and extended her hand.

Miranda stared at the tiny Band-Aid-colored square of cellophane-wrapped paper in her palm. "Is that . . . ?"

"Suboxone," Devin nodded. "I get a few strips from time to time. Go ahead. Take it. It's a peace offering."

Preemptive warmth dripped from her brain stem like a golden dollop of honey, rolling down her spine, radiating outward, setting millions of cells ablaze with the promise of imminent relief. Slowly, hypnotically, she reached out her hand.

Her buzzkill inner narrator shattered the moment. *Peace offering for what?*

She froze.

Who cares? she thought. "Peace offering for what?" she said.

"For the other night."

Miranda frowned. "The other night?"

"Yeah," said Devin, dope suspended in palm. "After lights out. The stuff I said to Amity."

It took a second to register. She glanced back at her cellmate, remembering the terror from that night, the tears, the mumbling, the rocking, the cruel voices wafting down the hall. *Mommy, it's cold in here.* Her voice hardened. "Maybe you should make your peace offering to Amity, then."

"No thanks," Amity shook her head. "I don't like drugs."

Miranda turned back to Devin who shrugged and bounced the cellophane in her still-extended hand, silently restating her offer.

She stared at it for a moment, then swallowed and heard herself say, "I don't either."

17

November 5, 2019. Worst birthday ever. Her teeth chattered, her knees trembled, her skin was covered in goosebumps. She nodded off, startled awake, then nodded and startled again, uncertain whether it was exhaustion or hypothermia that kept pulling her under. She felt like Rose at the end of *Titanic*. A Rose with no Jack. A *Titanic* with an alternate ending. One where Jack said, "Save yourself, bitch," and swam like Michael Phelps for the nearest life raft.

She just wanted to get back to her cell, back to her bunk, back to her itchy wool blanket. Meanwhile her inner narrator riffed on the telling details of the holding tank, taking literary snapshots for a future memoir.

The cell reeked of dried bleach on a dirty mop. A haggard woman snored next to her on the bench. Muffled male voices tumbled through the vent, intermittent shouting and maniacal laughter. A twelve-by-twelve plexiglass window on a steel door looked out into the medical lobby where nurses and guards sipped coffee from Styrofoam cups.

She had no idea why she had been summoned to Medical. Medical attention would have been nice a few weeks ago, back when she was vomiting on herself and staggering to the toilet every twenty minutes. But that storm had finally subsided. There was no need to see the doctor now. She didn't even want the Elavil that half the women on the sixth floor were prescribed, those little blue pills that were hoarded and snorted after lights out. Amity had it right: drugs suck. Drugs had cost her everything—her future, her freedom, her father.

The men in the next cell grew more raucous as the morning wore on. It sounded like someone was rapping. A dull thudding beat came pounding through the cinderblock, barely rhythmic, annoyingly simplistic. *123 . . . 123 . . . 123 . . .* Some of the pauses were so long, she started believing the song had ended. But then *123 . . .* not. Her eyes became heavy despite the noise. Her last thought before drifting away was of her dad. She wondered if he was on the other side of the wall. She hoped not. He hated rap.

Keys. Voices. The metallic slide and crack of a bolt unlocking. The door swung open. "McGuire!"

Miranda opened her eyes. A petite brunette in lime-green scrubs and matching Nikes tapped her foot in the hall. Beside her, a hawk-nosed guard twirled his keyring. "Come on, Christmas." He sucked his teeth. "We ain't got all day."

The nurse touched his arm. "I'll take it from here." She smiled at Miranda. The overhead fluorescents were not kind. A smattering of open pores, caked with make-up, peppered her cheeks and stretched across the bridge of her nose. "This way."

Miranda followed her down a corridor lined with offices—cramped windowless rooms with shabby desks and fake plants. 1980s-era health department PSA posters, yellowed and curled at the edges, were taped to the walls. A talking pink scrotum gave cheery, step-by-step instructions on self-screening for testicular cancer, a sinister-looking syringe with devilish eyebrows warned never to share needles, a chorus of germs and bacteria sang the praises of handwashing.

They passed an empty break room with an overflowing trash can. Coffee brewed on a cream-splattered countertop. Its rich aroma followed them down the hall.

A door on the right was propped open with a dustpan. The nurse walked inside, pulled a fresh layer of paper over the exam table, and motioned toward a scale in the corner. "Let me get your weight first, then I'll take your vitals."

Miranda stepped onto the calibrated platform and watched the digital display rifle through a litany of numbers before finally making up its electronic mind. *126.9.* The nurse was staring at her. She cleared her throat. "126 pounds."

Her inner narrator scoffed.

"Come have a seat."

The paper crackled as she climbed onto the exam table and settled in. The nurse separated the Velcro on the blood pressure cuff. Miranda held out her arm.

"Your blood test results came back," she said as she fastened it over her arm and fiddled with the buttons on the monitor.

Miranda glanced at the photo ID that hung from her pocket. *K. Salters, Registered Nurse.* "Blood test? I haven't taken any blood test."

"Sure you have," she smiled. The machine whirred. "Everyone has their blood drawn at intake."

She tried to remember. Couldn't. It occurred to her that on the night of her arrest, her blood was saturated with Girl Scout weed and almost two years of pharmaceutical-grade opiates. She wondered if this could be used against her. The cuff on her arm began to tighten.

Nurse Salters selected a file from a nearby cart. Lime-green fingernails flipped through computer-generated pages. "You're nineteen?"

"Today," said Miranda, staring at the rising numbers on the blood pressure monitor. She remembered the words *systolic* and *diastolic* from her anatomy and physiology class. One represented the highest arterial pressure of the blood; the other, the lowest. But she couldn't remember which was which.

"Oh, happy birthday. Plan on being in here long?"

She shrugged. *Did anyone?*

"The reason I'm asking is because I was looking over the lab results from your blood test and your hCG level was pretty high, like . . ." She glanced down at the file. "32,000 high."

Miranda looked up from the monitor. "I don't know what that means."

The nurse reached over and patted her knee. "Well, in nonpregnant women the number is usually zero."

The Velcro was suddenly a boa constrictor wrapped around her bicep, squeezing precious life away. Then, with a hiss, it released. Her laugh was an octave higher than normal. "Are you saying that you think I'm pregnant? That's . . . that's preposterous!"

Preposterous? Her inner narrator smirked. *It's preposterous that you would use the word preposterous. You sound old. You sound British. You sound like Victoria.*

The nurse shook her head. "No this is pretty accurate. We just need to figure out how far along you are. When was your last period? That's when we count from, even if fertilization occurred two weeks afterward. Weird, I know. Some man probably invented it."

This could not be happening to her. Not here. Not now.

The nurse was smiling. All teeth and pores. "So when do you think it was?"

"My last period?"

She nodded.

"I don't know. Maybe the beginning of September?"

The nurse clicked her pen.

"But I've been irregular from . . . medication."

"What kind of medication?"

"Opiates," she said in a small, defeated voice.

"I see." She made a note in her chart. "Well, I'm going to have food service send you up a sandwich every night with the evening meal. Since you'll be eating for two."

"I'm still not convinced—"

"And," the nurse closed the file. "I've scheduled an ultrasound with an outside doctor for next week so we can pinpoint how far along you are."

She sat there in stunned silence doing the mental math. Hazy, drug-soaked memories of intimate evenings with Nick swelled and popped in her mind, one after the other. Most times he used protection—she insisted on it—but there were exceptions; that one night at the beach, in the Seville Square parking lot, under the gazebo during a thunderstorm.

She exhaled and looked up at the ceiling. It was almost comical the way her life was detonating all around her. Almost.

"Don't look so sad." The nurse patted her hand. "This may turn out to be the greatest birthday you've ever had."

PART TWO
Third Trimester

18

Grease was on. Again. She pulled her pillow over her head in an attempt to block out the soundtrack. Resistance was futile. "Summer Nights" penetrated the hard, plastic, fire-retardant covering and bled straight through the thin layer of stuffing, right into her eardrums. *"Well-a, well-a, well-a. Huh! Tell me more, tell me more. Did you get very far?"*

"Please, God," she groaned into the pillow. "Just kill me now."

Her body ached, she had a vicious case of heartburn, and it was difficult to tell if the rumbling in her belly was merely gas or if the baby was practicing karate. She swung her legs over the side of the bed and padded over to the sink.

The water was a suspicious milky white, but it wasn't like there was an alternative. She held the button and let it run for a minute before washing her face. In addition to the painful pimple that had taken up residence on her forehead, it felt like two more had broken the surface of her cheek overnight. Pregnancy brought on more acne than high school.

"Stop touching it," Amity admonished from the top bunk. "You're making it worse."

"It's cruel to deprive women of mirrors." She squinted into the rusty piece of steel and flicked her toothbrush beneath the silty water. "Does it look bad?"

Amity shook her head. "You look so pretty . . . your skin, your hair. Look at your fingernails."

She stopped brushing long enough to glance at her nails.

"Mine were like that too when I was pregnant with Gabriella."

The awkward silence was quickly broken by the next song on the soundtrack. She walked over to the cell door and glanced down into the dayroom. Carli, Amy and the new girl, Summer, were standing in front of the TV, singing and acting along with *Grease*. Her inner narrator rolled her eyes, *Meth Head Theater presents* . . .

Amity leaped from her bunk and came to stand beside her. She watched the performance for a moment, then glanced at Miranda. Eye contact was all it took. They both erupted in laughter.

It felt good to see Amity smile. With her jury selection looming, she had been noticeably distant and withdrawn lately. Attorneys and psychologists asking questions about Gabriella probably weren't helping. Her heart broke for her cellmate and the tiny life she took.

"Hey," Amity grabbed her hand. "I thought we were laughing. Are those tears?"

Miranda wiped her eyes. "Uh uh."

"Yes they are." Amity hugged her. "Are you getting hormonal on me, Miranda McGuire?"

"No," she sobbed. "Maybe."

"It's okay. We probably don't need to be laughing so hard anyway." She took a step back and reached for Miranda's swollen belly. "We wouldn't want to hurt little Cameron."

She smiled through her tears. "Why do you keep calling him that?"

Amity shrugged.

Downstairs the television zapped off abruptly, followed by heavy footfalls across the dayroom floor. "How many times are you dumbass bitches gonna watch Grease?" Nebraska's angry voice boomed from the rafters. "Don't touch the TV no more. I'm sick of y'all waking me up with this cracker shit."

"Gawd," Carli Higginbotham protested in her privileged Gulf Breeze whine. "That was, like, so utterly rude."

"Nah," Brass countered from her cell, already back in her bunk. "Rude would be slapping the shit outta your dizzy ass. Facts."

Amity shook her head and mouthed, "I hate her."

Miranda was about to go into her standard snowflakian *it's not good to hate/she's had a rough life* monologue when Officer Woodley's staticky voice erupted from the PA system.

"McGuire, Orange Nine Low, step out for an attorney visit."

Her eyes widened. She pointed at herself. "Me?"

"You're the only McGuire I know." Amity smiled. "Do not start crying again."

"Oh my God!" She darted around the cell. "I'm so un-prepared. I had no idea this would happen today. Do I look fat?"

"You look pregnant."

"Shit!" She frowned into the rusty mirror again and fluffed her hair. "I don't know what to say."

"Just tell the truth," Amity said. "Tell him you're inno-cent."

Poor little Amity, her inner narrator sighed. *Here she is facing a life sentence and still able to put her fears aside to coach you through your anxiety.*

She buried her face in her cellmate's curls and kissed her soap-scented head. "What would I do without you, Amity?"

"You'd be late for everything, that's for sure." She reached up and straightened the collar of her jumpsuit. "Now go."

Miranda was almost to the stairs when she remem-bered something. She turned and ran back down the tier.

"Hey!" Amity exclaimed as she skidded through the cell doorway, already breathless. "I didn't mean for you to run. What if you hurt Cameron?"

She lifted her mat, grabbed the Bible, and dusted it off on the way back out the door.

Amity danced out of her way. "Why do you need that?

"For good luck," she said over her shoulder.

A harmless little lie in the great scheme of things. And much less complicated than the truth.

19

The bars rolled shut behind her. She stood waiting in the cage, hugging the Bible to her breast. Through the vertical slat of plexiglass, she could see Ms. Woodley in the officers' station, her face bathed in the soft white glow of her computer screen.

With the TV off and most of the women in their cells, the pod was unnaturally quiet. She glanced behind her. Across the dayroom Nebraska was standing over the toilet located just inside the doorway of her cell, peeing like a dude.

She caught Miranda looking and flashed a smile. "Sounds like a horse pissin' on a rock, don't it?"

Miranda quickly looked away.

The toilet flushed. "Beat on the damn door! That's what I do. If not, you're gonna be standing there all day. Facts."

She wondered if Officer Woodley had ever used her taser on a pregnant woman. Instinctively, she lowered the Bible in front of her stomach. The baby kicked.

Finally, the orange steel door rattled open. She stepped out and looked around before hesitantly walking over to the officers' station. Ms. Woodley was playing Spider Solitaire. She took a swig of coffee, swished it around her mouth and swallowed. "What in the hell are you staring at me for? I ain't the one that's here to see you." She jerked her head toward the short hallway. "Your attorney's down there."

She nodded and took a step in that direction.

"Hey McGuire. Whatcha' got there? Is that the Good Book?"

She showed her the cover. "Yes ma'am."

"Got mine right here." The sawed-off guard held up a pocket new testament. "Read it every day. Gotta stay armed with the Word, right?"

Miranda glanced at the holstered taser on her side and nodded.

"Well, get on back there." She adjusted her crotch and turned back to her computer screen. "I'm sure Mr. Tipton is a busy man."

Evidently so, her inner narrator remarked as she headed down the dim corridor. *Three weeks till the docket date and he's just now getting around to the initial interview.*

She could see him through the doorway at the end of the hall; briefcase open, padded elbow of his corduroy jacket resting on the desk, his head propped in his open palm. A shaft of sunlight illuminated a boyish cowlick.

"Um . . . hello?"

He pushed back his chair and stood. "Ms. McGuire?" he extended his hand. "Colton Tipton, Assistant Public Defender. I've been appointed to represent you in Judge Banaski's courtroom next month."

His palm was warm, his lashes were long, his smile produced quarter-sized dimples in his clean-shaven cheeks . . . that is, if he was even capable of facial hair.

He looked like half of her freshman class. She could picture him doing a keg stand. Shirtless. Which was fine for a frat party. Not so much for a court of law. Especially when she was fighting for her life.

He nodded at the Bible. "Do you bring that with you everywhere?"

She ignored the question. "How old are you?"

He crossed his arms and leaned against the table. "How old are you?"

"I'm nineteen," she said, "but I'm not the one who'll be cross-examining witnesses and stuff."

"Yeah," he inspected his nails, "I don't think there's going to be any cross-examination."

"Why not?"

"Because I don't think there is going to be a trial."

Hope bloomed. She suddenly realized how attractive he was. "Are they dropping my charges?"

"Why don't you have a seat."

His words barely registered over her hammering heart.

"Come on," he motioned to the empty chair across the table. "We have a lot of ground to cover and I still have three more clients to see before lunch."

She eased into the seat. "You didn't answer my question."

He grabbed a legal pad from his briefcase and twirled his pen. "I'm twenty-seven, okay? Finished law school last year, passed the bar, did my due diligence in county court before being promoted to the circuit court level in

December. I inherited your case when Kilgore got disbarred for ethics violations. Does that answer your question?"

She shook her head. "Not *that* question. You said they might be dropping my charges?"

"I didn't say any such thing." He glanced at his watch. "I told you that I don't think there is going to be a trial."

"Why not?" She absently rubbed her belly.

He continued to stare at her for a moment as if weighing great lawyerly ponderances in his mind. A little boy in a suit playing grown-up. Finally, he dropped a thick packet of paper on the table between them. "This is your discovery. I filed a motion for it in January. The state finally responded last week."

She leaned forward and pulled the stack of paper toward her, unsure of what she was looking at.

"Go ahead. Open it," he said. "Read. That's the entirety of the evidence in your case. Unfortunately, it's substantial. Lab reports on the heroin, Nexis results on the firearm. The sworn statement of the arresting officer who found them in your purse after you consented to a search." He shook his head. "For future reference, never consent to a search when you're carrying drugs and a weapon on your person. In fact, never consent to a search under any circumstances."

"They weren't mine."

"What else? Forensics reports, fingerprint matches, photos of the crime scene, photos of the evidence . . ."

She began to cry. "They weren't mine."

"Whoa. Hey. Hang on a minute. Ms. McGuire? Please. Don't . . . do that." He ran his fingers through his hair. "Shit."

"My name is not *Ms. McGuire*," she sobbed. "It's Miranda, okay? Stop calling me that. I'm too young to be Ms. McGuire, too young to be in jail, too young to be . . . pregnant!"

"Look, I'm sorry." Again, with the hair. "Should I—"

"Oh God!" she wailed, her face hot with tears. "You look like Nick."

"Who's Nick?" He nervously glanced down the hall at the officers' station.

She went forehead first into the soft cover of the Bible on the table, shielding her face with her arms. "Nick is a liar and a user and a selfish piece of shit." Her words ricocheted from the book. "And a charlatan and a thug and an illiterate loser."

"And I remind you of this guy?" he said. "Wow. Thanks. I'm flattered."

". . . and a freeloader and a noisy eater and a terrible lover."

"Do you want to discuss your case? Or is this a bad time? Should I come back?"

". . . and a weapons-grade asshole!"

"Okay." He snapped his briefcase shut. "I'll come back when you're not so—"

"Hormonal?" She watched him from the sliver of space between her forearms.

He gave the ceiling a *why me?* look. "I didn't say that."

"Try back in three months," she sniffled. "The baby should be born by then."

He found her eyes in the crease. "You have a court date in three *weeks*. We really need to go over this stuff."

"Fine." Her muffled voice was an octave lower in her cage of flesh. Decidedly unfeminine. She didn't care. Femininity was the least of her concerns at the moment. "Let's do it."

He stared at her for a few seconds. Perhaps waiting for her to emerge from her shell and sit up. When this didn't happen, he sighed and unlatched his briefcase. "You're charged with trafficking in the amount of 28 grams of heroin while in possession of a firearm."

The leather-bound King James was cool and reassuring against her cheek. "I'm aware of my charges."

"Then you already know what's at stake. Life imprisonment. And there is no parole in the Florida prison system."

He was bluffing. Had to be. What she intended as an unconcerned chuckle instead exploded from her lungs in maniacal laughter, rocketing her back off the table and upright in her chair. A string of snot hit the back of his briefcase. This, too, was hilarious. Everything was. The fact that he looked like Nick, the fact that she looked like The Exorcist, the life sentence she was facing, the baby she was carrying, Officer Woodley adjusting her fupa, Nebraska peeing standing up . . .

"Are you okay?"

"Sure," she giggled once the laughter diminished. "Never better."

Translation, her inner narrator dryly observed, *I'm a neurotic, hormonal, emotional, disgusting, bloated wreck.*

"Shut up!" She pounded the table.

He raised an eyebrow. A crescent moon over a still black lake. Both attorney and client froze, suspended in the moment, the echo of her outburst pulsating between them. Until suddenly, something stirred beneath the water. He clicked his pen and began jotting something on his legal pad.

"I wasn't talking to you," she said.

He glanced up at her without pausing. Beneath the Gregorian hum of the air conditioner, she could hear his Uni-ball whispering and slashing across the page. Whispering incriminating observations. Possible outright lies.

"What are you writing?"

He cleared his throat. "Well, I think we may need to have an evaluation done."

"Um, you're a little late. I've already been evaluated and diagnosed."

"And?"

"And I'm pregnant." She gave her best Victoria smile. "You'd know this already if you'd come up here after arraignment like everyone else's public defender. But I guess you were too busy doing keg stands."

"What?" He laughed. "I don't drink. *Yet.* I may need one after this. Look, I apologize for not coming sooner. Like I said, I inherited you from a colleague who is no longer with the office and my caseload was already over-loaded."

The baby kicked as if to say *whatever*. She rubbed her belly. "That's no excuse."

He shrugged. "Wasn't intended to be. It is what it is."

She winced. Of all the trite clichés and mindless phrases in millennial vernacular, nothing annoyed her more than *it is what it is*. Except for maybe *at the end of the day*.

"But even though we got off to a late start, I'm here now. And I'm all caught up on your case. Not to kick Kilgore when he's down, but it may be fortuitous that you were reassigned to my caseload. He's been in the office for a couple of decades and was probably jaded after handling thousands of cases. With me, you may not get that level of trial experience, but you get boundless energy. I'll fight for you. That's all that matters, at the end of the day."

"Oh my God. Seriously?"

He nodded. "And just so you know, the eval I'm requesting has nothing to do with your pregnancy. I want a mental health professional to come talk to you. Competency may be an issue. With the mountain of evidence against you and the potential life sentence that a guilty verdict would bring, we'll take all the help we can get."

She worried the Bible cover with her thumbnail, raking it against the corner of the book. "That's the second time you've mentioned life. Are you trying to scare me? The detective said I was only facing 25 years."

Only? Her inner narrator sounded off. *Have you lost your mind?*

"That's without the enhancement." He met her eyes and quickly looked away. "The firearm bumps it from a first-degree felony to a life felony."

This cannot be happening.

"Can I just volunteer for the electric chair?"

"Florida stopped electrocuting prisoners a few years ago. Most states lethally inject these days."

She knew this. It was actually 29 states plus the federal government, now that the Trump administration had directed the Department of Justice to begin carrying out executions again. Her former life was constructed of similar statistics and talking points. But that time and that girl felt light-years away. Pills and picket signs. She used her jumpsuit sleeve to wipe away the remaining tears. "Lethal injection sounds great right now."

"Don't talk like that. What about . . . ?" He glanced at her stomach.

She followed his eyes. "Oh, I'm not keeping it. Even if I get out, it's going into foster care."

He, her inner narrator corrected. *He is going into foster care.*

Miranda shrugged.

"Well," he cleared his throat again, "I may have a little good news."

She looked up. "Go on."

"So we've already established that the trafficking charge carries a mandatory minimum of 25 years in prison. The firearm enhancement bumps this up from a first-degree felony to a life felony. If we go to trial and you're found guilty—which I believe you will be in light of the overwhelming evidence stacked against you—the judge will have no other option but to sentence you accordingly. Doesn't matter that you're a college student, doesn't matter that you're pregnant, not even your clean criminal record can help you. If the state proves their case beyond a reasonable doubt and the jury convicts, the judge must and shall hand down a guideline sentence pursuant to the Florida statutes."

"Wow," she said, "that is good news."

He leaned back in his chair and smiled. "But there is one way around a minimum mandatory. One way a judge can sentence you below the guidelines. Really, the only way," he paused for effect, clearly waiting for her to inquire what this path might be. He brushed an invisible speck from his khakis. She didn't bite. Finally, he blinked. "It's called an uncoerced plea agreement."

"Seriously?" His credibility began to plummet. She shook her head, exasperated. "All that for a plea deal? I've been on the sixth floor for almost five months. Believe me, I understand the concept. What are they offering?"

He shifted in his chair. "Do you understand that they have all the leverage in your case? That we're lucky the state is even making an offer?"

She rolled her eyes. "Come on. Enough build up. Out with it."

Fingers. Hair. "And you're aware that I'm required by law to present you with the offer whether I think it's a good deal or not. Which, in this case, I do. And I would strongly advise you to take it."

She crossed her arms and waited. The baby kicked.

He nodded, obviously pleased with himself. "The state is offering to reduce the trafficking charge down to simple possession in exchange for a plea of nolo contendere which is Latin for—"

"No contest. I know what it means. Again, I've been in jail for five months. Some of the women in my pod have been to prison three, four times. The girl in the next cell just signed an 18-month deal for manufacturing meth. Just tell me the offer."

"Well, if you'd stop interrupting . . ." He pushed up his coat sleeve, glanced at his watch, adjusted his tie. A little boy playing *I know something you don't know.*

Why couldn't she have been assigned a woman public defender? Or a balding middle-aged man? Anyone but this maddening Nick clone in corduroy and khaki.

"Ten years," he said, "with credit for time served. I negotiated it myself. I tried to get adjudication withheld on the firearm but couldn't get them to bite. The only point I could really press is your clean criminal history. All in all, I think it's a really good deal considering what you're facing."

She was silent.

"What do you think?"

She stared at the packet of papers in front of her. *The discovery*, he called it. The cover sheet had her name in bold. **State of Florida v. Miranda McGuire**. The entire state with all its power, *versus her*. She chewed her lip.

"Is the public defender's office in the same building as the state attorney?"

"Our offices?" he said. "Sure. Right across the hall."

She nodded to herself. "Do you go to the same bar together after work?"

What was left of the boyish smile slid from his face. "I told you I don't drink."

"What about office parties, softball games, double dates, stuff like that? Is it, like, one big family?"

"What exactly are you implying, Ms. McGuire?" His tone was brisk.

She shifted gears. "I don't think I'll sign your deal."

"I think that would be a colossal error on your part. It may not be on the table tomorrow."

He was full of shit. Every woman on the sixth floor who had ever done any time, from Nebraska to Bianca to Heather Wilcox—the new girl who was back from prison on something called an evidentiary hearing—were all in agreement on one thing: you never jump on the first plea bargain.

Especially when you're innocent. Even the habitually negative and combative voice in her head agreed.

"Ten years is a long time." She opened the Bible and flipped through the pages until she found the business card. It was lodged in First Corinthians. "May I use your pen?"

Instead of passing her the one he was twirling between his fingers, he reached into his briefcase and grabbed a gnawed Paper Mate, no doubt reserved for incarcerated clients. "Here you go." He rolled it across the table, a quizzical expression on his boy-band face.

She flipped the card over and wrote on the back, deliberately foregoing her normal looping cursive in favor of stark legible block letters. After dotting both i's and crossing both t's, she stared down at her handiwork.

Nick Archiletta

She might as well have been staring at a random name in a phonebook. Who was he? A stranger. Someone who used her for sexual pleasure and a place to crash and whom she used for access to the pills that enslaved her. There was a scientific term for relationships like this in nature. Symbiotic? Mutualistic? She tried to remember but got Amity's voice instead. *Jail blocks my brain waves.* Didn't matter. The term no longer applied anyway, whatever it was called. There was nothing mutually beneficial about being pregnant and facing a life sentence for someone else's bullshit. She wanted out. Immediately. And she felt zero guilt for what she was about to do. Her only regret was that she didn't do it five months ago.

She pushed the card across the table.

He frowned at it. "Who's Nick Archiletta?"

"He's the person you should be trying to persuade to sign a deal for prison time. He's the one who should be sitting in this chair. Worried sick. Facing a life sentence. Pregnant!" She felt her emotions churning again. She forced herself to breathe. "Well, not pregnant, but . . . this stuff was his. I hate guns. I think they should be banned. The way the gun lobby has infiltrated congress is—"

He held up the card. "So what is it you want me to do with this?"

Her eyes narrowed. It was suddenly clear. "You're a Republican, aren't you?"

"I'm . . . not into politics." He glanced at his watch again. "Look, I really need to go. I'll let the prosecutor know that you reject the plea bargain. They'll probably say they're ready for trial, but I should be able to get a continuance by requesting the psych evaluation."

"A continuance? For how long?"

"Depends on the next open docket. I'm guessing three months." He stood, gathered his papers and placed them in his briefcase. Then he flicked the business card up and down against the leather. "And this?"

She rubbed her belly. The baby kicked. "Would you call the detective on the front? Sandifer? Just give him that name and tell him Miranda McGuire is ready to co-operate."

20

Family Feud was on the TV. This meant it was after 5:00. Almost time for the trustees to bring the food carts up. Her stomach rumbled in anticipation. She remembered the candy bars her dad sent when she first came in. She was just giving them away. She'd give anything for a Milky Way right now.

Dad. Her heart pulsed with pain at the thought of him. She wondered if Colton Tipton was representing him too. She hoped not. Her father didn't have an ace in the hole like she did with Detective Sandifer. He was going to need quality representation. Not some fresh-out-of-law-school frat boy with dimples and baby fat.

A warm gust of breath tickled her earlobe and swept across her cheek. "When did *Family Feud* become so racist?"

She turned and found herself looking into the hollow eyes of Heather Wilcox. Eyes that didn't exactly radiate intelligence. When coupled with her slack jaw and the downturned corners of her mouth, the effect was that of a dimwitted day laborer from a Steinbeck novel.

"Racist, how?"

"Oh come on," she dug a tattooed finger in her nose, "you don't see how they pit a white family against a black family on every show? The other guy wasn't doing that. The fat white guy that was asking the questions before I went to prison. What was his name?"

Her back ached. "I have no idea."

On the TV, a third red X appeared over a squeaky blonde's face. *Bonk!* Her family consoled her as the host moved across the stage to where a black family huddled.

Half of the women in the pod celebrated. Half were silent. Divided equally along racial lines.

"Come on," urged Nebraska from the other end of the bench. "You got this."

A tall ministerial man with world-weary eyes leaned over the microphone. His voice was rolling thunder, so deep that Miranda couldn't make out what he said. *Olive Oil?*

Her know-it-all inner narrator scoffed. *Clearly, he said carnivore.*

"Good answer!" Bianca clapped. "Good answer."

The host pointed up at the big board. A plaque flipped, the fifth and final slot. *Baltimore.* The studio audience applauded, lights flashed, music played. Nebraska high-fived and hugged Bianca as if her team had just won the Super Bowl.

Heather shot her a sidelong glance. Her expression said it all. *Gimme a freaking break.*

All throughout the lightning round Miranda watched without watching, her thoughts dominated by the complicated issue of race. The filtering system in her brain was not programmed to sort by skin color. She sorted by vibration, gender, party affiliation. Before Heather pointed out their differences, the opposing families were just people on television. Were Nebraska and Company rooting for the family that more closely resembled themselves? Possibly. So what? It felt harmless, natural, certainly not racist. So then why did it feel so repulsive to imagine herself doing the same thing?

The credits rolled. The losing family returned to the stage to exchange hugs and handshakes with the winners. She didn't sense any racial tension. Just two American families smiling and practicing good sportsmanship.

She resisted the temptation to smirk at Heather. There was no need to gloat. She could hear her dad lecturing her after Ms. Rhodes gave her detention for talking back in the fifth grade. *Would you rather be right? Or be happy?* If Heather insisted on viewing the world through the Trumpian prism of divisiveness, that was her business.

Nebraska bounced off the bench just as Barenaked Ladies launched into the *Big Bang Theory* theme song. "All right bitches." She walked over to the TV. "Y'all know the drill. *World News* time."

The dayroom began to clear. Women muttered under their breath as they walked away.

"I know y'all wanna kite me up outta here," she said as the nightly news anchor's concerned face and perfect hair filled the screen. "I know y'all are plottin' on me. I got some request forms if y'all need 'em. It's Nebraska. Like the state. Make sure you spell it right." She swaggered back to her spot on the bench gripping invisible testicles, a rap artist on stage.

Miranda scanned the top tier for Amity. It had almost become a game to seek out her cellmate when Nebraska was being oppressive, like a private joke that required no words. Just a quick glance to register the most recent act of tyranny. She found her leaning against the railing in front of their cell. The tattered knees of her long john bottoms and lint-ball-covered sports bra waffle-ironed through the mesh. Her top lip curled in disgust. At the start of Fall semester, if someone had told her that by Spring she would be six months pregnant, sitting in jail, facing more time than her dad who was also in jail, and that her closest confidant would be a girl awaiting trial for killing her own infant daughter, she would have laughed in their face.

"Hey," another gust of warm breath, this time powered by a thunderous protest, "I was watching that!"

Nebraska leaned forward to see who was sitting beside Miranda. Deep lines appeared in her forehead. Her jaw twitched, her nostrils flared. "I don't give a fuck what you was watching. It's 5:30. We watch the news in here. Every day. Facts."

"Yeah?" said Heather. "And who made that rule?"

"I did," Nebraska smiled, amused by this challenge to her sovereign dominion. "My pod, my rules. You don't like it? Roll your shit up and go beat on the glass. I'm sure Officer Woodley can find you another cell."

Tension crackled in the air like electricity, flowing freely from both ends of the bench, flowing straight through Miranda who was sitting in the middle.

A palpable hush fell over the pod, an expectant silence that seemed to balloon in the slow passage of seconds. Bulging, heaving, swelling with anticipation until it was popped by the pinprick of Amity's voice. "Um, Miranda? Did you want me to braid your hair?"

She looked up at the top tier. Her cellmate's eyes burned with urgency. Adrenalin flooded her bloodstream. The baby kicked.

Heather stood and stretched. Her arms were a collection of shitty prison tattoos—a rosary draped over praying hands without fingers, an unshaded flower, her name in slanting cursive. "Whatever," she said in her monotone drawl, "you can have your little TV. I've got one at the house."

Nebraska shot to her feet. "Are you sayin' I can't afford no TV?"

Heather shrugged. "You said that, not me. But Daddy always said that a hit dog'll holler." She pronounced Daddy like she was from Molino. *Deddy*.

Nebraska pounced, grabbing a handful of hair and yanking it toward her explosive hooking fist, over and over like a cymbaleer in a high school marching band. On the other end of the crushing blows, tattooed arms windmilled and flailed as Heather's fingernails ripped powdery white slashes and bloodlines across her face. They banged against the TV and crashed to the floor.

A static spike erupted from the PA system, followed by Officer Woodley's voice. "Everybody to their cells now. Jackson! Wilcox! Break it up!"

"Come on, Miranda!" Amity called from upstairs. "She's gonna roll the doors. You'll be locked out."

She couldn't move. It was as if she was strapped to the bench, paralyzed, unable to look away from the savage brutality that was unfolding in front of her. The two women grunted and cried out as blows were dealt and absorbed. Blood gushed from Heather's nose and smeared her face. A thick plait of hair affixed to a chunk of Nebraska's scalp landed near the toe of Miranda's croc, tossed from the swarm of elbows, fists, and knees that were rolling around beneath the TV. A few feet above, David Muir cast his somber eyes on America and reported that the stock market was plummeting. *"The Dow dropped more than 2500 points this week while the S&P 500 fell 11.5 points, the Market's worst five-day skid since 2008."* His words provided a surreal soundtrack to the violence on the floor.

Movement on the other side of the plexiglass. A platoon of deputies. The outer door slid open, the bars rolled. They stormed in, weapons drawn. Even to Miranda's untrained eye, the response was a little overkill. More *active shooter* than *girl fight.* Officer Woodley was at the head of the phalanx. The laser sight of her stun gun was trained on Nebraska's back. A red dot appeared between her shoulder blades. Oblivious, she continued to straddle Heather, simultaneously choking her and banging her head against the concrete.

The hook zipped through the air on a line and sank straight through her t-shirt. She arched her back and toppled over, convulsing. Heather attempted to sit up and caught one in the chest, right near the nipple. She too began to spasm as they pumped her full of voltage.

"What the fuck are you doing?" a stocky, dimple-chinned deputy barked at Miranda, taser leveled. "I know Officer Woodley instructed everyone to return to their cells."

A red dot appeared on her stomach. She instinctively covered her baby with her hands.

"Don't tase her," Amity yelled from upstairs. "She's pregnant!"

Officer Woodley knelt next to Nebraska and removed the handcuffs from her belt. "Get on up to your cell, McGuire." She snapped the restraints over cast-iron wrists. "Before you get hurt."

Dimple-chin reluctantly holstered his taser.

Beware of the gung-ho rookie, her inner narrator cautioned. *How many times has this fresh-from-the-academy, itchy-trigger-finger archetype appeared on Dad's police shows?*

She walked sideways, back flat against the wall, until she passed him. Then she climbed the steps as quickly as her pregnant body could move.

They were dragging Nebraska through the door by the time she reached her cell.

"Well," said Amity, "that's the end of that."

"Good riddance," smirked a voice down the tier.

Miranda glanced in that direction. Long elegant fingers twisted and twined nervously through the bars. *Summer?*

"For sure," Carli Higginbotham agreed. "Two words to say about that—bye bye."

"I'ma tell her what y'all said when she comes back." Bianca called out from downstairs.

"Gawd," said Carli. "What did we say? I didn't say anything."

"Hey Brass! You hear me boo? I'ma shoot you a kite through—"

"Shut the fuck up!" Dimple-chin exploded, laboring with Heather's weight as he gripped her shackled ankles and staggered behind a wiry man with black gloves and sergeant stripes. They carried her like a piece of furniture while she moaned through swollen lips, dazed from the voltage and blunt force trauma.

"They're not coming back." Amity shook her head. "Not after that."

Nebraska's plait was laying beneath the television. An officer must have kicked it there. The floor around it was streaked with blood. Residual evidence of the violence. She wondered how much more had soaked into the concrete and walls over the years. The sixth floor had only recently switched to females. For the previous three decades it housed some of the most dangerous, high profile male criminals ever to be arrested in Pensacola. She wondered what a CSI forensic black light would reveal. The place would probably light up like a rave.

Amity gently brushed the back of her hand against Miranda's swollen belly. "I can't believe you would expose little Cameron to such danger."

Why do you insist on calling him that? She almost said. *He doesn't have a name.* But just as the words were forming, David Muir interrupted with breaking news.

Something called the Coronavirus had erupted in a place called Wuhan China and was spreading across the globe. Cases in Italy tripled to 3000 and the death toll spiked to 100. France was reporting 300 cases and five deaths. Spain was preparing for the worst. There was talk in Ireland of cancelling the St. Patrick's Day parades. In America, eight people linked to a Seattle nursing home had died and the virus had spread to sixteen states. The President was calling it a hoax, a ploy by the Democrats. *"Much less deadly than the flu which killed 37,000 Americans last year."*

For the first time since the 2016 election, she hoped he was right.

21

The shackles sawed through her socks and gnawed into her ankles. With cuffed wrists, she reached down to adjust them but the baby was in the way. Bending forward stole her breath.

"I thought shackling pregnant women was illegal," she yelled toward the front of the van.

The tiny Central American woman in the next seat stopped praying and looked at her quizzically. The tall blonde in the front row turned and nodded. "I'm pretty sure that *is* the law." Almost beautiful, her teeth were broken and rotten, ravaged by crystal meth.

The passenger side transport officer shook her feathered eighties mullet left and right and looked back at Miranda through mirrored Oakleys. "The law says you can't be shackled *while in labor.* Are you in labor?"

There was no sense in dignifying such a snide rhetorical question with an answer.

"Didn't think so." She exchanged glances with the driver, a thick-shouldered man whose wrinkled bald head resembled a shar-pei. "Until that day comes, the only requirement by law is that you be handcuffed in the front so that you're able to break your fall, should you take a nasty spill . . . which might be in your future if you keep telling me how to do my job."

Miranda stared out the window. The shotgun houses, overgrown lots, and *Beware of Dog* signs of the East Pensacola avenues rolled by like a John Cougar Mellancamp video. Two boys wrestled in a front yard, a woman in pink curlers checked her mail, an airplane made a small white incision in the indigo sky. Just another Monday morning in the American South. No evidence of the apocalyptic pandemic that was rumored to have begun rippling across the country in amber waves of pain. But it was coming.

Spring break was not officially cancelled but the rest of the nation was wagging its sanitized finger at the Sunshine State; outraged at those thoughtless college kids who had descended on the Gulf Coast to get drunk and rub suntan lotion and Covid-19 all over each other, frowning at the local businesses who wouldn't shut their doors, scolding everyone from the county commissioners to the governor for enabling this reckless behavior by dragging their feet.

Most of the country's institutions were already turning off the lights. The NCAA basketball tournament had been scrubbed, along with every other major sporting event and concert for the foreseeable future. *Social distancing* was becoming a viral catchphrase. The disease feasted on large crowds. She figured her beloved UWF would be closing its doors any minute, as well as every other school in the state. The courts couldn't be too far behind.

The women of Blue Six were already gossiping. Each night after lockdown new and exciting buzzwords wafted through the vents and carried down the cellblock. Words like *emergency release, nonviolent offenders, ankle monitors* . . . Amity was convinced that Miranda would be shortlisted for any such mass exodus. She made some valid points: clean record, college student, female, pregnant . . . Still, Miranda had her doubts. It would be nice to get her public defender's expert opinion on the matter, although labeling Colton Tipton's opinion as "expert" was probably a stretch. At any rate, emergency release due to a global pandemic felt like a longshot. Her luck wasn't that good. She just hoped he had spoken with the detective. That was her ticket out.

The M.C. Blanchard building is a 40-year-old structure in downtown Pensacola that occupies the city block where Government and Main streets intersect with Spring and Baylen. Its six stories are home to the august court of the First Judicial Circuit as well as the Ernest E. Mason Law Library and the Escambia County Clerk of Court. Miranda caught glimpses of it through the window, flashing between the trees and the passing vehicles before emerging in full as the van turned onto Spring Street.

A horn blared. Brakes squealed. She lurched headfirst into the thin padding of the next row. Her cuffed hands reflexively shielded her belly. "Ai, Dios Mio!" the woman next to her cried as a silver BMW swerved then straightened, almost plowing through a woman and two children who were crossing the street.

Miranda could see the driver checking his rearview as he sped off, sunglasses on the tip of his nose, yapping away on his Bluetooth.

"Flipping lawyers," growled the guard with the sharpei head. "He almost mowed down that poor family. Probably coked out of his mind."

"I doubt it," said the pretty methhead in the front row. "Nobody does coke anymore. Maybe some really good molly."

"I shoulda called his tag in is what I shoulda done."

As the van accelerated toward the back parking entrance and sally port, Miranda watched the little family gather themselves and hurry across the street toward the courthouse. The woman moved with the dogged perseverance of a low-income single mother. An exhausted soldier carrying on. She hefted the younger of the two children, a little girl with a purple pacifier, while the elementary-school-age boy ran ahead to scatter the pigeons and stomp mud puddles, tie flapping in the wind.

She wondered where they were going. Traffic court? Misdemeanor court? More likely, drug court. Or maybe the father was one of the inmates currently staggering off the larger, more crowded male transport bus just ahead. She could see them across the parking lot, filing into the building under armed supervision. The line was never-ending. She was surprised that many people could be crammed inside one vehicle.

So much for social distancing, her inner narrator smirked as the van rumbled toward the loading dock.

Getting off was an ordeal, standing to move down the narrow aisle, ducking to avoid the low ceiling, small steps to keep the shackles from yanking against her swollen ankles, all while dealing with the constant aching and soreness in the muscles and ligaments that supported her ever-growing belly.

The tiny immigrant woman paused at the van door to adjust her own shackles. Then, before stepping onto the metal foot stool, she turned and adjusted Miranda's too. The relief was instantaneous.

"Let's go, Guatemala," said the guard with the mullet. "Random acts of kindness ain't gonna save your bony ass from getting deported."

Miranda was fuming as she followed the older woman out of the van. A gloved hand clamped on her elbow as she stepped onto the stool, guiding her firmly down to the pavement. The assistance was neither wanted nor needed. She glared into the mirror-tinted Oakleys. A bloated, pasty, untweezed redhead glared back. Self-loathing washed over her like a bad odor, rendering her speechless.

"Problem Biggun?" snarled the mullet.

She wanted desperately to say something withering, something mean, something hurtful. But all she could come up with was, "Trump is going to lose!"

The woman frowned. "Uh . . . okay. I'll let my girl-friend know. I'm sure she'll be thrilled."

Wow, her inner narrator deadpanned. *You really told her. Way to go for the jugular, Miranda.*

The baby echoed her sentiments with a roundhouse.

"Well, as much as I'd love to stand around and talk politics," the guard tapped her G-shock, "I need to get you crackheads into Judge Banaski's courtroom before her honor has an aneurism. That old battle-axe is heartless enough when she's *not* cranky, and nothing grinds her gears like having to wait. Last time we got seated after nine, she threw the book at every single inmate that came before her."

Miranda glanced at the digital display on her watch. *9:25.*

The guard noticed her looking and smiled. "Oops, sucks to be in your shackles."

The bowels of the building were as soundless as the caves at Fort Pickens. It was like walking through a nuclear bunker. She could faintly hear the Hispanic woman mumbling prayers just ahead of her and the air whistling from the shar-pei's nostrils as the pitiful procession moved deeper down the maze of corridors. Exposed pipes, caked with dust, ran overhead. Naked fluorescents splashed harsh light on the walls making the thick green latex paint appear wet. Tinted bubble cameras tracked their movement. Locked doors buzzed open and slammed behind them as they passed through.

The hallway reeked of sweat and, oddly, bologna. For the first time since the second trimester, the smell of food did not make her hungry. Just the opposite. She felt nauseated. Something stirred at the far end of the corridor, a distant hum that swelled as they drew near.

"All right, ladies," said the mullet when they reached yet another steel door. "Time for your thirty seconds of fame. Ready?"

She waved up at a camera. The door popped, and the hum became a roar. On the other side of the plexiglass, at least a hundred men stormed across the holding cells and pressed salivating shouting faces against the windows.

"Oye Mamacita!"

"Damn, look at that fine ass ho! I bet she'd suck up everybody in here for a shot of ice."

"Sheeit, not me. Not with those teeth. Looks like she been chewing on rocks."

"There she go y'all. Snowbunny Red. Why you look so sad baby?"

"Pregnant pussy! You know that shit is good . . ."

Six months ago, such disgusting language would have made her a nervous wreck. After two years on the sixth floor, Amity still returned from her court dates in tears. But Miranda had become desensitized to the crude comments during her monthly trips to the Health Department where she was escorted past the crowded holding tanks on the way out and coming back into jail. She learned to block it out, keep moving, and never, ever, look inside the cells. This last lesson came via a gigantic uncircumcised penis.

"All right, knock it off!" boomed Shar-Pei. "You're acting like a bunch of flippin' animals."

Momentary silence, followed by mumbling, followed by:

"Man, fuck that cracker! Check out the redhead's ass . . . I like that old Mexican bitch . . . Lemme see them titties baby! Don't be like that . . . Hey Snowbunny Red, look what I got for you . . ."

Crates of bag lunches were stacked by the wall. The mullet grabbed an armful and began handing them to the line of women as they passed. The bologna odor wafted from the damp bag, so powerful that she could almost see it, a pinkish processed meat steam that curled vaporously up toward her nose.

"Miranda!"

She vowed to become a vegetarian once the baby was born.

"Miranda!"

They were nearing the end of the primate section of the zoo. The guard stood beneath a camera and fluffed her mullet in the distorted reflection. One of the animals was pounding on the glass a few inches from her face.

"Miranda!"

Interesting, her inner narrator observed. *They stopped calling you Snowbunny Red. I wonder how they know your—*

"Andy!"

Only one person called her that. She turned slowly toward the muffled voice. Amid the hardened and tattooed faces that were shoving and jockeying for position, her dad held his ground.

He looked thin. Gaunt. His county jumpsuit hung from the sharp right angles of his shoulders like an extra-large shirt on a wire hanger. His bushy gray beard could not conceal his sunken cheeks. Months without sunlight made him look much older than his 46 years. Tears welled in astonished eyes as he pointed at her immense belly.

It was the first time she remembered seeing his fingers clean, with no evidence of grease or nicotine stains. This was somehow more heartbreaking than his emaciated appearance. Like a defining part of him had been amputated.

She swallowed and nodded, forcing a smile through tears of her own.

"Move it Biggun!" said the mullet. "You can talk to your sugar daddy when you get out."

He made a Taylor Swift heart with his hands, something an adamant little fourth-grade version of herself taught him through the window of his truck in the school drop-off line. She tucked the bag lunch under her arm and raised her handcuffs in an attempt to complete the father/daughter ritual, but the guard snatched her forward by her sleeve before she could get her fingers assembled.

"Are you deaf? I said let's go."

She shook free in the doorway and turned back. "Love you!"

He smiled and elbowed the young man beside him. "That's my daughter! I'm going to be a grandfather!" Gold teeth shone back through a forest of dreads.

A Bronx cheer erupted from the holding cell as the mullet slammed the door . . . followed by mausoleum silence. "You ladies can blame McGuire here when Judge Banaski starts passing out time like Mardi Gras moon pies." Her frown lines pulled into grin. "Hope your kid enjoys foster care."

Her cruelty fell on deaf ears. Miranda's thoughts were on her dad. Even as she departed the intestinal underbelly of the building and filed through a side door into a hushed world of soft lighting, oaken pews and burgundy carpet.

The Honorable Judge Banaski wore the ornate white lace collar on her robe à la Ruth Bader Ginsburg and appeared to be close in age to the iconic liberal justice. The similarities stopped there.

"I hereby remand you . . ." she paused and glared over at the ragtag group of female prisoners being seated in the jury box before turning back to the woman who stood before her. ". . . to the Florida Department of Corrections for a term of eighty-four months—"

"Eighty-four months?" The woman exploded, clinching her Walmart dress in her fists.

"With credit for time served—"

"Did I hear her right?" She towered over her wincing attorney. "I couldn't have heard her right."

A murmur rippled through the gallery. The bailiff, a sleepy-looking man with salt and pepper hair, made eye contact with the deputies. The woman's voice and mannerisms were familiar, but Miranda couldn't place them.

The waspish old judge continued, unperturbed. "I'm going to recommend substance abuse treatment while in prison and—"

"I can't believe this bitch just gave me eighty-four months. That's like five years!"

Judge Banaski raised her gavel in both hands and slammed it down with the fury of Thor. "Order! One more outburst like that and so help me God I will—"

"What? Send me to prison?"

Her attorney resembled Woody Allen. "Miss Applewhite . . . please."

"Bailiff!" roared the judge.

Applewhite. It clicked as the bailiff and deputies converged. *Rhonda Applewhite. The ranting prostitute who was shooting up on the toilet in the holding cell back in October.*

"I told you I was an addict!" she bellowed as they muscled her toward the side door. "You sentence me to rehab and release me back to the street to wait for a bed to come open? The fucking waiting list is six months long! What did you expect? You knew good and goddamn well I was gonna violate probation! I was dopesick for Christsake! Get your fucking hands off me!"

The door banged shut behind them.

"You have thirty days to appeal this sentence." The judge scribbled a note on her calendar before turning to the clerk. "Who's next?"

"State versus Theodore Tankersly."

A rotund man in red suspenders and a matching bowtie came bounding down the aisle. "Ted Tankersly. That's me, your honor." As he neared the bench Miranda could see the sweat pouring over his jowls into his collar.

He looked like a salesman. Or maybe a bookkeeper. The writer in her wondered what his backstory was. What events transpired in his life that led him to be standing before Judge Banaski, sweating profusely in a bowtie. Someone obviously had big hopes for him once upon a time. No one names her child Theodore expecting failure. Theodore was a thoughtful name. An ambitious name. She imagined some expectant mother back in the seventies dreaming big for the little life that was growing inside of her, wishing him intelligence, kindness, wealth, height, strength, leadership . . .

"Ahem, Ms. McGuire."

She turned to find Colton Tipton leaning against the jury box, cologned and gelled and dressed for court.

His eyes searched hers. "Are you okay?"

Besides the fact that these shackles are too tight, the guard with the mullet is a first-class bitch, I'm terrified of what the future holds, there's a tiny human being inside of me pressing his feet against my ribcage, and I just saw my dad for the first time since I was arrested?

"I'm fine."

He slid into the seat next to her and nodded hello to the other women. "I'm sorry they brought you all the way down here for this. We're going to ask for a continuance to get the psych eval ordered. The state won't object. This is just a formality." He paused as Judge Banaski removed her glasses and leveled a cocked finger at Theodore Tankersly. "Probably for the best we don't have to face her today. She's on a rampage."

Miranda alternately slid the handcuffs up and down each wrist. "Did you . . . um . . . make that phone call?"

He gave her a blank look. "Phone call?"

No. Fucking. Way. "I gave you a business card. Detective Sandifer?"

"Oh right, right, my bad. I have so many people on my caseload, the faces kinda run together."

My bad, her inner narrator dryly remarked. *Two words you never want to hear from your attorney.*

"Well this is the face that asked you." She would have kicked him if she wasn't shackled.

"I didn't mean it like that," he stammered. "Your face obviously stands out."

She exhaled and looked at the ceiling. "Did you or did you not call Detective Standifer?"

"Yes. We spoke on the same day I came to see you."

Across the courtroom, Judge Banaski was ripping poor Theodore a new one.

"And?" said Miranda.

"And I did what you asked. Even though I'm still not convinced it was ethical. What was the guy's name again?"

"Nick . . . Archiletta." *Your twin.*

"Right. Well he ran it through the NCIC and FCIC and there were no hits."

Theodore Tankersly was blubbering. The courtroom tilted and slowly began to spin. "What does that mean, no hits?"

"It means," he said, "that your Nick was either using an alias or that he's never been arrested before and therefore not in the database."

"That's impossible!" She stomped her foot.

A stunned silence fell over the courtroom. The judge spun in her chair. "Counselor, if you cannot control your client, I will hold both of you in contempt. This is your one warning." She stared them down for a long moment before finally turning back to Theodore.

Nick's last words throbbed in her head like a migraine. *"I just can't get caught slippin'. With my record I'd never see daylight again."* He was either lying about his record or he had been lying about his name all along. Most likely the latter. She felt cheap. Like some dirtyfoot on Maury who didn't know who her baby's daddy was.

"I'm sorry," whispered the frat boy, straightening his tie. "I tried to press him but he blew me off. Asked me why he should waste his time chasing ghosts when he had a slam dunk conviction with you."

She felt like she was going to throw up.

"The state is still offering ten years."

22

Sleep was getting more and more difficult to come by. Her pillow was about as soft as a dictionary and half as thick. Her mat was no better. Her cozy apartment with its queen-size bed, fluffy comforter, and stack of pillows and stuffed animals felt continents away. It was impossible to get comfortable in her bunk. Everything ached. Lying on her belly was out of the question. It hurt to lie on her side, and Ms. Brenda—the nurse at the health department who gave her the prenatal vitamins—told her not to lie on her back because the weight of the uterus would press against some obscure vein and decrease blood flow. *"Bad for mommy and baby."* She spent most nights half-propped against the frigid back wall of the cell, wrapped in her itchy wool blanket, fading in and out of consciousness.

Gradually she was becoming aware of the patterns and tendencies of the tiny human being that was sharing her body. She could tell when he was asleep, when he had hiccups, when he was stretching. Some nights when she caught herself craving food that she wouldn't have dreamed of eating seven months before—a leathery jail hot dog, for instance—she was certain the baby had found a way to invade her consciousness and place his order. As if the one-room efficiency of her body was not clamorous enough between herself and the bickering voice in her head, now there was another roommate to deal with.

Roommate? Her inner narrator smirked. *More like squatter.*

The morning sun climbed the narrow window. A sliver of light widened into a shaft and began its slow march across the cell floor creeping up the wall into her bunk. She watched it bleed over her knees, watched it scale the slopes of her swollen belly and breasts, watched until it was stabbing into her eyes, forcing them shut.

Officer Woodley's voice crackled over the intercom. "Line up for rec."

Recreation was a rarity on the sixth floor. When they bothered to call it at all, they called it so early that there were very few takers. Most of the women were full from the predawn breakfast and sleeping soundly in their bunks.

"Hey Amity," she tapped the overhead steel. "Wanna get some fresh air?"

A swath of blanket drooped in front of her face then was quickly yanked back up as her cellmate rolled over and mumbled a refusal.

"Well, I'm going," she decided.

She hadn't been to rec once since she was arrested. The yard was for mingling and she stopped being a social butterfly in high school, the year her wings were clipped with pain meds. But with the coronavirus making its presence felt up north and new rules being implemented every day, she knew there may not be many more opportunities. Flinging the blanket aside, she pitched and rocked to her feet and slipped on her crocs.

"Careful with Cameron," Amity mumbled from under her blanket.

"Stop saying that!"

"Last call," Officer Woodley rasped over the speaker.

"I'm coming, I'm coming." She hurried down the tier to the top of the stairs.

Bianca Bradshaw was waiting by the door, the only other woman from her wing who was going out. Her jumpsuit appeared to be even tighter than usual. She had been passing notes with a girl across the hall. Miranda had caught a couple of glimpses of her through the glass. She was the polar opposite of Nebraska with delicate features, a slender frame, and the lithe movements of a ballerina. Aside from signing through the window when Ms. Woodley wasn't working, the only opportunities to see each other were at rec and church. Bianca was glowing with excitement and anticipation. Miranda thought of a saying she had heard many times during her stay on the sixth floor, usually when boyfriends stopped visiting and families stopped sending money. *Out of sight, out of mind.* Poor Nebraska.

A bolt of fear struck just as the bars were rolling shut behind her. *What if I have to go to the bathroom?* It seemed like she was peeing fifty times a day lately. As soon as she managed to get up from the cold and unforgiving steel seat, she felt like she had to go again. If only pooping were so easy. Opioid blockage was remedial math compared to the calculus of third-trimester constipation. It had been two days and counting since her last bowel movement. She breathed deeply in . . . and exhaled as she stepped through the orange steel door.

"How long is rec?" she asked Bianca. ". . . Bianca?"

"Hmm?" Bianca was locked in on the ballerina. "What?"

"How long will we be outside?"

"An hour," she said without looking. "If we're lucky."

They fell in line outside of the officers' station where Ms. Woodley was checking off names. It was strange seeing her in a mask. There was something dystopian about uniformed guards with their faces covered. Something sinister and apocalyptic. Especially since none were given to the inmate population.

"Nguyen, gotcha. Go stand by the door."

A fidgety Vietnamese girl with a pixie cut spun on her heel and hurried down the hall. Frances Montgomery was next, the only woman who had been on Blue Six longer than Amity, followed by a surgically enhanced blonde with vacuous adult film star eyes.

"Happy Halloween," said Ms. Woodley. It was late March.

She checked off the *other* redhead on the sixth floor—though green-eyed and therefore not a member of the rarer *blue-eyed* MC1R sorority—followed by a biracial girl with freckles, followed by a goth chick whose raven hair was shaved on one side, followed by Bianca's new boo who was named *Fountain,* followed by Bianca who received a knowing smirk, followed by Miranda.

"McGuire, you ain't going to rec."

She knew better than to argue. She had to pee anyway. It felt like the baby was using her bladder as a trampoline. She turned and took a step toward her wing.

"Hang on," said Woodley. "I ain't refusing you recreation. They just called you for a visit is all."

A visitor? She glanced in the direction of the interview room where Colton Tipton, Esq., tried to convince her to sign ten years of her life away. "In there?"

"Not in the Corona era, darlin'. Aintcha' been watching the news?"

Not since you shot Nebraska with a stun gun.

"Downstairs," she said. "Through the glass. Line up with the rest of the girls and the rec escort will drop you off. It's on the way."

The rec escort turned out to be the transport officer from court with the wrinkled bald shar-pei head. "Whoa. Somebody looks like she's ready to pop." His eyes were smiling over his mask, a black hexagon with a gold Saints fleur-de-lis in the center. "How far along are you?"

She squeezed in front of the goth chick as the elevator doors hissed shut. "Thirty-one weeks."

He squinted at the ceiling, doing the math in his head as they descended. "So, almost eight months. I remember my wife at eight months with our daughter. She made me go to those dang Lamaze classes with her. All that breathing and counting and practicing for the big day. Know where I was when little Hannah came screaming into the world? Chain-smoking outside the hospital, that's where. Sweating bullets. It changed my life forever though. Made a man out of me. Maybe it'll do the same for you."

Yeah, her inner narrator added, *maybe it'll make a man out of you—a callous, heartless, selfish, stupid man, devoid of emotion and bereft of conscience. That way you can use and abuse and abandon with impunity. Maybe it'll toughen you up so you can survive prison.*

"I'm not going to prison," she blurted.

"You're not?" He held the elevator door as they filed into the hall. "That's a blessing. Mommas belong at home with their babies, not rotting away in cages."

"Amen," said Frances Montgomery.

"Come on." He removed his keys from his belt. "Your visitor is waiting, and I need to get these ladies to the recreation yard. With this corona thing taking over, who knows when we'll run it again."

23

Small white wire formed geometric diamonds in the window, interwoven chain-link dental floss that ran between the thick sheets of safety glass and served as an extra layer of protection against disgruntled and sometimes violent inmates.

She lowered herself onto the circular stainless stool as the bars clanged shut and locked behind her. On the other side, a jovial man with dancing eyes and a neon green tie was waving. His face was the color of chronic hypertension, and tufts of white hair exploded from his ears. His surprise seemed sincere when he noticed the phone. He banged his palm against his forehead and picked it up, affecting a theatrical listening face, blinking rapidly as he mouthed the words *hello . . . hello . . .*

She reached for the receiver and wiped it on her sleeve before raising it to her ear. He reacted in mock fright, mimicking her sanitation process then beaming as he introduced himself.

"Ms. McGuire? I'm Dr. Silverstein."

Of course, he was. She thought of some of the shrinks that she and her dad had encountered on the way to his bipolar disorder diagnosis. Why was it that so many mental health professionals were wack jobs themselves? Maybe it was that Nietzsche thing: too many years staring into the abyss.

"Silverstein?" she said. "Is your first name Shel?"

"Like the great children's author and poet?" His unruly eyebrows swam to the center of his forehead. "Sadly, no. But I have been a sort of *Giving Tree* in my time. My ex-wives can attest to that. Ouch."

Her intuition rated him as harmless. He reminded her of another doctor. Dr. Livingston, the eccentric poet emeritus at the university. She manufactured a polite smile.

"So," he leaned toward the glass conspiratorially, his animated eyes shifting left and right, his voice dropped an octave. "Tell me, have you been locked up long enough that you find me attractive?"

She tried not to giggle, but holding it made it worse. Strain of effort caused her to pass gas. This proved to be the tipping point. Laughter exploded from her lungs, big hearty McGuire laughter, resulting in spittle on the glass and pee in her underwear.

"I'll take that as a maybe." His eyes crinkled as he unzipped his attaché case, a weatherworn leather relic littered with stickers. Plastered over the others was a shiny red, white, and blue rectangle that read *Bernie 2020.*

"How's Bernie doing?" she asked when she was able to breathe again.

"After Super Tuesday?" He removed a stack of papers. "Dead in the water. He hasn't conceded yet and he's not mathematically eliminated but . . . it looks like it's going to be Biden."

"Anyone is better than what we've got."

"Obviously," he said. "Trump has most Democrats looking longingly back at the good old days of George W. Bush. You're too young to remember him, but trust me, he was no beacon of freedom."

"Oh, I know all about W." Doctor or not, this guy needed to know who he was dealing with. "The mismanagement of Katrina, the invasion of Iraq for nonexistent WMDs, the no-bid contracts awarded to Haliburton, which was the former company of his Vice President, Dick Cheney . . . should I go on?"

"I'm tempted to say yes." He cocked his head as if viewing her from another angle. "But unfortunately, I have a court appearance over in Milton at eleven. How old are you, young lady?"

"I turn twenty in November."

"You're obviously a college student?"

"West Florida."

"Argonauts. My alma mater. Political Science?"

She shook her head. "I was an English major."

"Was?" He raised an eyebrow.

"Well, I kinda came to jail . . . and got pregnant."

"Hopefully not in that order."

Big salty hormonal tears were streaming down her face before she even realized it.

"Hey. Hey." He touched the glass. "Come now. It's not that bad."

"It's . . . horrible," she sobbed. "Unbearable. I didn't do anything, and my attorney still wants me to sign a deal for ten years. Everything aches. I didn't ask for this little ball of elbows and feet and knees in my belly. I don't even know his father's real name. My bed is hard. I can't sleep. The food sucks, the guards are mean, and look at me! I'm a fat, disgusting train wreck!"

"Come on," he said, "don't say that about yourself."

"Why not? It's what you're thinking!"

"It most certainly is not. I think you're a beautiful, intelligent young lady. If my little Tabitha grows up to be anything like you, I'm going to be the proudest grandfather on the panhandle."

"Whatever," she sniffed, "you don't even know me."

"Oh, I know you plenty. I know you're a pissed-off redhead Irish Scorpio who looks to be weeks away from dropping a defensive tackle. I know you're scared shitless. Who wouldn't be? Childbirth is scary enough on this side of the glass. Doing it in captivity, in the midst of a global pandemic no less, would be terrifying. This tells me you're brave. And you're obviously bright. Oh, and you're a Democrat which means you generally err on the side of kindness and empathy." He smiled his Doc from *Back to the Future* smile. *Roads . . . ?* "Now, did I nail you or did I nail you?"

She shifted on the stool. "How'd you know I'm a Scorpio?"

The long hairs on his eyebrows seemed to prickle like ant antennae. "I was raised by a band of Gypsies."

"Really?" She wiped the tears from her cheeks. "My bunkie is a Gypsy. Although she prefers the less offensive Roma."

"No, not really. You told me you were born in November. It was either Scorpio or Sagittarius. I just guessed."

Duh, her inner narrator took a swipe. *You're so freaking gullible sometimes.*

"Hey, whoa, come on," he pleaded. "No more tears. Tell me, uh, tell me where you got your political chops. Did you watch a lot of *The View* growing up?"

"Whatever! Try Rachel Maddow and George Stephanopoulos."

"Your parents must have been big on politics."

Wiping away the tears was a losing battle. She let them fall. "I don't have parents. Just a dad. And even though he had a *Jeb!* bumper sticker on his truck and claimed to be a Republican, he didn't know the GOP from the GDP. He was too busy working on cars and going back and forth to the casinos in Biloxi."

Dr. Silverstein nodded as if he had made the two-hour drive along I-10 West himself a time or two. "Craps?"

She shook her head. "Blackjack. He was convinced he could count every card in a six-deck shoe. He lost more than he won. Not just money either . . . He was gone a lot back then. I had the house to myself. More importantly I had the remote to myself. For some reason I gravitated toward the Sunday morning roundtable shows over cartoons. I was a weird kid. I liked to pretend I understood all the verbal sparring. It was fun to repeat some of the more eloquent phrases and mimic the mannerisms of these beltway insiders. Then, little by little, I started grasping some of what they were saying. Of course, it helped that it was 2008, Bush was on his way out and Hillary was looking like the next president. The first female president."

He smiled and smoothed a sticker on his attaché case. "If only she could've found a way to slam the door on a certain young black senator from Illinois."

She realized she was no longer crying. "At the time, I remember being more interested in whether there was ever a redhead in the oval office. That was my own little oppressed demographic. Especially at Suter Elementary."

"And was there?"

"George Washington."

"Ha! You sound like one of Trump's cabinet members. Alternate facts and revisionist history. Washington's hair was definitely not red."

"He powdered it."

"Really." He appeared to be genuinely astonished by this revelation.

"Well he may have gone gray by the time he reached the White House. Thomas Jefferson was a redhead until the day he died."

"Jefferson was a redhead?"

She nodded. "So were Martin Van Buren and Andrew Jackson. Calvin Coolidge's nickname was Red—I hate it when people call me that—but you can see why if you ever look at his official portrait. Who else? Oh, Eisenhower."

"Fascinating."

She paused and squinted through the glass. "Are you patronizing me because I'm a hormonal mess? Is this some psychology trick?"

"Not at all," he chuckled. "I just can't believe I'm doing a criminal psych evaluation on you. If we were in my office, I'd be offering you a job."

"Christopher Columbus had red hair and freckles, too. Though no self-respecting ginger would ever claim him. Jefferson and Jackson are baggage enough."

He had seemingly forgotten all about his court appearance across the bay. "So, as a young woman, as a girl, were you upset when Hillary lost?"

The baby stirred. She braced for the inevitable morning military press he performed on her ribcage, like a power lifter pushing up. She closed her eyes as the pain came . . .

"Are you okay?"

. . . then exhaled and nodded as it subsided.

"I was upset when she lost in 2016 for good reason. We elected a Twitter troll as president. But not in 2008. Every time Obama was on TV, whether on the debate stage or in interviews, it was like he was teaching a master class on foreign policy or constitutional law or the American dream. And he was doing it in a language that even an eight-year-old girl could understand. Maybe that's because he had a daughter my age. Anyway, I campaigned for him with a lemonade stand in front of our house. I even got my dad to register as a Democrat so I could use his vote. I don't know if you can tell in my current bloated condition with this ugly county jumpsuit, but I'm a force of nature when I want something."

"No, I can absolutely see that," he said. "You're making me want to get out and vote right now and it's not even April."

"My dad ended up betting on Obama to win it all that year. This is when Hillary was still the frontrunner. Even before she got nervous and floated the vice presidency offer. Remember that?" An image pulsed in her mind, of landslide victory results pouring in on the TV, of a little redhead in pigtails hopping up and down on the couch while her father chain-smoked beside her. "That acceptance speech in Chicago . . . wow, historic. I've got chills just thinking about it. And I got a four-poster bed out of the deal. Did you know that people gamble on elections?"

"I've heard," he mumbled absently into the receiver, grinning as if he wasn't quite sure what to make of her. "Have you ever taken an IQ test?"

"I'm a little above average. Enough that I was in gifted classes in elementary but not so much that I could coast through high school without trying. I've always made good grades. Why?"

"Just curious. Let me ask you this—do you think if it was an equally eloquent Republican that hooked your attention all those years ago, someone as bright and charismatic as Obama, someone just as passionate about his ideals, only they were *conservative* ideals, do you think your values would be different?"

"Are you implying that I'd be sitting here with a MAGA tat on my knuckles if Sarah Palin was articulate enough to put a positive spin on mass incarceration, melting ice caps and corporate greed?"

"Whoa," he laughed, "I really did knock it out of the park with my pissed-off-redhead-Irish-Scorpio analysis. But no, I am not implying that you are fickle, my dear. I guess it's just that the further I get into exploring the human mind, the more I realize that we are all just consciousness. Consciousness experiencing itself."

"Whatever, Deepak Chopra. Did you smoke a joint before you came in here? Don't tell me. Girl Scout cookies, right?"

He frowned but went on. "From vast inner space we latch onto these thought forms, these concepts and ideologies, and we pull them around ourselves to create a sense of identity. *I'm a Democrat, I'm a Christian, I'm an American, I'm a psychologist.* These are just outfits, uniforms, jerseys we wear. Deep down, we are pure consciousness. Everything else is illusion."

The baby kicked. "Hey, I'm not the one with a Bernie sticker on my . . . man purse."

"I prefer attaché case." The laugh lines and crow's feet of his face briefly touched when he smiled. "And just because it's all a grand illusion doesn't mean you shouldn't play your part with gusto."

"Donald Trump is not an illusion. He's real, he's ripping this country apart, and he's running for reelection. That doesn't keep you up at night? Even if he loses, there's no reason to believe he'll go quietly. There's a much better chance of him igniting armed protests in the streets. When has he ever accepted defeat? When has he ever acknowledged he was wrong? From his low inauguration turnout, to his pitiful response on this corona thing and every Ukrainian arm twist, hurricane sharpie, hush money payout, and inner circle indictment in between, all he's done is lie and pervert and incite and corrupt!"

"Don't get yourself all worked up, Ms. McGuire. Please. We probably shouldn't be talking politics anyway—"

"Let me finish."

"Come on. Look at your hands. They're trembling. All this stress can't be good for the baby—"

"I DON'T GIVE A DAMN ABOUT THE BABY!" She closed her eyes, gathered herself, exhaled. "What I mean is . . . I don't want the baby. Like everything else that has happened over the last year, it was a mistake. He's going into foster care as soon as I deliver. And he'll be adopted as soon as a home is found."

"I understand." He looked away.

"So, Republicans . . ." she paused and stared down at the gnawed fingernails on her hands. They *were* trembling. "Republicans are constantly going on about *what the founders intended*, calling themselves strict constitutionalists and even forming factions like the Tea Party in resistance to government overreach. Yet they kneel before a tyrant like Trump. And if he loses in November and he declares the election results illegitimate because he thinks millions of illegals voted against him or some other ego-driven crackpot conspiracy theory, if he refuses to cede power, those same so-called patriots will applaud him even as he takes a wrecking ball to the country they claim to love. Hypocrites!"

"Don't you think that's a little severe? Not to fuel this conversation any further but, most conservatives—"

"You don't think they're hypocrites?"

He stared at her. "I think they are mostly good people with different opinions. Different values."

"Yeah, if you consider galloping hypocrisy a value," she snorted. "Conservatives are anti-abortion but pro-capital punishment. They claim *all life is sacred* when it's convenient and dismiss the whole *thou shalt not kill* thing when it's not. They rail against government intrusion, yet they want Roe v. Wade overturned so the government can force poor teenage moms to have babies. Then when those same babies are born into poverty, they vote against aid to dependent children and against raising minimum wage. Republican senators like McConnell and Graham claim to be good Christians but do they ever follow the teachings of Christ when dealing with the poor? Never!"

He glanced at his watch.

Hey Elizabeth Warren, her inner narrator intervened. *Ever heard of non-verbal cues? Take a breath and dial it down a notch. You lost him five minutes ago. Time to get off the stump.*

She shook her head, refusing to let it go. "They don't care about Jesus. Unless they can namedrop him to get some votes. No, Republicans worship at the altar of big business. And big business loves nothing more than cheap labor. That's why they vote against raising minimum wage year after year. They're all about paying workers peanuts while raking in ginormous profits and passing the social costs like health insurance and welfare and poverty along to the taxpayer. That's capitalism to them. Billions of dollars a year in subsidies to big oil is capitalism to them. But let some poor mom try to feed her kids by applying for food stamps and they label that *socialism*. Unbelievable."

"I agree one hundred percent . . . with fifty percent of what you just said." He chuckled at his own cleverness. "But may I ask you a question?"

She rubbed her belly. "That's what you're here for, right?"

"Well, this is off the record, so to speak. I'm just curious. You're obviously somewhere left of Trotsky in your politics. Especially the women's rights stuff. And you've been very . . ." He searched her face as if the word he was seeking would appear on her forehead via predictive texting. ". . . direct about your intentions with the child you're carrying. This is none of my business but, why didn't you abort? I know you have that option, even in here."

Her hand fell still. The baby sensed it and attempted to kick it away. An image of her dad in the downstairs court holding tank pulsed in her mind. Pale, bearded, tired.

"My father is Irish Catholic," she quietly explained. "I've broken his heart enough."

"I understand," he nodded.

More tears. The faint reflection in the glass was hideous. He gathered his papers and stacked them on the Formica, intentionally avoiding her eyes which was fine with her.

"I need to get some info from you. School history. Employment-history-type stuff. It's really just a formality, though. You are clearly competent. The most competent inmate I've ever interviewed."

Look at you, her inner narrator cracked. *Most competent inmate. Little miss overachiever. You've still got it, Red.*

"That's a good thing, right?"

"Sure," he said, "a clean bill of mental health is always good . . . unless you were planning on using insanity as a defense."

24

22,000 deaths. And every day the number seemed to jump another couple thousand. New York was being especially ravaged with close to 900 dying a day. Images of body bags piled in refrigerated morgue trucks, chaotic hospital hallways lined with gurneys, and empty wind-swept city streets were broadcast over the airwaves each night. The evening news was no longer a point of contention. Every woman on the sixth floor gathered around the TV at 5:30 p.m., drawn to the grimness like onlookers at an accident site. The showers emptied, the phones swayed vacant on silver cords, even the kiosk was abandoned. At least until the daily death toll was announced.

Miranda always stayed until the anchor signed off. There was so much to absorb, so much going on. Scientists across the globe were in an arms race to develop a vaccine, unemployment was skyrocketing, food lines unspooled for miles, bidding wars for masks and ventilators between states were erupting, all while the president gloated that his *huge* TV audience was outperforming *The Bachelor.*

She trudged back up the stairs to her cell. Even though she was unwavering in her desire to give the baby up, she could not help but wonder about the unraveling world it was being born into. What would America look like in the year 2100, on his eightieth birthday? What would the planet look like?

The dirty bottoms of Amity's feet were the first thing she saw when she entered the cell. They extended from the blanket as she laid on her stomach, writing. Envy stirred in Miranda's chest, flickering like the fluorescent on the tier. It felt like decades had passed since she had lain on her stomach, and even longer since she had written. She grunted and groaned as she performed the sequence of moves necessary to load her stiff and expansive body into the ever-shrinking space of her bunk.

A baby cried on the TV downstairs. She felt its piercing wail in her swollen nipples, where yellow colostrum leaked into the maxi-pads she had recently begun stuffing inside her 36 DD county-issued bra. She rested her head against the back wall and tried to catch her breath. Everything was so achy and sore.

FML said her inner narrator. The baby concurred with a mule kick exclamation point. Miranda was never a fan of trite internet acronyms, but as she lifted her shirt and gazed down at what appeared to be a tiny heel and toes imprinted in her abdomen, jutting from the skin, she had to agree. *FML* was pretty accurate. No other three letters so perfectly encapsulated the catastrophic convergence of what was going on with her body, what was going on with her life, and what was going on with the world.

"Hey Miranda," Amity's voice floated down from the top bunk. "How do you spell *thighs*?"

The footprint vanished from her belly as if washed away by the tide. She traced its tiny afterimage with her finger. "T-h-i . . . g-h-s."

The fact that Donald Trump was occupying the White House in the midst of a global pandemic was more *FTW* than *FML*. But then *FTW* could have been the subtitle to his campaign slogan: *Make America Great Again . . . Fuck the World*. Now his base was getting exactly what they voted for. The dismantling of the administrative state. Unfortunately, that dismantling included the National Security Council's pandemic team and a chunk of the

Centers for Disease Control's budget for three years running.

"What about *throbbing*?" said Amity.

She frowned at the overhead steel. "Throbbing? T-h-r-o-b-b-i-n-g. What are you writing up there?"

"Nothing."

She wondered if the rabid right were experiencing buyer's remorse, if only in the dark mancaves of their hearts. Scandals and lies and misspelled words on Twitter were one thing, but overflowing hospital morgues and sprawling unemployment lines were much more difficult to dismiss as fake news.

"Nipple," said Amity, "one p or two?"

"Oh my God," Miranda slammed her palm down on her mat. "Seriously?"

Amity swung her legs over the side of the bunk and dropped to the floor. "You know I'm not a good speller."

"Two p's." Miranda looked away as her cellmate pulled down her thermal bottoms and sat on the toilet. "What's up with the mask?"

"Heather Wilcox left her bra drying on the rail when Nebraska beat her up. Nobody else claimed it so I put it under my mat." The sound of her urine tinkling against the bowl filled the cell. "Then all these guards started showing up with masks. But they're not passing them out to us . . ."

"So you made your own."

"Yeah." She stood and flushed the toilet.

"Out of Heather Wilcox's bra."

"I saved the other cup for you."

"Thanks," Miranda smiled, "I always wondered what Heather Wilcox's sweaty nipples smelled like . . . That's nipples with two p's."

Amity crawled in next to her and gently touched her belly. "Hey Cameron," she said in baby talk. "It's your Auntie Amity."

"Why do you insist on calling him that?"

She shrugged. "He likes it."

Miranda shook her head. "So you still haven't told me why you need help spelling all these smutty words. Are you writing erotica up there?"

"Nah," said Amity, "just a sexy letter."

"To whom?"

"I traded Saturday's and Sunday's breakfast trays to Summer for a pen pal. She gave me an auto parts salesman in Bellview named Brock Fisher. She said he's a stage five creeper. Do you know what that is?"

"No idea," said Miranda.

"Me neither. But supposedly if I write him something dirty, he might put money in my account. That's how Summer gets her commissary."

"Yeah? Well Summer better be careful. There are some weird people in this world. One of those stage five creepers might turn her into a lampshade when she gets out."

"A lampshade?" Amity scrunched her nose as she pushed off the bunk and walked over to the window. "I don't get it. I just want to get us some more candy bars."

Miranda studied her tiny profile in the bruised and violet back glow of dusk. Heather Wilcox's bra strap cut an equator through her thick curls. Rosary beads rattled against the mesh. Her spinal column notched a serrated line from the nape of her neck to the waistband of her tattered thermals.

Her trial should have begun in March. She was in the middle of jury selection when the system ground to a halt due to corona. The delay was probably a blessing for Amity. The prosecutor in her case had already pulled a fast one by asking the pool of prospective jurors if anyone present opposed capital punishment due to political or ideological reasons. A moot point since the State was not seeking the death penalty in her case. But by excusing all who raised their hands, the field was limited to a rogue's gallery of religious fundamentalists and Fox News parrots. This seemed like a dirty trick to Miranda, especially since Amity's only hope was mercy.

She sucked in her breath and turned from the window. "I can't believe it!"

Miranda rubbed her belly. "Is the lady in the Jeep flashing her boobs again?"

"Nuh uh," her voice took on that airy mystified tone from the first night. "It's a sign. Come look."

"Just tell me."

"I can't." Amity pressed her forehead against the mesh and stared out into the twilight. "Words won't capture it. You have to see."

That's what she always says, her inner narrator grumbled. *Remember the heart-shaped cloud? The Cameron's catering truck? Her grandmother's face in the pancake?*

"Come on Amity. I just got comfortable."

"Hurry!"

It was no use. The girl was a force of nature when it came to signs from the universe. Miranda rocked and huffed and performed the sequence of moves necessary to extract herself from the pizza oven that was her bunk.

"Thanks for the assistance, Nostradamus."

Amity leaped from her perch on the small metal desk and grabbed her hand, pulling her toward the window.

"Much better," said Miranda.

"Do you see them?"

She scanned the amethyst sky for UFOs and shooting stars. "What am I looking for?"

"Down," said Amity as she nuzzled in next to her, "straight down."

A swarm of bioluminescence rollicked over the ghost-weed and confederate jasmine that grew behind the paint and body shop on the side of the jail.

"Lightning bugs." Miranda smiled, suddenly eight years old again, barefoot in the backyard with a mason jar.

"Tita calls them forest stars." Her voice was slightly muffled behind the bra cup. "They're magical."

"I wouldn't go that far. They may be magicians but they're not magical. They just pull off their little trick to lure prey and seduce mates."

Like Nick, her inner narrator said, *or whatever his name was.*

Amity's breath escaped the mask and fogged the window. "Not the red ones. Not the fireflies."

"All of them," said Miranda. "They don't even produce heat. That light we're seeing? It's cold light."

"It's still a miracle. Words can't make it not. I've been in this cell over two years. I look out this window every day. Sometimes for hours. I've never seen a firefly down there. You haven't either. Tell the truth."

"No," she conceded, "I have not."

Amity reached over and seized a lock of red hair, twining it around her finger. "It's a sign."

"Of what?" said Miranda. "The apocalypse?"

She shook her head, still mesmerized by the swirling lights below. "Luck. The universe is sending you a message. This is going to be an amazing year for you."

Miranda watched the last vestiges of color bleed from the sky. "Well it has definitely kicked off with a bang."

25

The Health Department was only a couple of blocks from the jail. She could have walked it were it not for the shackles and the soreness and the tiny human being taking up residence in her body.

There was only one transport deputy this time, some-one's grandmother with a smoker's hack and a cannon holstered to her belt. Apparently 36 weeks pregnant posed so little threat as a flight risk that the sheriff opted to use the extra manpower elsewhere. For a brief mo-ment she allowed herself the fantasy of making a break for it. *Tuck and roll Miranda!* The camera crew of her im-agination zoomed in on a hobbled and round redhead waddling down corona-deserted streets with a cop car hot on her trail, the harrowing chase reaching top speeds of one mile per hour.

"You know what? I'm over it!" The deputy shouted through her floral-print mask into a flip phone as they pulled into the Health Department parking lot. "If Beatrice is too much of a Namby Bambi to leave the damn house, I'll get Morris to sit in . . ."

Miranda pressed her face against the warm glass and located the sun. Although the dark tint diluted its blind-ing white glow, she could still feel its immense power. A lyric from Young the Giant's "Cough Syrup" rattled faintly from a transistor radio in her mind. *A dark world aches for a splash of the sun.*

". . . so I'll make him a cheat sheet!" She gunned it down the narrow alley beside the building and braked be-side a nondescript gray door. "Look, I gotta go. Let me get situated and I'll call you back."

Miranda was well acquainted with the building and the door and the people behind it. This was her eighth visit. Once every four weeks till week 32, then again two weeks ago at 34. Now she anticipated coming once a week until it was over.

They used the side entrance so the good people in the lobby weren't depressed and shocked by the sight of a handcuffed pregnant girl in a county jumpsuit. She thought this was a stupid and out-of-touch practice considering that most of the Health Department clientele were poor people who had either been to jail themselves or loved someone who had. Anyway, the parking lot and lobby were almost empty due to *essential medical personnel only* corona rules.

The deputy slammed her door, walked over to the paint-speckled intercom and pressed a button. Then she returned to the car. Miranda dragged her body across the cracked brown vinyl and waited behind the driver seat.

Spring flooded in. "You ready dear?"

Birds, air, grass. She swung her shackled feet out over the curb.

"Up you go." She was surprisingly strong for a woman her age.

"The shackles are tight," said Miranda as they short-stepped toward the door.

"I've got them locked on the loosest setting." Perfume emanated from the dangling skin on her throat. She winked. "Tell you what. I'll take 'em off when we get inside. Handcuffs stay on though. I don't wanna lose my job."

The door opened and a statuesque brunette with warm, intelligent eyes, a white lab coat, and a pink mask motioned them in. "This way, Ms. McGuire."

"Hang on." The deputy knelt at her feet.

Miranda assumed the position. Some things were mechanical after seven months. She placed her cuffed hands against the wall.

"Left foot," said the deputy. She raised it slightly. "Right foot." Same thing. The relief was instantaneous. She wondered who invented shackles. Probably slavers.

Lab Coat was watching. The name Marcia was embroidered over her heart. "You appear to be carrying well despite your circumstances. Six pounds is standard at 36 weeks. I'm guessing he's somewhere closer to seven and a half. Might have a little sumo wrestler on your hands."

"How'd you know it's a he?"

"I was just looking at your ultrasound."

"Where's Ms. Brenda?"

"New York. Volunteering. She's on the front lines of this corona thing. I'll be delivering your baby. If that's okay."

"Are you a doctor?"

She shook her head. "CNM, Certified Nurse Midwife. But you're in good hands. I've been delivering babies for over a decade. Step into my office."

The deputy poked her head inside, saw no doors or windows or armed accomplices and said, "I'll wait out here. Give y'all some privacy. I've got a few phone calls to make anyway."

Miranda glanced around her office. She was obviously new. A few unpacked boxes were stacked in the corner. Contemporary Country twanged from a digital clock radio on the shelf, next to a small carved wooden Buddha and a framed certificate acknowledging that she was a board-certified nurse midwife.

"How long do you have to go to school to become a midwife?"

She led Miranda to a sofa that occupied the space where a metal file cabinet once stood. "It took me a little over six years. You have to be a registered nurse first. Then there's an extra two to three years of schooling with an emphasis in Ob/Gyn care."

The couch cushion was soft enough to make her want to cry. It almost seemed designed to absorb the pressure on her uterus. But after so many months of sitting on steel, even an Adirondack chair would feel luxurious.

"I'm surprised you're not wearing a mask." She maneuvered behind her desk and tapped on her keyboard. "Is the jail not providing them?"

"Only for the guards," said Miranda. "I've heard rumors that we're supposed to get some soon. Maybe after Memorial Day."

"Mmm." More keystrokes.

There was a silver-framed picture next to her computer, of her and a buzzcut woman doing shots in Paradise. She caught Miranda looking. "That's my best friend, Lana. She's a cancer survivor. We were celebrating in the Caribbean." She pointed to the other end of the desk. "That's me and my daughter in Hawaii." Then, the bookshelf. "Turks and Caicos." On the end table. "That's me in Bali." Her eyes smiled above her mask. "Yeah, I read *Eat, Pray, Love* a couple of times. Don't judge me."

"I love Elizabeth Gilbert."

Miranda Kerry McGuire, you are forbidden to cry in front of this woman. Do you understand me? Pull it together.

She frowned at the screen and reached for her Starbucks cup. "I know you're probably sick of these questions . . . I just need to update . . ." She yanked her mask around her chin and drained the cup. "Now why on earth would they . . ."

A hazelnut gust washed over Miranda. She closed her eyes.

The midwife was staring at her when she opened them.

"Are you okay?"

She nodded, swallowed. "It's just been a long time since I've smelled Starbucks."

"You poor thing! What do they feed you in there? I've had two babies myself and delivered hundreds. I couldn't imagine being pregnant without fruit and nuts and brownies and ice cream."

"I get an extra peanut butter sandwich every night."

"Peanut butter and jelly with milk?"

"Just peanut butter. With water from the sink." It was actually a hardened greasy dab of sugarless peanut butter squished between two pieces of stale bread.

Her face hardened. "Seriously?" She shot a quick glance at the door, then reached down into her bag. "Do you like cheesecake?" Before Miranda could answer, there was a Tupperware container in her lap. "I was just going to leave it in the break room anyway. The fork's clean. Eat as much as you like."

Miranda managed to be dainty and polite for the first heavenly bite. After that, the baby took over. She was debating licking the Tupperware dish when the questions began.

"You're not diabetic, are you?"

Miranda shook her head. "That was the kindest thing anyone has ever done for me. Thank you."

"You're welcome. Have you had any major injuries over the last few years?"

"I hurt my back in high school."

"Did it require surgery?"

"No."

Just a pain med script that led to addiction that led to desperation that led to having sex with a stranger who carried a gun and dealt drugs that led to jail and pregnancy that led to me sitting here licking cheesecake from my teeth . . .

"Any family history of heart problems, strokes, seizures?"

"No."

"Are you allergic to anything?"

"Handcuffs."

Another smile.

"So your estimated due date is coming up. Do you have any problem with June the second? It's a Tuesday. I just wanted to ask you before I notified the jail. If there's a conflict, a relative's birthday on that day for instance, I can easily schedule it for another weekday. Can't do weekends though. Brownsville Medical Center keeps less ancillary staff on the weekends so elective inductions are only scheduled Monday through Friday."

"June second is fine."

She leaned back in her chair. "This is your first baby, I assume."

Miranda nodded.

"Are you facing a lot of time?"

"No," Miranda lied. Suddenly humiliated in the face of this successful woman with her degrees and her cheesecake and her well-loved children and her pictures of exotic locations.

"Do you have someone who will care for the baby until you resolve your legal issues?"

She stared at her hands. "I'm not sure if . . . I mean, it's complicated."

"Not sure of what? Not sure if you're going to keep him?" Her voice was excruciatingly kind despite her obvious incredulity. "Miranda—may I call you Miranda?—you're 36 weeks pregnant. You're going to have to decide. No one from DCF has come to visit you?"

"Once." Tears slid over her cheeks and dove down her face. "But then all this corona stuff happened."

"Poor thing." She grabbed a box of tissues, walked around the desk, and sank down next to her on the sofa. "This year has been tough on everyone."

"Year of the firefly." Miranda blew her nose.

Her look was half smile, half frown. "Why do you say that?"

"It's just something my cellmate, Amity, told me."

Her eyes widened. "Amity Davenport is your cellmate? I've been following her case on the news. Is she really that vicious in real life?"

"Amity? Vicious?" Miranda used another tissue to wipe away the tears. "She's about as vicious as a box of kittens. They're probably going to lock her away forever. But they could let her out tomorrow and she would still be tormented for the rest of her life. She didn't mean to kill her child."

"Hmm." The midwife searched her face. "Postpartum?"

She shook her head, unsure of how much of her friend's case she should discuss with a stranger. Finally she just said, "terror," and left it at that.

The guard poked her floral print mask through the door. "Everything kosher in here?"

Miranda nodded.

"Yes ma'am," said Marcia the midwife.

She left the door cracked. Her perfume lingered even as her voice trailed off. *". . . it's just Pinochle for crying out loud. Tell her I'll bleach the damn table . . ."*

"I don't want this baby," said Miranda. "I want him to have a good home. A good life. I can't give him that. I can't even give myself that."

All it took was a pat on the leg. The human contact was more than she could handle. She began to sob uncontrollably. The midwife wrapped her arms around her and pulled her close. "Shh . . . it's okay. Just a very difficult situation, that's all. The hormones aren't helping either. You're going to be just fine. Both of you."

"I lied," she managed to get out. The sadness was suddenly suffocating. "I'm in big trouble. I might go to prison."

It was the first time she acknowledged the possibility out loud.

"I can't believe you don't have a case manager to hold your hand and walk you through this. What, were they just going to show up at the hospital and have you sign a bunch of waivers and release forms? Where's your mom?"

"Dead," Miranda said. *Might as well be.*

"How about your dad?"

"He's on the fourth floor of the jail, I think."

"Jesus."

Her embrace was soothing. Maternal. When she pulled back to search Miranda's face, there was a powerful urge to resist. Such warmth in a cold world was rare.

"Are you sure you want to give him up? How will his dad feel about all this?"

Miranda stared at the wall. "I don't even know his father's real name."

The cuffs sawed into her wrists as the midwife took her hands. The shot of pain was a welcome diversion. "I'm a single mom. A lot of my friends are too. I deliver healthy happy babies to single moms all the time. Even if you have to go away for a little while, you can still . . ."

Miranda shook her head, hardened her heart.

"Okay," she sighed. "If you're sure. I have a friend at FFN. I'll give her a call. It's probably too late to vet an adoptive home he can go straight into, but they have a *foster to adoption* program there. The transition should be relatively seamless."

"Thank you." Relief trickled into her crushed heart. "For everything."

The midwife stood and straightened her lab coat. "We need to get you a mask though. It's too dangerous, for you and the baby, to not wear one."

Miranda watched her open the bottom drawer of her desk and grab an N95. "Do you have an extra? I can put the second one right over the first. No one will know."

She looked skeptical. "These are extremely difficult to come by. Dr. Fauci and Dr. Birx are saying they should really only be used by medical professionals. Why do you need two?"

"My cellmate is wearing a dirty bra over her face."

"Amity Davenport?"

"Yes ma'am."

Reluctantly, she reached back into the drawer.

26

The iron bars ground and groaned their way across the front of the cell, culminating in a powerful *crack* as the bolt slammed into the locked position for the evening. The annoying fluorescent that flickered over the tier like a Seville strobe mercifully zapped off. In ten minutes, the cell lights would shut down too. The peanut butter sandwich from two hours earlier remained heavy on her breath but light on her stomach. Breakfast was still eight long hours away.

Amity sat on the desk, back to the window, swinging her bony legs. "You're starving, aren't you? Want me to get you a waterburger?" Without waiting for an answer, she hopped down and snagged Miranda's cup from the end of the bunk.

Waterburgers were a running joke between the women of Blue Six, a way to make light of the hunger pangs. She filled it to the rim.

"Ugh! Amity . . . What are you doing to me? I'll be up all night peeing."

Her friend carefully handed her the lukewarm cup. "You'll be up all night peeing regardless."

"True." She took a sip.

Amity began pacing in front of her bunk, one foot in front of the other. "So, a hundred thousand people since March. That's a lot, isn't it?"

Miranda knew what she was up to. Her cellmate loved to hear her rant about Trump. She didn't bite this time. She just nodded. "Mm hmm."

Amity held out her hands for balance, as if taking a field sobriety test. "Do you believe in reincarnation?"

"What?" The abrupt shift caught her off guard. "I don't know. It's possible, I guess."

"Not, like, if you're bad then you'll come back as a frog. I'm talking about people . . . about souls . . . returning."

Miranda folded her hands over her stomach. The baby kicked them away. She let them fall to her sides. "No, I know what you mean. I think Einstein is the one who said *energy doesn't die but is merely transferred.*"

Amity stopped walking. "I don't get it."

"Well, I mean, if we are energy . . ."

"Oh, right." She grabbed the top bunk and swung her face down in front of Miranda's. "And do you believe it?"

Miranda shrugged. "Who am I to argue with Albert Einstein?"

Not being nitpicky, her inner narrator interjected, *but Buddha may have had something to say about reincarnation too . . .*

"Do you ever wonder if one of those hundred thousand people who died from the coronavirus is already back in your tummy? Living inside you? Living inside Cameron? Waiting to be born again?"

Miranda massaged the bridge of her nose. "Why do you insist on . . . ugh never mind. No. I do not think that is possible. Cam—damn it!—*This baby* was conceived in September, long before anyone died of the virus."

"Oh yeah," she said. Long pause. Then, "Maybe it could be Gabriella."

Palpable sorrow filled the cell, real as the walls. The air was heavy with it. Heat lightning flashed outside the window.

Radio static crackled from the far end of the tier. The distinct clop and squeak of Ms. Woodley's boots approached. Amity snapped out of it. "Mail call! Do you think Brock Fisher wrote me back?"

"Who's Brock Fisher?"

"The auto parts salesman that Summer sold me for two breakfast trays. Remember? It's been two weeks since I mailed him a letter."

Ms. Woodley appeared at the door with a small stack of envelopes. She peeled the top one off and stuck it in the bars. "Don't get too excited, McGuire. It's just a return to sender. Look at that big red finger right there. Might as well be flipping you the bird. Oh well, better luck next time."

Amity snatched it off the bars as soon as she walked away. "When did you write a letter?"

"I haven't written a letter since I've been in this cell. You know that. I give you all my indigent supplies to trade for food."

She frowned at the envelope. "Victoria McGuire, isn't that your mom's name?"

"No. It's not. May I see my mail please?"

"Sorry." Amity climbed in next to her and handed it over.

The letter was addressed to her mother. Although Victoria had been Victoria Echelhardt for almost fifteen years. The address was *910 Oliver*, her childhood home, but the return address was her own name with the jail post office box. She might have questioned her sanity were it not for the handwriting. Definitely not hers. Strangely familiar, but not hers.

As soon as she opened it and unfolded the unlined county stationery, everything clicked into place. She glanced at the envelope once more, smiled and shook her head, then began to read.

Hey Andy,

Surprised? Come on . . . you of all people should know the power of McGuire ingenuity. How's my favorite princess holding up? What a mess, right? Especially on this end. I thought I had a pretty good plan, but Mike Tyson said it best—"Everybody has a plan until they get punched in the face." Pretty humiliating though. Maybe I'll get put on the World's Dumbest Criminals website. One day you can show my grandbaby (My grandbaby!) what a pinhead Granddad was. ☺ It was so good to see your pretty face the other day. You look like your momma when she was carrying you, all rosy and radiant. I know I look like shit. Hope you're not worried. It's nothing a good Marlboro and a Bud Light can't fix. I'm assuming the father is that little wannabe thug that never wanted to come in the house when you stopped by. Hard to imagine someone who's too scared to look a girl's dad in the eye, sticking around during tough times. Don't worry about it. We'll get by. Same way we did when your mom took off . . . What a crazy year so far! I used to think you were overreacting with all the Trump stuff. I should have listened to the smartest girl I know. Remember when you saved us in 2008? ☺ I lost the house, Andy. I'm sorry. Not just for that. I'm sorry for failing you. You were a little bundle of potential from the first day you came home from the hospital. A better man could've molded and guided that potential far beyond the Pensacola city limits. Instead, look at us—stuck in this bad dream. I'll make it right. For you and for the baby, I swear I'll make it right. Just hang in there. And wash those hands!

I love you—Me

She refolded the letter and placed it back inside the envelope. Oddly, not crying. Although there was tightness in her chest. Her heartstrings groaned from the tension.

Amity was a different story. "Who's Mike Tyson?" she sniffled.

Miranda glanced over at her friend. "No idea."

"I don't get it." Amity lay her head on her shoulder. "How did he . . . ?"

She pointed at the envelope. "I grew up in this house. I'm sure the bank foreclosed on it when he came to jail. He knew the letter would be turned around and that the mailroom probably wouldn't bother reading it since it was stamped *Return to Sender*. That's my best guess."

Amity sighed. "I love your dad."

The cell light shut off just as the final thread snapped and the grand hormonal piano of her heart fell screaming to the empty street below, exploding on impact.

"It's okay." Amity rocked her in the dark as she convulsed with tears. A role reversal from a similar night eight months earlier. "Everything is gonna be just right."

27

June 2, 2020. She knew it was going to be an adventure as soon as her favorite transport officer appeared at the bars of the holding tank, trademark mullet highlighted for the occasion.

Someone's been to Fantastic Sams, her inner narrator smirked.

Her Oakleys were wrapped tight around her thin face, perched atop her bird nose. A pair of shackles were draped over her shoulder and an American flag tattoo rippled from her leathery skin beneath her uniform sleeve.

"Morning Biggun." She clicked her handcuffs. "Ready to have a baby?"

Traffic was light for a Tuesday, even in the Corona era. They pulled into Brownsville Medical Center just after

7:00 a.m., a ranch-style building done in brown stucco and orange terra-cotta with a fountain in the circular driveway.

"Pretty swanky for this side of town," said the mullet as they drove around the back. "I think there used to be a titty bar here."

"Fascinating," said Miranda.

Classy, said her inner narrator.

A few of the younger nurses gawked as she jangled through the door in shackles and an oversized county jumpsuit. "Put your mask on, please," said a woman behind the desk, a Donna Brazile doppelganger in starched white scrubs. Despite the *please* it was obviously not a request.

"Shit." The deputy reached beneath her Dog the Bounty Hunter mullet, spun a black mask around her neck and snapped it over her mouth. "You'd think I'd remember this damned thing by now."

Donna Brazile's real name was Marlene, the charge nurse at the clinic. She led them down a hallway to a room with framed paintings of sunflowers on the walls. "Marcia should be in around nine. Go ahead and change into this gown and we'll start the IV and get you hooked up to the fetal monitor. There's some forms and waivers I'm going to need you to sign as well."

Mullet spun her keys on a crooked finger. "All right Biggun, let's get you out of all this county jewelry. You ain't gonna take off on me, are you?"

Miranda leaned over the bed and assumed the position while the shackles were removed, then she turned and offered her wrists.

Nurse Marlene pointed toward the bathroom. "You can change in there."

"Just leave the door open." The deputy strolled over to the TV and started mashing buttons. "Does this thing work?"

The cotton gown smelled like fabric softener and was warm against her skin, a welcome change from the restrictive, chemical-boiled, polyester jumpsuit that felt more like a religious penance than an article of clothing. The baby did his regularly scheduled morning military press against her sternum. She leaned against the sink as the pain subsided.

Enjoy it while you can, Cameron, her inner narrator sneered. *You don't know it yet but there's an eviction notice hanging on your door.*

"His name is not Cameron," she muttered.

"Need any help in there?" the nurse called.

"I'm okay." She neatly folded her jumpsuit and tucked her bra and panties inside, then she walked back out into the small delivery room.

Two more nurses had entered while she was changing. A young black woman in yellow scrubs was fooling with the fetal heart rate monitor and positioning the IV while an ancient white woman with sea green eyes laid out a syringe, vials, and alcohol pads. Deputy Mullet had rolled a wheelchair in front of the TV and was watching *Good Morning America.*

"That's my niece, Aisha," said Marlene, "and this is Ms. Bonnie. We've delivered a few babies with Marcia over the years. Everything's going to be perfect. Don't you worry."

She eased into the bed. Compared to the hard and lumpy mat in her cell, it was like sinking into a cloud.

"I know them pillows feel good," said Ms. Bonnie in a Cantonment drawl. "I'll bring you some extras once I get done taking your blood."

Aisha gently worked some type of elastic belt around her back, tightened it around her belly and checked the monitor while Ms. Bonnie expertly wrapped a tourniquet around her bicep.

"Why are you drawing blood?"

"Precautionary," said Marlene. "In case you need a transfusion. Now I need to ask you some questions . . ."

She answered on autopilot. *Family history, surgical history, medical history, gynecological history, are you Diabetic? Epileptic? Hypoglycemic? Asthmatic? HIV positive? Are you currently taking any medications? Are you allergic to anything? Have you come in contact with anyone known to have Covid-19 in the past 14 days?* As she monotonically rattled off every *no ma'am* and *yes ma'am,* it occurred to her that this day would be the last day of the endless appointments, awkward double-takes and redundant questions. It was all coming to a head.

Like the disgusting pimple on the side of your nose.

She flinched, blindsided by her inner narrator's casual cruelty.

Ms. Bonnie returned with two pillows while Aisha secured the IV with a piece of tape. Miranda glanced over at the monitor. "*FHR* is the baby's heart rate?"

Soft brown eyes blinked kindness in her direction. "That's right. Hear that beeping? His is good and strong," said Aisha. "The other one, *CTX,* monitors your contractions. How far apart they are, how long they are lasting, and the effect they are having on the *FHR*. Not much happening right now but once Marcia puts in the catheter and starts the Pitocin, things will get going. You'll see."

Her eyes calcified into flint as she stared across the room. Miranda followed her granite gaze to the TV, where police were firing tear gas and rubber bullets into a crowd of peaceful protesters outside the White House. She watched in horror as they waded in with batons, bludgeoning picketers and press corps alike to establish a perimeter. The images were like something from the old Soviet bloc, some strongman authoritarian government, even modern-day Hong Kong, *not* the United States of America. The next scene in the loop was the President and members of his cabinet marching across hazy Lafayette Square, followed by footage of Trump posing with a Bible outside of St. John's Episcopal Church.

Miranda was disgusted, she was shocked, but she was also jealous. People were finally waking up, finally uniting, and she was missing the moment, pregnant and in jail.

"Are people protesting in Pensacola?"

"We had a candlelight vigil last night. By the George Floyd mural at Graffiti Bridge." As if on cue, images of the deceased flickered on the screen, culminating in the Minneapolis police officer kneeling on his neck. She shook her head. "He looks just like my dad. I still have nightmares about when they did that to him right in front of our house."

"Is your dad . . . deceased?"

"No, he's alive. He's serving a life sentence. He's been in prison since I was nine. But the Innocence Project is looking at his case."

"My dad's in jail too," said Miranda.

The deputy spun round in the wheelchair. "Well this is awkward."

"I need to make my rounds," said Aisha. "I'll be back to check on you in a little while. But Ms. Bonnie will take good care of you while I'm gone."

"Good morning!" Marcia breezed into the room and headed straight for the sinks. She looked over her shoulder as she scrubbed her hands. "Any problems getting settled in?"

"No ma'am."

Cities burned, police cars were flipped, and monuments fell on television. She frowned as she snapped on a pair of latex gloves. "Do you want me to change that to something less stressful? *Animal Planet*, maybe?"

The deputy sat up straight and fluffed her mullet, clearly in awe of the pretty midwife. "I love *Animal Planet*. Chimp Eden is my favorite. What channel?"

"It's okay," said Miranda. "I never get to watch *Good Morning America* at the jail. It's a luxury to see what's happening in the world."

"I don't know if I'd call it a luxury." She pulled a shield over her surgical mask and rolled a stool to the foot of the bed. "Let's see what Planet Earth's newest resident is up to this morning. Are you experiencing any pain?"

"Not really." Her hospital gown slid up over her knees. "No more than usual."

The deputy appeared over Marcia's shoulder. "I'm supposed to handcuff her to the bed, but I figure I've got the situation under control. Unless, of course, you feel threatened."

Marcia pulled the gown back over Miranda's knees. "I'm sorry. What was your name again?"

"Cindy." She dug her thumbs in her belt. "Cindy Tucker. Officer Cindy Tucker, or just Cindy if you'd like."

"Thank you, Officer Tucker—"

"Ouch."

"—we're trying to keep this environment as sterile as possible for both mom and baby's sake. I understand that you have a job to do and leaving the room is out of the question, but if we could just get a little bit of privacy. Especially while I'm performing the exam."

"Oh yeah, sure," she winked. "I'll be right over here if you need me."

Marcia shook her head and turned back to Miranda. "Bonnie, would you raise her a little bit?" The older woman reached for a panel on the side of the bed. Slowly, she ascended. At least her torso did. "Perfect. Here hon, slide your feet into these stirrups . . . that's it. When it's time to begin pushing, these are going to be your best friends."

Miranda wished she had removed her socks when she changed out of her jumpsuit. The holes were humiliating.

Marcia lifted her gown again and probed gently.

She winced. Ms. Bonnie placed a steadying hand atop hers and nodded reassuringly.

"I know, I know," said Marcia. "This will be over in a sec. Let's see. Dilated one centimeter . . . fifty percent effaced, negative two station."

Ms. Bonnie released her hand and scribbled the information on a notepad. "Got it."

"Okay, so what I'm going to do now is insert this balloon catheter into your cervix while Bonnie starts the Pitocin through the IV—"

"What channel *is Animal Planet?*" Officer Tucker shouted from across the room. "It's 33 on my TV at the house but this looks like *Fox News.*"

God help us, said her inner narrator.

Marcia ignored her. "Contractions should start strengthening pretty soon. Not sure how much you learned about this in school, but basically contractions cause the cervix to soften and become thinner. When I perform your cervical exam and note the effacement, this is what I'm referring to. Right now you're at fifty percent which is normal."

Fox & Friends blared from the TV. "How do you turn this damned thing down?"

Marcia shot Ms. Bonnie a pleading look and the older woman hurried over to adjust the volume.

"Contractions also cause the cervix to open or dilate. You're at one centimeter now. Once you reach ten, the baby will be moving from the uterus to the vaginal canal. I have a feeling you know all of this already . . ."

"Some of it."

"Physiology class?"

She shook her head, smiled. "TV."

"*ER*?"

"*Grey's Anatomy*."

"Mmm." The midwife's eyes crinkled above her mask. "Well, just in case Dr. McSteamy failed to brief you on stationing, this is the way we track the location of the baby's head. He's at negative two right now. When he's engaged at station zero, the largest part of his head will have entered the pelvis . . . plus five means he's coming out."

Although she had been carrying the baby for forty weeks, there was still something unnerving, if not terrifying, about the idea of a head in her pelvis. She kept telling herself not to worry, that women had been doing this since the dawn of time. She thought of Victoria, and how twenty years earlier her mom and dad skidded into

Sacred Heart parking lot, already in labor. Was she nervous? Was she scared?

Ha! Nervous about what? She didn't want you any more than you want this baby.

For the first time in months, Miranda found herself craving painkillers again. "Are you going to give me an epidural?"

"The anesthesiologist will. He'll be around in a few hours. You should be over three centimeters sometime after lunch."

Her stomach growled. "Lunch?"

"Mine, not yours. You'll be dining on ice chips for the duration. At least until this little dude decides to join us." She glanced over her shoulder at the frosted mullet in front of the TV. Then she lowered her voice. "I did bring you a sub for afterwards. Hope you like turkey and avocado."

"Thank you."

The masks were awkward. Even in a hospital. They forced eye contact by eliminating two thirds of facial focal points, forced people to lean in a little closer to hear. An awkward intimacy. Corona had made the world into one giant masquerade.

The world was a masquerade long before corona, her inner narrator scoffed. *You were just too naïve to realize you were at the ball.*

Marcia continued to search her face. "So . . . I've been in contact with Karen Tate from the Foster to Adoption Program. There's a family on standby as long as . . ."

"I'm not going to change my mind."

"No, I know that. You've been pretty consistent as far as your intentions are concerned. What I was going to say is . . ." She cleared her throat. "Jeez, this sounds horrible. She said there's a family willing to take him and potentially adopt him as long as he's not handicapped or, I guess, black. Apparently there's a checklist of what they're willing and not willing to accept."

"I see," said Miranda.

After a pregnant silence, Marcia held up her hands. "Look, I deliver babies. That's what I'm good at. All this other stuff is not my area of expertise. I'm really just trying to help."

"Well, he's definitely not black," said Miranda, "and as for handicaps, you've seen the ultrasound. Was there anything abnormal?"

"Nothing."

Miranda rubbed her belly. The baby was uncharacteristically still, possibly gathering his strength. The calm before the storm. "Do I get a checklist of what *I'm* willing and not willing to accept in potential adoptive parents?"

"I would imagine so." Marcia removed her gloves and stood up. "But again, not my area of expertise. She'll be here tomorrow. You can ask her."

"I really only have one stipulation."

She walked around the bed to check the monitors once more. "What's that?"

The baby's heart rate *beep beep beeped* over a paid political ad on the TV.

"That these people, whoever they are, be barred from adopting my child or even fostering him until someone better comes along. I'd rather he grow up in an orphanage than be contaminated by their stench."

28

Contractions came on like menstrual cramps, rolling waves of pain that gathered and built and shattered and subsided. Intense enough to make her whimper.

The mullet whipped around. "You okay over there?"

She nodded, swallowed, breathed. Sweat trickled down her temple.

By noon, they were three minutes apart. The guard shut off the TV and moved her chair over by the bed.

By one o'clock she was no longer whimpering, she was cursing like Nebraska Jackson.

Her catheter fell out an hour later. Marcia performed another cervical exam. "Five centimeters, eighty percent effaced, negative one station."

"Got it," said Bonnie.

"Please," she gasped. "Get me some fucking morphine."

Marcia reached out and pushed a sweaty strand of hair from her face. "The anesthesiologist will be here in a minute, hon. Just try to focus on your breathing. All this is normal. You're going to be fine."

She had to restrain herself from biting the midwife's finger off. "Tell him to hurry the fuck up already!"

"Okay," Marcia smiled, the embodiment of calm and patience. "Okay."

I like this chick, said her inner narrator. *Very professional . . .*

Miranda beat the bed with her fists. "Please don't start talking. I cannot deal with this right n—"

Another contraction took her breath away.

She was on her feet when the anesthesiologist walked in, leaning over the side of the bed, rocking, swaying, anything for a little relief.

"I told her she shouldn't be up," said the guard. "She wouldn't listen. She gets more and more difficult with every contraction."

"Let's see if we can remedy that." A Godlike voice filled the room, deep and masculine. It was difficult to locate him through the blinding thrum of pain, but she imagined him as handsome. "Now, I'm going to be threading this needle and catheter into your spinal cord, so I'm obviously going to need you to be very still. Up you go."

She sensed more than saw Aisha helping her back into the bed along with Officer Tucker.

"Excellent," said the handsome doctor. "Now, deep breath on the count of three. One, two, three . . . and exhale."

A shot of lightning went through her body. She vomited over the railing.

"Hey!" The guard protested. "These are brand new boots."

"I have some clean towels over here," said Aisha.

As the lower part of her body disintegrated into tingly numbness and the pain thudded away, she leaned back in the bed and tentatively touched herself. Only pressure remained.

"How you doing?" the manly baritone voice inquired. Her hero.

"Much . . ." she turned and came face to face with a short, bald, bespectacled man in his sixties. "Better."

"Excellent." He smiled. "Redheads always pose a challenge. Specifically blue-eyed redheads like yourself. That same mutated MC1R gene that raises your pain threshold can also make you resistant to anesthetics."

"Raise her pain threshold?" The bleached-blond mullet fanned out over Officer Tucker's narrow back as she wiped the puke from her boots. When she came up for air, the slack skin of her face was wine red. "Hell, she's been moaning and groaning for hours."

"A clear indication of her level of discomfort." He set a small beige cartridge with a red button on the bedside table and studied her through Rooseveltian glasses. "I gave you a little extra, Ms. McGuire. If the pain returns just press this button. Good luck to you both."

Aisha lingered, hovering over her, wiping her mouth, checking the monitors, refilling her cup with ice chips. She was humming a slow jam while she worked. The melody was familiar. *Halo?* Miranda intended to ask but she dozed off while the words were forming in her head.

She awoke feeling disoriented. And wet. The guard was snoring softly in the chair next to her. She leaned over to read the time on her G-Shock. *8:12 p.m.* "Officer Tucker?"

No answer. The fetal monitor beeped with the persistence of an alarm clock only with none of the annoyance. Just the opposite. She found it strangely soothing.

"Ms. Tucker?"

The guard opened a resentful eye. "What?"

Embarrassing as it was to admit . . . "I think I have to poop."

She stretched, yawned, and pushed her lanky body out of the chair. "Hang on. I'll get the nurse."

Three minutes later she returned with the cavalry.

"Her water broke," said Bonnie as Marcia scrubbed her hands. "Sheets are soaked."

The midwife lowered a shield over her surgical mask while Aisha arranged spotlights at the foot of the bed. "Feels like you need to poop, huh?" She lifted the wet gown. "Ten centimeters, plus three station. Crowning."

"Got it." Bonnie scribbled down the info then raised the bed until she was sitting straight up.

Marcia stared at the monitor. "Okay, on this next contraction I want you to push for a ten count. Can you do that for me? Just push down into your bottom. Ready? PUSH!"

". . . two . . . three . . . four . . ." Aisha counted.

"Come on!" Marcia urged. "Dig your heels in, tuck your chin, and push!"

". . . seven . . . eight . . . nine . . ."

Her muscles tensed; she squeezed her eyes shut. A sheen of sweat exploded across her forehead.

"Good, now take a breath and we're gonna do it again. Ready? Push!"

She strained, grunted, gritted her teeth. The pressure was a massive gravitational force between her thighs. Although safely sealed off from the pain, she could still feel it stretching her.

"One more," said Marcia. "You can rest between contractions. Gimme everything you've got this time, okay? PUSH!"

". . . two . . . three . . . four . . ."

She clenched the sides of the mattress and channeled every ounce of down force her body could generate.

"That's it girl!" shouted the guard. "PUSH!"

". . . six . . . seven . . .eight . . ."

Despite the titanic struggle, she was hyperaware of everything around her—the smell of antiseptic and latex, the clinking of metal instruments, the baby's heartbeat broadcasted loudly over it all, plunging when she pushed, racing when she rested.

"I don't like this setup." Marcia glanced at Aisha. "Will the end of the bed break away?"

The nurse nodded.

"Let's do that."

Miranda watched as a third of the bed collapsed and disappeared.

"Much better," said the midwife, eyes on the monitor. "On the next contraction, I want you to reach under your legs and pull them back toward you as you push."

"Like a yoga pose." The guard peered over her shoulder at Miranda's illuminated genitalia. "Damn them lights are bright."

Marcia stiffened but remained focused on the monitor. "Think of your legs as levers."

"Like those slot machines in Biloxi," said Escambia County's finest. "Only instead of a bucketful of quarters, you get a baby!"

"No. Actually it's nothing like that." Marcia frowned back at the guard. "And would you please keep your mask on."

"Damn it." She fumbled for her mask.

"In fact, I saw some surgical scrubs and caps in the cabinet over the sink. If you insist on standing over here, you need to dress accordingly. We're trying to keep this area as sterile as possible."

Bonnie wandered over with a stack of towels and began draping them over her knees. Aisha was humming again. The same song she was humming after the epidural.

"Is that Beyoncé?"

The nurse shook her head. "Keisha Cole."

The baby's heart rate slowed as the pressure built. She grabbed a swath of cloth from her knee and mopped the sweat from her face.

"Here we go," said Marcia, "hands under your legs, remember? Ready? PUSH!"

". . . two . . . three . . . tuck your chin!"

"Why does that matter?" Miranda gasped.

"If you're talking, you're not pushing." Marcia shouted at her vagina like a drill sergeant. "And I *need* you to push during these contractions. Now come on! Dig deep! Push into your bottom!"

She tucked her chin and gave it everything she had. The ten count felt like an eternity.

"Okay, breathe."

Bonnie darted in and dabbed a towel between her thighs. It came away bloody.

"Take her leg," the midwife said to Aisha before looking around for the guard. "Can we get your assistance over here?"

"Ten-four." Officer Tucker stepped forward, mullet tucked in her surgical cap, papery blue scrubs concealing her deputy uniform.

"See how the nurse is holding Ms. McGuire's leg? I want you to take the other and push it back toward her on the next contraction. Gently. Can you manage that?"

"I think so."

"Just mimic Aisha. She's done this a few times." The baby's heart rate plummeted. She glanced at the monitor. "Okay, here we go. PUSH!"

She shuttered her eyes and strained. A galaxy of stars rippled across the inside of her eyelids. She could feel herself stretching as the women shouldered her knees back towards her chest. Marcia pressed latex gloves against her pelvis and perineum, almost massaging them.

"Tuck your chin!" the guard bellowed. "Push into your bottom!"

Aisha smiled but never wavered in her relentless count. ". . . seven . . . eight . . . nine . . ."

"Here he is," said Marcia. "He's coming out. PUSH!"

The baby's heart rate slowed to a crawl. Miranda glanced at the monitor.

"Don't worry about that," the midwife implored. "Let's go!"

Her muscles ached from the effort. She braced for another round; clenching, straining, struggling.

The guard's eyes widened as she looked down, her sun-ravaged face suddenly ash white.

"Push!"

Marcia continued massaging with her palms. "Come on Miranda. Almost there. Give me everything you've got."

Sweat poured into her eyes. She roared like a power-lifter. "AAGGHH!"

"Holy shit," the guard muttered.

"Okay, hang on," said Marcia. "Rest a second. The difficult part is over. Little pushes from here on out."

Aisha ceased counting. Officer Tucker's mask expanded and collapsed over her mouth in short hyperventilative breaths. Bonnie selected a bulb syringe from the utensil tray and stood next to Marcia. When Miranda ventured a glance down at her stadium-lit vagina, she saw that the midwife was gently supporting the small human head that was protruding from her body, just past the ears, face down, marbled and matted with amniotic fluid and blood.

"Come on, little pushes."

She watched in utter amazement as, inch by miraculous inch, her child was born.

Once the nose and mouth were accessible, Bonnie moved in and began suctioning the fluid with the bulb. When the chin popped out, Marcia had her rest again.

"The pressure of the birth canal on his chest will help to clear the remaining fluid from his lungs." She continued to support his head and neck while massaging Miranda to help her stretch. "The blood is yours, not his. There's a little tear. I'll put a couple stitches in after we get you cleaned up."

"It almost feels like he's . . . turning."

"He is. He's getting his little shoulders north and south for the final leg of the journey."

Bonnie continued to suction out fluid. "Nurses call this thing here a bulb syringe," she said as she worked. "Mommas and grandmas usually just call them booger suckers."

Marcia smiled. "Come on, big push."

A shoulder emerged . . .

"Keep going."

. . . then another.

Still cradling his neck, she slid her fingers beneath his armpit. Three more pushes and he was out, almost gushing into the world on a wave of amniotic fluid.

"That's beautiful," the guard whispered, before her eyes fluttered and she fell straight back. Her head hit the tiles like a bowling ball.

"Shit." Marcia handed the baby to Bonnie and knelt beside the deputy. "Officer Tucker? Can you hear me?"

Bonnie immediately placed the baby on Miranda's chest and began toweling off the fluid and blood and white waxy vernix. "He's cold. Your body heat'll warm him up. Let him nurse if you want to. There won't be any milk yet but there's plenty of nutrients in the yellow colostrum. Plus it soothes the baby and'll help to shrink your uterus back down. We like to call this time the golden hour."

Aisha selected a pair of hemostats from a tray of utensils. The umbilical cord had yet to be cut. Mother and child were still one.

She bent to smell his head. Big blue eyes looked up from her breast. Eyes that searched her own, eyes that mirrored her own. Her heart melted, swelled, soared. She was in love before he ever blinked. Love and something more—the singular urge to protect him at all costs, a primal instinct as old as time.

Bonnie suctioned his little nose again and showed her how to rub his back to stimulate those first deep breaths as Aisha clamped and cut the umbilical cord. This proved to be too much activity for the baby. He opened his mouth and formally proclaimed his displeasure loud enough for his granddad to hear him across town at the jail.

The guard blinked, sat up, and rubbed her head. The mullet spilled from the back of the surgical cap.

"Apgar," said Aisha. "I got all twos."

"Same here." Bonnie slid a cotton beanie over his head. "I was waiting on the grimace and respiration grades, but this little tirade took care of both. Perfect score."

The baby howled even louder.

Miranda patted his back. "Aww, it's okay. Are they upsetting you? Just lay your little head down right here. I know. I know . . ."

The baby stopped crying and stared up at her intently, as if their paths had crossed before but he couldn't recall her name.

Bonnie smiled. "He recognizes your voice. He ought to, right? He's been listening to it for nine months. It's probably a comfort to him in this big ol' bright scary room."

The baby frowned, sighed, and took a bulldog right on her stomach. It was the gooiest black poop she had ever seen.

The midwife helped the woozy guard into a wheelchair and walked over to the bed. "Mmm. Meconium. Looks like we got a healthy baby on our hands."

Miranda barely heard her, barely smelled the poop, barely noticed the nurses reaching over her, under her, around her. The world as she knew it had been condensed into the eight pounds of sweetness that lay helpless on her chest, exhausted from the journey. Everything that mattered before—court, corona, school, politics—seemed suddenly insignificant, washed away on a storm surge of love and oxytocin.

"We're going to need to birth the placenta," said Marcia. "It won't take long. Thirty minutes tops. But I like to be thorough, make sure all of it's there, monitor any blood loss. I'll put those stitches in too. Bonnie's going to massage your tummy a little to help the uterus begin the shrinkage process. I have to warn you, for most women this is not a pleasant experience."

"I'll be gentle," said the old nurse.

"I'll give you a little more Pitocin to stimulate the shrinkage as well. Meanwhile," she motioned Aisha over, "Aisha here will be taking good care of this sweet little bundle."

Miranda hesitated. "Can't I just hold him while you're doing all that stuff?"

"No," said Marcia, all business. "The baby needs to be measured, printed, tagged, given his Vitamin K and Hep B shots, put in a diaper, swaddled in a blanket, given his eye ointment."

Aisha lifted him from her chest. "I'll just be right over here at the warming station. You can watch us if you'd like."

As if she had a choice. As if there was any way she could take her eyes off her baby.

Marcia leaned closer. "Hey . . . it's probably for the best that you don't become too attached."

Too late for that, her inner narrator scoffed.

The guard rolled the wheelchair over for a better look. "Check out this handsome little butt-naked angel. All he needs is wings and a harp. What are you gonna name him?"

"Ms. McGuire has already made her intentions clear," said the midwife. "The baby's going to be placed in a loving home. I assume she'll just allow the—"

"Cameron," said Miranda. "His name is Cameron Patrick McGuire."

29

Midnight. He slept on her chest. She lightly brushed her fingertips around his tiny ears, over his cheeks, between his eyes, down his nose, across his mouth, marveling at the precision and craftsmanship of nature, the Cupid's bow of his top lip, the veiny translucence of his eyelids, the miniscule creases where his fingers bent at the joint.

God is real, her inner narrator whispered.

How could she argue? There was no way, not with a miracle breathing on her collarbone.

His little forehead wrinkled, his eyes twitched beneath the lids, his hand opened and closed. She wondered if he was dreaming. Could a baby dream on his first night outside of the womb? Or would his subconscious first need to be filled with stimuli? She could not stop touching him. She could not stop staring at him. He was the most beautiful thing she had ever laid eyes on. It was hard to believe that such perfection came from her.

Hours passed as she lay there mesmerized. Concussion Mullet swapped guard duty with Smartphone Granny. Bonnie was in and out checking vitals, changing ice packs, changing her pads, bearing 800 milligram Advil with OJ and graham crackers. Aisha rolled in a bassinet which she ignored, Marlene brought in a form she forgot to have her sign, hearing test lady came and went, then birth certificate lady, housekeeping lady, billing lady. At one point she realized someone was stroking her hair and looked up into Marcia's sad smile.

It was in this twilight of unaware awareness, this state of alert exhaustion where the ocean of dreams met the shore of consciousness, that she heard the ominous sound of heels approaching in the hallway. Somehow, she knew. She wrapped her arms around the baby and glanced over at the guard. Officer Tucker had returned. It was morning.

"Helloooo," trilled a middle-aged woman in a Stein Mart pants suit and yellow mask. "You must be Miranda."

The baby shifted, blinked awake, opened his mouth, and wailed. "Shhh." She patted his tiny back. "It's okay. Momma's got you."

"Karen Tate," the woman pulled her mask around her chin and smiled. "I'm from the Foster to Adoption Program."

Miranda ignored her.

The smile flickered to an awkward grin.

"It's okay," she continued to murmur in his ear, breathing in his scent, rocking. "Momma's right here."

"He's adorable." The woman held out her arms. "May I?"

Miranda felt her face harden into a snarl.

"No? Okay." She pulled up a chair and unlatched her briefcase. "I know how difficult this must be for you. A colleague of mine received a call this morning about some stipulations you have regarding child placement?"

She wished they would all just get out—this woman, the nurses, the guard, all of them.

"I want you to know that our organization will do everything to ensure that your baby is raised in a loving home." She removed a form from her briefcase. "And, of course, we will honor any preferences you may have."

Miranda glanced at the form. *Statement of Guardianship.* She closed her eyes, kept rocking her child, tried to rock it all away.

"Ms. McGuire?" The woman touched her arm. "Could I just . . . ?"

"Don't." Miranda bristled.

Her hand fell away. She glanced helplessly over at the guard.

"Look here, McGuire." The mullet stood shakily. "I know this is a shitty situation. But being nasty to this lady ain't solving nothing. Especially when she's here to help you."

"She's not here to help me," Miranda's voice cracked. "She's here to take my baby."

Cameron began to cry again.

"Stop it," said the guard. "Nobody's taking your baby. I've got a copy of the form right here." She reached in her back pocket. "See here? *Child Placement Plan for Newborn of Inmate*? This authorizes me to release the infant to one Karen Tate of the Foster to Adoption Program. That's your handwriting, your signature, this is what *you* wanted. So don't be rude to this nice lady just because—"

"It's okay," said Karen Tate. "I've been doing this for a while. It's not always seamless."

"I'm not putting him up for adoption." Miranda spoke into existence what she had known from the moment he was placed on her chest. "I go to court soon. I'll get him as soon as I get out."

Karen Tate stared at her baby. "These decisions are difficult enough in a lucid, clearheaded state, but under hormonal and emotional duress . . ."

"Oh, I was definitely hormonal and emotional over the last few months, when I thought I wanted to give him up. But I've never been as clearheaded as I am right now."

"Clearheaded or not," said Officer Tucker, "we need to be pulling into the jail sally port in less than an hour."

"Think hard about this. We have couples on our registry who can give him the type of opportunities that would be a struggle for a single mother like yourself to provide."

"Especially . . ." the guard rocked on the heels of her boots, "a single mother *convicted felon.*"

"I'm not a convicted felon," said Miranda. "Not yet. And I'm not putting my baby up for adoption. Those families might be able to provide him with opportunities, but no one will love him like me."

Cameron squirmed in her arms. She imagined it as a celebration dance. He paused and gave her that look again. *Do I know you?* Her heart swelled.

"Okay." Karen Tate smoothed her pants suit. "If you're positive this is what you want, we can assist you here as well. I should be able to get him settled into a good foster home by the end of the week."

Miranda watched as she placed the *Statement of Guardianship* back in her briefcase and brought out a *Temporary Legal Custody* form.

"Believe it or not," she smiled, "this has happened before."

Miranda squinted at the legalese while Cameron continued to familiarize himself with his arms and legs.

"It basically just gives our organization temporary custody of the child and allows us to apply for government assistance on his behalf until the legal guardian retains custody. In your case, this would be as soon as you get out of jail."

She wrapped her arm around the baby, bracing his head with one hand while she scribbled her name and the date with the other.

"Okay, well I guess that's it." She glanced at the signature before laying the form in her briefcase. "I'll go grab a copy of the certificate while you say your good-byes."

"Right now?" Miranda held the baby closer. Her breath shortened and her palms began to sweat.

"You take as long as you need, Ms. McGuire." She pulled her mask back over her mouth. "And, of course, my office will be in touch."

"Yeah," said the guard. "As long as you need. Just keep it under five minutes."

"Five minutes?" Panic set in. The baby sensed her distress and began to howl. They wept together. She tried to memorize his little face, the scent of his skin, the silken fuzz that covered his head, his tiny fingers and toes, the warmth of his breath, his weight on her chest. The time quickly evaporated.

"Come on, McGuire. We gotta go."

She held him tighter, kissed his eyes.

"That pretty little doctor left a care package for you along with instructions for use." She dug through its contents. "Something called Dermoplast to spray on your girly parts, a peri bottle to rinse yourself, Advil . . . I'll need to clear it all with the captain soon as we get back, but shouldn't be a problem, we just really need to get on the road."

All she could do was ignore her. She lifted her baby to her face, forehead to forehead. They stared into each other's eyes.

The guard grabbed him and began to tug. "Come on."

The baby screamed.

"Stop it!" Miranda cried.

"Just let go," the guard ordered.

The room began to spin, terrycloth slipped across her fingers. Suddenly she was clutching air.

"Jeez," the mullet muttered on the way to the door. "I hate this fucking job sometimes."

She could hear Cameron crying in the hall when the guard returned. Crying for her. She tried to get out of the bed, almost fell, but was caught in an iron grip.

"Easy now." Officer Tucker clicked her handcuffs. "Let's not make this situation any more traumatic than it already is."

Thirty minutes later, they were pulling into the county jail parking lot. She stared up at Grayskull from the squad car window, the desperation of her newborn's screams still echoing across the bombed-out rubble of her broken heart.

There is no God.

PART THREE
Postpartum

30

"Are you gonna eat today?" Amity set a tray on the end of her bunk. "It's your favorite. Hotdogs!"

Miranda stared at the wall, pillowcase damp with tears.

"Come on. Sit up." Her friend tugged at her limp arm. "You've gotta eat something or you'll die."

Death sounded appetizing; weightless, dreamless, soundproof death. Permanently offline. Do not resuscitate.

A spork pressed against her lips; two dice-sized canned carrot cubes and a sprout of nuclear green broccoli, bright enough to make her blink. It took more effort to resist.

"Yes!" Amity went back to the tray and reloaded. "Do you know the difference between broccoli and boogers?"

Chewing was endless and exhausting.

"Carli Higginbotham doesn't eat her broccoli." Another sporkful. "Sorry. Just trying to make you laugh."

Get her out of here, her inner narrator demanded.

Even the voice in her head was heavy and lethargic.

She lay back down while Amity was attempting to saw into the rubbery hotdogs with the dull plastic utensil. This time she refused to budge.

"I cut it into beanie weenies," said her cellmate. "Would you please just eat half? A couple bites? Miranda I'm worried about . . ."

She tuned her out. Listening required energy. *Everything* required energy. It took massive amounts of willpower just to stagger to the toilet at night. And when she reached it, she would just sit there and cry. Her vagina throbbed with pain. Milk leaked from her swollen nipples, milk on which her baby would never nurse. The physical discomfort was nothing compared to the crushing weight of guilt, of hopelessness, of inadequacy.

Somewhere deep inside her still lived an honor student who understood that everything she was experiencing could be reduced to molecules, brain chemistry, a predisposition for depression due to low serotonin levels magnified by the physical exhaustion of childbirth. But this knowledge was about as soothing and effective as Amity's small hands massaging her shoulders.

"It's gonna be okay," said her cellmate. "Lots of girls come back sad after they have their babies."

Sadness did not come anywhere near the soul of her condition, the emptiness, the inertia. All she could do was lie there and stare at the wall until sleep slid its gloved white chloroform hand over her mouth and tugged her back under.

It was some time after lights out when a male guard appeared at the cell bars. "McGuire! Front and center."

She opened her eyes and stared into a flashlight beam.

"Miranda McGuire?" He glanced up at the number over her cell.

She rolled over.

Amity leaped from the top bunk. Her bare feet slapped the concrete as she walked over to the bars. "She's not feeling good. Is there something I can help with?"

"Not feeling good . . . as in fever, dry cough, difficulty breathing?"

"No," said Amity, "as in postpartum. She just had a baby. Hey, don't you work in the infirmary?"

A burst of radio static ruptured the silence. He grunted. "For the last seven years, I have, ever since the new jail exploded, or imploded, whatever you wanna call it. Were you over there for that?"

"I heard about it."

"Damn gas leak. At the time I remember thinking that was about as terrifying as things could get. Then this co-rona stuff comes along."

"That's where I know you from," said Amity. "Blood pressure checks downstairs."

"Yeah. I need to get back to my post before the nurses start pulling insulin. I just volunteered to do Woodley's security check so I could find out about the baby. Do you know if it was a boy or a girl?"

"Miranda's baby? Who wants to know?"

"Her father. Patrick McGuire. He's been hounding me about it since he was moved downstairs."

"Her dad?" Amity gushed. "Tell him . . . tell him it's a boy!"

"A boy, huh? He'll be happy to hear he has a grandson. I'll let him know." A footstep, then, "Are you sure she's all right?"

"Mmm hmm. She's just recovering. It's hard. Hey, you said her dad moved downstairs? What for?"

His voice dropped a decibel. "Medical isolation. We just had 49 test positive for Covid. Most are asymptomatic. Most."

Miranda watched their shadows project on the wall. The cell grew quiet, motionless, as still as her childless belly.

"He may be headed for an outside hospital soon."

31

She trudged to the shower with cinderblocks tied to her feet, strapped to her back, hanging from her waist, dangling from her neck. Faceless strangers on the tier spoke her name as she passed. Someone touched her shoulder on the staircase. The world outside her mind was a tear-streaked blur, more sensed than seen. Inside was heavy and dark.

She stood beneath the shower and cried. Lukewarm needles of water beat the tears from her face, washing them down the drain with the blood and milk and dead skin cells. She remained there until count time. Then she dragged herself back up the stairs.

Amity was all over her as soon as the bars rolled. "You're soaking wet. Where's your towel? Are you still bleeding? That jumpsuit is dirty. Do you want me to brush your hair?"

It was easier to let her hover. Miranda plopped down on her bunk and went away while her cellmate tugged at her jumpsuit, dabbed at her with a towel, replaced the pads in her bra and handed her a clean one for her panties.

She went where she always went—back to the delivery room. To the howling little lifeform on her chest. To the moment before the cord was clamped and cut, when they were still connected. To those big blue eyes looking into her own. *Do I know you?*

"Miranda? You need to put that on so I can help you get into this clean jumpsuit."

She looked down at her hands. Dirty chipped nails picked at the pad. Wisps of the gauzy fabric unraveled and frayed.

"Come on," said Amity. "Ms. Woodley's gonna come through for count any minute. You know how she is about being dressed."

"I don't care . . . about Woodley." Her tongue felt thick, dry. She tried to recall the last time she uttered a word. Any word. *The health clinic?*

Amity smiled, touched her hand. "Yeah, you're right. Screw Woodley. Will you do it for me?"

She exhaled a heavy sigh and maneuvered the pad down the front of her panties. Then she allowed her cellmate to jostle her into the baggy jumpsuit.

Amity had moved on to her hair by the time the guard came through to count. She blew straight by. *"Nine, ten . . ."* Then backtracked. "McGuire, how we doing tonight?"

She willed the words out of her mouth. "I am—"

"Officer Tucker was just telling me how she helped deliver that young'un of yours." She raked her key against the bars. "That must've been a real shindig. Least you got outta here for a while, right?"

Memories curb-stomped her heart. The smell of his skin, the fuzzy softness of his head, his tiny nose, his clasping fingers, his perfection, his vulnerability, his tears . . .

"Put your mask on," she said before walking away.

Amity reached for the N95 at the foot of the bunk and tried to pull it over her head. She pushed it away.

"Come on, Miranda. I'm wearing mine."

She always wore hers. She slept in hers. But Miranda already felt like she was suffocating. The last thing she wanted was a mask. Waves of guilt washed over her, ripping open wounds, dousing them with seawater. Her shoulders racked with silent sobbing.

"Okay." Amity massaged her. "Okay."

She could feel herself sinking again, descending into darkness, black as Rorschach blots, dense as coastal fog.

"I have a surprise for you!" Amity ran to the bars, looked down the tier, then placed a foot on Miranda's bunk and vaulted herself up top.

Her frenetic energy was exhausting. It was like living in a cell with a moth. She could hear her upstairs rummaging, flipping back her mat, knocking over cups, humming, talking to herself in little bursts of encouragement. *"Come on, Am. They're right here somewhere . . . Aha! Now where are those Q-tips?"*

A yellow Bible tract fluttered down in front of her face and came to rest between her feet. The words, *Wages of Sin,* were emblazoned over a crude rendering of a man sitting on the floor of a cell. His back was against the wall, head on folded arms, arms on bended knees in the universal pose of despair. Miranda knew it well. Her body naturally gravitated to the position now that her stomach was quiet.

Amity dropped down from the top bunk and sat crosslegged at her feet. She folded a clean towel in half, then folded it again before laying it on the floor beside her. Next, she began setting items on top of it—an orange cannister of *Murray's* hair grease, a plastic spoon, a couple of Q-tips. Last, she produced a pad, bit a chunk from the end, and used her fingers to tear into the cottony center.

Miranda felt no curiosity, only fatigue. She watched from beneath heavy eyelids as Amity reached for her foot . . . and paused.

"Wages of Sin? What's this?" she grabbed the tract, scanned the back, and smiled. "Oh, it's mine." Then she crumpled it up and shot an airball at the toilet. "I read it already . . . scary."

Miranda moved to lay down.

"Wait!" Amity tugged at her foot. "I haven't even started yet. Here." She hopped up, grabbed the pillow and placed it behind her. "Just lean back. This won't take long."

Reluctantly, Miranda settled back against the flat pillow and watched as her cellmate began wedging maxi-pad stuffing between her toes.

"This is the closest I could get to cotton balls. You're not ticklish, are you?"

Her dad's voice echoed from a bolted storage unit in her mind. *If you're a good little girl . . . like you say you are . . . then you won't laugh when I tickle your feet . . .* Nothing in her body or soul felt capable of being ticklish. Not anymore, not ever again.

Amity unscrewed the lid from the plastic container of Murray's and stirred the contents with the spoon. "This isn't hair grease obviously." She replaced the spoon and selected a Q-tip. "It's floor wax. I got it from the trustee. I think she likes me." She dipped the Q-tip inside then held it over the top. Milky liquid flecked with silver dripped back into the canister. "See the glitter? That came from Brock Fisher's card. I scrapped it off." Her smile lit the cell, the smile of a girl who was clearly pleased with her own ingenuity.

Hot tears streamed down Miranda's cheeks as she watched her cellmate paint her toes in glittery white. She felt unworthy of such kindness. Her dad's voice again: *. . . this little piggy had roast beef, this little piggy had none . . .* She wondered if Cameron would ever get to experience his grandfather's take on this classic.

Amity redipped the Q-tip and looked up. "Do you like it?"

What she intended as a nod convulsed into a sob.

"Well, I think it looks beautiful." She inspected *to market* and moved on to *stayed home.* "Have you ever heard of havening? Ms. Amber taught me about it when I was on suicide watch last year. She compared it to hacking into a computer and changing stuff around. Except the computer is your brain." Amity glanced up from her toes, saw that she was listening, and set the Q-tip on the container. "What you have to do is hug yourself. Like this. And rub your arms up and down, up and down. I know it looks dumb. But if you do it, and breathe slow through your nose, it'll trick your brain into releasing oxycontin which makes you feel better."

Somewhere in the darkness of her being, a flicker of a smile stirred. "Oxytocin," she gently corrected.

Amity went back to work on her toes. "I'm just telling you what Ms. Amber said. She's gone anyway. The new mental health lady, Ms. Boyd? She just wants to put you on more medication."

"Hey Amity?"

Her brow was furrowed in intense concentration. She answered without looking. "Yeah?"

"Thank you."

32

"Nite bitches." Laughter on the tier. Toilets flushed. Cell bars rattled and rolled. She glanced at the window. Nightfall smoldered beyond the mesh and plexiglass. Somehow she managed to sleep through another day.

Look at the bright side, her inner narrator yawned. *Most new moms average an hour or two of sleep per night. You've been logging eighteen to twenty since you returned from the hospital.*

She fell back onto her pillow as if absorbing a physical blow. Ironic that the coldest voice in her world did not belong to some mean girl prisoner or sadistic guard but instead resided squarely in the center of her skull.

Amity's inverted face appeared over the side of the top bunk. "You missed the news again. You would've loved it tonight. Trump had a rally in Oklahoma, and nobody came. He looked so sad getting off that plane. I almost felt sorry for him."

"Ahem." Ms. Woodley glowered through the bars.

"Yay! Mail call!" said Amity. "You got anything for me in that stack?"

The grizzled guard scratched her nose with her palm. It made a wet clicking sound inside of her mask. "I don't know, Davenport. Are you gonna continue to bad mouth the President?"

Amity shook her upside-down head. "No ma'am."

In another life Miranda might have staunchly defended her cellmate's right to express her political opinions. It all seemed so trivial now. A colossal waste of energy. Not just politics . . . pills, school, writing, even hopes and dreams. Life itself. One gigantic exhausting drain. She rolled over.

"Hang on there, Sleeping Beauty," Woodley rasped. "Your busy little bunkie ain't the only lucky winner tonight. Got something here for you too. This'n ain't a return to sender neither."

Miranda watched her slide a manilla envelope between the bars. She felt no enthusiasm, none of Amity's excitement. Her inner weather remained inveterate and undeviating. Guilt and self-loathing stretched beyond the horizon.

Amity leaped from the top bunk and landed in a crouch. "I'll get it."

"Not without your mask, you won't."

"Oh yeah." Amity spun around and grabbed the N95 that was hanging from her bunk. "I thought I had it on."

Woodley rolled her eyes, scratched her nose again. "How'd you get a nicer mask than me anyway?"

"Miranda brung me one back from the hospital. You can have it if you want. I still have my old one. I made it out of Heather Wilcox's bra." She plucked both envelopes from the bars and glanced at the smaller white one. "Yesss!"

"Hmpph." The guard studied Miranda. "I wonder what else she brought back from her little field trips."

"All kinds of stuff!" said Amity. "Pain killer spray, a squirt bottle for after she pees—she's not supposed to wipe. And they gave her some way better pads than the granny pads the jail passes out."

I know what we didn't bring back, her inner narrator murmured. *I'll give you a hint . . . he weighed eight pounds, eight ounces.*

Miranda faced the wall.

"She sure has been acting strange," said the guard. "I might need to do a cell search pretty soon. Some of my unconfirmed sources have been telling me about all the Suboxone that's been floating around here recently."

Amity was quiet for a moment. "We don't do drugs."

"That's what they all say, and besides you don't have to do them to sell them. Y'all forget I know what you're in here for. See that computer out there in the officers' station? It's got all your information on it."

"I'm in here for an accident," said Amity.

"Hmmph." She marched off.

Amity waited till she was a few cells down the tier, then danced over to her bunk. "Brock Fisher wrote me again! And you got a letter from somebody named Marciaaaaa . . . Viajera?"

"I'll read it tomorrow," she mumbled into her pillow.

"'Kay," said Amity. "I'll just put it right here."

Papers rustled next to her head. Amity vaulted up into her bunk and tore into the letter from her pen pal. Down the wing, Miranda could hear Ms. Woodley spreading more correctional cheer. She closed her eyes. The baby was right there, breathing on her collarbone, making those soft little gurgling noises.

"He sent me an *ICare* package!" Amity's voice rang out.

"Hope he got your ass some Colgate," Keisha from downstairs fired back.

"I want my cut, Amityville," said Summer.

"Y'all quiet down!" Woodley shouted. "It's bedtime."

Miranda rolled onto her back and stared up at the steel underbelly of the top bunk.

Amity's voice dropped to a whisper and wafted down through the crack. "You get half of my candy bars."

The lights on the tier dimmed. The overhead fluorescent would soon follow. She glanced to her immediate right. The manilla envelope was wedged beneath her mat and hung over the side of the bunk. She watched it bob in the downdraft of the vent.

"He wants to sign up for a video visit!" Amity breathed. "I've never had a video visit."

She closed her eyes. The envelope remained. A butterscotch afterimage pulsing in her mind.

"I've never had *any* visits," her cellmate continued to babble.

She inhaled, exhaled, reached over, grabbed the envelope. Her name was written in an elegant green font above the jail's P.O. Box. She stared at the letters that formed *Miranda McGuire,* stared so long that the familiar words began to look foreign. All those lines and loops equaled a person and the person was supposed to be her, but there was no connection. The experience was similar to staring into her own eyes in the bathroom mirror as a little girl. She felt detached. Dislocated.

Her fingernail was chipped and jagged and still bore traces of the glittery floor wax that Amity had applied the week before. She dug it beneath the piece of scotch tape, popped the envelope, and slid out its contents.

The first thing she saw was the footprints, one on either side of the page. She traced each cherubic toe, the valleys and ridges of the ball, the tiny cracks and swirls of the heel. Those same little feet that kicked in her belly for the duration of the third trimester and sought traction on her sweaty stomach moments after birth.

"Would you ever date a fifty-year-old?" Amity hopped down from her bunk. "Like if he was really nice and wrote you letters and worked at an auto parts store?"

Miranda ignored her. The top of the page said *Certificate of Birth* in Old English script. Below it was a picture of the driveway, fountain and foremost building of the Brownsville Medical Center complete with palms, stucco archways, and Spanish tile roofing.

Thought you might want a copy of this for your records, read a yellow sticky near the bottom. *Stay strong and keep your chin tucked. You have so much to live for. I wish both of you the best of luck. Love, Marcia.*

"Who's Marcia?" Amity wiggled in beside her.

"Nobody." She removed the Post-it and stuck it on the overhead steel.

This is to certify that Cameron Patrick McGuire was born to Miranda Kerry McGuire and _____ on this 2nd day of June, 2020.

"Hey!" Amity gushed. "Cameron! I knew that was his name."

The lights clicked off. Miranda carefully replaced the birth certificate in the envelope and slid it beneath her mat. "I really wish you wouldn't read my mail."

"Why not?" Big owlish eyes materialized in the darkness. "You read mine."

"No I don't."

"Well you could if you wanted."

"I don't want to."

"Why are you being so mean?"

"I'm not being mean."

"Yes you are." She stomped her foot. "Ever since you came back from the hospital, you've been so . . . so cold."

Miranda closed her eyes. "I lost my baby, okay? Just please—"

"I lost mine too."

"No Amity. You killed your baby. There's a difference."

A poisonous silence fell over the cell, irrevocable and terminal.

"I'm sorry," she immediately said, hating her voice, hating her knee-jerk cruelty, hating herself. "I didn't mean that."

Amity rose slowly, a sorrowful shadow in the darkness. And like a tendril of smoke, she vanished up into her bunk.

33

The Asian girl in the elevator kept slinging her bangs over the swollen purple slit of her right eye. Miranda remembered her from the one time she attempted to go to rec and instead wound up in a psych evaluation. Her name was Nguyen unless you were Ms. Woodley, in which case it was *Nugent*. She lived across the hall.

"Hey, I remember you," she said in a voice that was more South Alabama than Saigon. "You was just prego not too long ago. Was it a girl or a boy?"

The guard who was escorting them downstairs glanced over at her. A gold sheriff's star was steam-pressed on his forest green mask.

"Boy," she mumbled, inspecting her crocs.

"Is my shiner making you uncomfortable? It's ugly ain't it?" She slung her bangs defiantly. "I've had worse. My baby's daddy was a wannabe MMA fighter and a roid head. He sent me to Sacred Heart more than a few times over the years. This ain't shit."

"What happened this time?" asked the officer. "And don't tell me you slipped in the shower."

Miranda closed her eyes as they descended. Their muffled voices echoed down the corridors of her brain. It was as if they were talking on the other side of the elevator doors.

"Nah, I got jumped by some bitches on Red side. They quarantined my pod last week because Frances Montgomery came back from insulin with a fever. All of a sudden, I'm getting blamed for bringing the Wu-flu from China. First of all, I'm Vietnamese. There's a difference. Second, I've lived in Myrtle Grove my whole life!"

The elevator trembled to a stop. The doors hissed open. "Well maybe your lawyer has some good news for you," said the guard. "This way ladies."

Miranda trudged behind them, her feet as heavy as her heart. Had life always been such a slog? Maybe it was just the jail—the concrete, the steel, the drab paint scheme, the smell. It was all so debilitating, designed to convey hopelessness. Head down, she moved forward. One foot in front of the other. Images haunted her every step. The baby wailed, milkless, motherless. Her father lay dying on a hospital bed alone. Amity cried herself to sleep.

The guard swung open a steel door and frowned back at her. "Are you all right?"

She nodded.

"Well come on, catch up. Your attorney is waiting."

As she crossed the hall to where they were standing, it occurred to her that this was the same place she talked politics with the psychologist. She felt the baby kick and longingly caressed her belly. Cavernous silence awaited her hands. Lifeless as a desert highway.

Her public defender was on the opposite side of the plexiglass, tie loosened, hair gelled, a Blue Wahoos mask concealing his dimpled chin.

"Heyyy, you got Tipton?" Nguyen slung her bangs and waved with her fingers. "Lucky girl. I had him in misdemeanor court last year. So cute, and smart. I've got Turnbull." She rolled her lone visible eye. "Ever had him?"

Miranda shook her head.

"Old alcoholic perv . . . wouldn't know the law if it bit him on the—"

"Let's go," said the guard. "You can chit-chat when you get back upstairs."

The bars slammed behind her. She sank onto the metal stool. She could hear Nguyen's crocs slapping the waxed linoleum as she wandered over to the next cell. Tentatively, she picked up the receiver.

"Wow, you look different . . . skinny." He left his mask on. "Did everything come out, you know, healthy?"

She stared down at her toes. The last remnants of Amity's pedicure sparkled patchily from her nails. "Yeah."

"Excellent," he said. "That must have been really difficult to go through in here."

She shrugged.

"Are you okay? You look pale. I saw on the news where there are more positive cases popping up in here every day."

"I'm fine," she said.

How's your dad? her inner narrator smirked.

"Well I'm glad to hear it." His eyes conveyed sincerity. "These are dangerous times. The governor may have been a little premature in declaring Florida open for business."

She picked lint balls from the lap of her jumpsuit.

"Okay, down to business." He pulled some papers from his open briefcase and stacked them on the Formica. "I have here the results of Dr. Silverstein's competency exam and he finds no evidence of psychosis. Neither at the time of the offense nor at the present in your ability to stand trial . . ." He paused, read a little more to himself, and tossed the papers back into his briefcase. "So, there's that."

She should have been interested and engaged, should have been anxious, if not hysterical. After all, her life was hanging in the balance. Instead, she was only numb. Part of her felt like she deserved all the misery and misfortune that fate could heap on her plate.

She glanced up at him. He no longer resembled Nick. It was difficult to even conjure an image of Nick to compare him to. Strange that the father of her child and the spineless jellyfish responsible for her sitting in jail had a face so indistinguishable, so unremarkable, that she could not retrieve it from memory. The synaptic glue that held his features together in her mind had weakened from neglect, the image produced was distorted, pixelated. Like a blurred boob on a Jerry Springer rerun.

"The State is still offering ten years." He stared at her. "I tried to talk them down to eight, but the prosecutor won't budge. I thought maybe with this current Covid logjam, we'd have a little negotiating capital. Some of my other clients have benefitted from it. I don't think there's been a trial since March and the system is getting more and more congested with every arrest. Unfortunately, your case is such a slam dunk. It's the 775 enhancement that's killing us. They already feel like they're bending over backwards for you by offering ten years for a first degree PBL."

Her breath was warm in her mask. Her eyes felt heavy. She wished she could lay her head on the cool Formica until he finished.

"PBL means punishable by life," he clarified. "Sorry. I spend so much time in zoom conferences with judges and other attorneys discussing habeas corpus and certiorari and PDRs and PSIs . . . sometimes I forget that civilians don't speak Latin and legalese."

Civilian? her inner narrator scoffed.

"Oh, and the 775 enhancement? That's actually 775.087, Section 2. The firearm reclassification statute. Your trafficking charge falls under 893.135. I forget the subsection for 28 grams of heroin. But my point is that I know your case well. I've gone over it multiple times since our last meeting and I just don't see—"

Miranda lay her head on the Formica.

"Shit," he mumbled, "not this again."

"I'm okay. Just exhausted. Continue."

He hesitated. "I was just going to say that I really don't see a lot of, uh, options moving forward other than, you know, signing the, um . . . hey, it's really awkward talking to your head. Or not awkward but maybe surreal. Absurd. I mean, don't get me wrong, it's a nice head, an interesting head. Very . . . red. But it's difficult to hold a conversation with . . ."

She slid her palm between her cheek and the cool surface and stared up at him through the plexiglass.

"There you are. Much better. Are you sure you're okay?"

"Positive."

"Look, you don't need to make a decision right now. No one is going to jury trial anytime soon, but as your attorney, I strongly advise you to consider the State's plea offer. The case against you is open and shut and there is no reason to believe that Banaski will treat you any differently than every other armed trafficker found guilty in her courtroom."

Her shoulder throbbed from holding the receiver to her ear. She balanced it on her face, closed her eyes.

"Are you . . . high?" He looked around before leaning toward the glass and whispering, "Are there drugs in there?"

With Herculean effort, she forced an eye open. "I don't do drugs."

"Well I'm not judging you either way. I'm on your side. Listen, I know ten years sounds like an eternity. But when did you get arrested? I know it was last year . . ." He dug around in his briefcase.

"October."

"Last October," he said. "So, coming up on a year. You'd get credit for all that, plus time off for good behavior, and when you factor in all the talk in Tallahassee about prison reform, you could very well be at work release in a few years. Definitely no more than seven. How old are you again?"

She didn't answer.

He went back into his briefcase. "November fifth, 2000. So you'll be twenty in a couple of months. I'm twenty-eight. Do I look old and decrepit to you? You'd be younger than I am right now when you came home."

What home? said her inner narrator.

"I thought you said they weren't having court."

"I said they aren't holding trials right now. Docket dates are a different story. You can plea out in video court and be on the next bus out of this place." He closed his briefcase. "Or we can wait until the courts reopen and take our chances with a jury. You already know my feelings on this but if a trial is what you opt for, I will do everything in my power to provide a vigorous defense. You don't have to make a decision right now. We've got a couple weeks. Just think about it."

The long trek back up to the sixth floor was a streaky haze of bright fluorescent lights, passing guards, and sinister overhead cameras. The antiseptic smell of the hallway infiltrated her mask as Nguyen's voice droned and twanged in her ear. She craved her bunk the way she once craved K4 Dilaudids: achingly, hungrily.

The orange steel door rumbled shut behind her, a moment later the bars rolled open. The women in the dayroom watched and whispered as she dragged herself up the stairs. None of the faces were familiar.

The pod was unnaturally quiet for a Monday afternoon. *Divorce Court* blared from the television, but it rang hollow in the absence of competing voices and only highlighted the surrounding silence. A carnival barker on an empty midway.

She plodded along the tier. Vague shapes parted to allow her passage. Soft tissue brushed against her. A sad smile swam into focus then quickly disappeared. The iron finish line of her cell door was only a few steps away. It occurred to her that Amity was not out front, not watching TV, not leaning against the railing in her trademark sports bra and tattered thermal bottoms. She turned toward the cell entrance with a sinking feeling.

The top bunk was empty. No linen, no property, only rusted steel. Amity's mat was rolled up at the head of the bed with the pillow resting on top of it.

She heard footsteps behind her. A hand brushed her shoulder.

"They packed her up a little while ago," said Summer. "Suicide watch."

34

Frances Montgomery's glasses were held together by Saran Wrap and foggy from the breath that escaped her mask. She kept pushing them back up on her nose as she hunched over the pocket Bible in her lap. Her trembling finger flew over the words, line after line, page after page, as if she was frantically seeking salvation and the window was closing.

Miranda watched her from across the holding cell while the girl next to her talked her ear off, annoyingly modulating the ends of her sentences so that each sounded like a question.

"My public defender? Mr. Tipton? He thinks I should sign a deal for a year and a day in prison? But that's like, sooooo long? I already missed Caleb's second birthday. Could you imagine if I missed his third?"

She blinked, and in the space of the blink her baby's eyes searched her own; innocent and vulnerable. He deserved better. It wasn't his fault that his mother was an addict and a prisoner. She hoped he landed in a loving home.

"I'm hoping for Keeton? The drug program? Have you ever been there?"

Miranda shook her head and got up. Her foot was asleep. She could feel the other women's eyes on her as she staggered across the cell.

"Um, sorry?" the girl called behind her. "Social distancing? Like, I get it?"

Social distancing. Was there a bigger oxymoron within the crumbling walls of the county jail? She was already about as distant socially as one could possibly be. Distance in the physical sense with her cloistered cage high above Fairfield Drive, but even more secluded mentally, emotionally, in the dark trenches of her mind.

She walked to the front of the holding tank and gripped the bars. Her shadow projected weakly onto the cinderblocks across the narrow hall. Though murky and opaque, she could still fill in the details. A dandruffed, slump-shouldered, broken thing stared back at her.

During her ten-month stay on Blue Six, her wing had flipped multiple times. Women were always getting in fights, bonding out, making trustee, going to court, going to prison. The unit was in constant flux. Amity was the only mainstay, and now she was gone too. But in each manifestation, there was always that *one girl*: unwashed, despondent, shattered. As she stared at her silhouette, it dawned on her that the title was now hers—she had become the damaged girl on the wing.

Pounding boots echoed in the hall. Her shadow was gradually overtaken. "Well dammit if it ain't Biggun." The mullet jangled her keys. "'Cept you ain't big no more. You getting outta here today or what?"

Miranda shrugged as the holding cell door swung open.

"I know you wanna see that young'un of yours." She turned to the guard beside her. A gaunt middle-aged woman with thinning hair. "I delivered this one's baby a while back."

"I heard about that."

"All right ladies," said Officer Tucker, "line up out here on the wall. Montgomery, put that Bible away. Cameras are watching, so from this point forward I want you to maintain social distancing and keep your masks on at all times."

The other guard slammed the door behind them.

"Lead the way, McGuire," Tucker frowned, "and regardless of what happens in court, I want you to take a shower when you get back upstairs. You smell like shit."

Slowly, she made her way down the narrow corridor while the other women followed at six-foot intervals. Her arm brushed the wall. The thick paint felt grimy against her skin. She wondered if Covid could transfer from surfaces to pores. She leaned into it.

The male tanks were at half capacity. But that didn't stop the lewd comments from spewing through the bars like raw sewage.

"Aw shit. Check it out y'all. The pussy parade is coming!"

"Damn bitch, whatthafuck happened to you?"

"She had my baby. That's what happened. Bring that little ass over here, Red. Lemme give you another one."

"She looks like she got AIDS."

"Show me them titties, ho!"

She remembered her first night in jail, walking the same hallway, passing the same holding cells, hearing the same comments, feeling outraged, mortified, terrified . . . Now she felt nothing. She heard the words, even braced for the sting, but the hurt never came. It reminded her of the epidural. Not just the numbness, but the awareness of pressure; the sense that trauma was happening on some level, but feeling walled off from the pain.

The hallway ended at a massive steel door. As she stood there waiting, a piece of prose from her old life thundered over the loudspeakers in her mind, echoing across the dry riverbeds and canyons where she walked alone. Something about returning to where she started and knowing the place for the first time. *Eliot? Kipling?* English Lit felt light-years away.

This was her reality now—the steel, the plexiglass, the inhumanity, the unchecked testosterone thundering through the bars to her immediate left.

"Look over here bitch. Check out what daddy's got for you . . ."

With dead eyes, she turned toward the voice, laughter exploded from the holding cell. Hard faces stretched in the shadows. One of them had diamond encrusted teeth and an eyepatch. Something in her memory stirred. He held a finger to his lips. *Shhhh . . .*

"If y'all don't shut the fuck up . . ." Ms. Tucker jiggled her key into the lock. "I will personally make sure that every one of you remain in that tank until tomorrow morning. Court or no court. So if you enjoy sleeping on steel, keep bumping your damn gums."

The feisty guard snatched off her Oakleys, shook out her mullet, and stared the raucous cell into silence. When order was established and the alpha acknowledged, she put her sunglasses back on and held the door open. "Go ahead, McGuire." The women filed into the main hallway of the jail behind her.

Gucci! Her inner narrator nudged. *Everything's Gucci!*

Miranda glanced over her shoulder. The door slammed. She wondered if the wannabe thug, sperm donor was in there with him. Maybe Nick was one of those faces in the holding cell; contorted in laughter, leering, catcalling, clutching his crotch. It was possible. His image remained a darkened silhouette in her memory, a deleted profile pic on a dead page. Maybe she overlooked him in the murk.

Doubt it, said her inner narrator. *He'd be hiding on the toilet if he was in there.*

Wherever he was, he had no idea that he had a son. That was the lone silver lining. As long as the artist formerly known as Nick remained ignorant—or at least indifferent—to his son's existence, Cameron would never fall victim to his toxic influence, his selfishness, his cowardice . . .

And in a few minutes, barring any unforeseen circumstances, he would be safe from her as well.

She vaguely remembered video court from her first morning in jail—newly jumpsuited inmates packed thigh to thigh in rows of hard plastic chairs, a dour-looking judge on a television monitor holding conversations with people off screen, a tired public defender in an ill-fitting suit pleading a conveyor belt of defendants "not guilty," hustling guards replenishing vacated seats with warm bodies . . .

Covid changed everything.

Aside from the handful of women scattered across the first two rows and the tall, freckled guard adjusting the camera, the room was empty.

"All right ladies," said Ms. Tucker as they shambled down the aisle. "We're gonna maintain our social distance. I want five chairs between y'all. That means four to a row, two on each side of the aisle. But staggered, so you ain't sitting directly behind each other. That would defeat the whole purpose."

"All rise," announced the freckled guard. "The Honorable Claire Banaski presiding."

Miranda looked around to see if all the other women were getting up. They were. She was already worn out from the walk over. The thought of standing when she just sat down was exhausting, not to mention ridiculous.

"Be seated," said Judge Banaski as Miranda was struggling to her feet.

She plopped back down and leaned right to see around the massive human being sitting three seats over on the next row.

"Clerk?" said the judge from the television screen, more Zoom meeting than criminal court proceeding.

"State versus Hailey Braddock, Your Honor," said a high-pitched nasally voice off camera.

"Um, right here? Not sure what to do? This is my first time?"

The freckled guard made a *come here* motion with his hand. Annoying vocal inflection girl pushed back her chair and stood. The bald Amazon in front of her sucked her teeth, glanced back over a hulking deltoid, and scowled like Nebraska Jackson. Then she smiled.

"Well, well, well, Snowbunny Red. You finally had that baby, huh? You just gonna sit back there and not say nothin'?"

Miranda glanced across the room at Officer Tucker. She was busy pantomiming submission techniques to her coworker.

"You shaved your head."

"Facts," said Nebraska. "I caught lice when I got off lockdown. Don't tell Bianca. She messin' with anybody up there?"

Miranda tried to remember if Bianca was still on Blue Six.

"She is, ain't she? I heard she was talkin' to some skinny bitch on Red side. Fuck it. These crackers 'bout to send me down the road anyway. Do you know how many bad bitches are at Lowell? I ain't got time for all that drama in my life. Facts."

The television screen was Brady Bunched into four quarters. Judge Banaski was top left, top right was dark, the prosecutor glowered beneath the judge, and her very own frat boy PD beamed from bottom right. He reminded her of a first-time contributor to the Powerhouse Roundtable on *This Week with George Stephanopoulos.*

"I saw your little dizzy-ass bunkie in the psych cell the other day."

"Is she okay?"

Nebraska shrugged. "I don't know. I didn't talk to her. But she's in the psych cell so probably not."

". . . no Amity. You didn't lose your baby. You killed her. There's a difference."

The scab that encrusted her heart was ripped again. She stared down at her hands, gnawed nails on twined fingers. A shadow stretched across the floor, seeping toward her. Officer Tucker was standing at the end of the row.

"Zip it, McGuire. You too Jackson. Y'all can exchange phone numbers after court."

Nebraska watched her walk away. "I can't stand that bitch."

Across the room, Hailey Braddock raised her right hand in front of the television monitor and solemnly swore to tell the truth.

"So whatchu down here for?" said Nebraska. "You 'bout to cop out, ain't you?"

Miranda looked to see if Tucker was still watching. She was.

"Man, fuck that bitch. We're looking at time, Red. Her petty ass rules don't apply to us. Look, I don't blame you for copping out. My auntie is doing life in the Feds for armed trafficking. You can't play with that charge. These crackers'll bury your ass." She jerked her massive head toward the video screen, "'specially nasty Banaski."

Hailey Braddock returned to her seat with a smile that no mask could contain.

"Um, so she gave me probation? Maybe this is our lucky day?"

"Shut up bitch."

A group of male inmates was ushered in and seated across the back five rows. "Quietly," Tucker admonished.

"Clerk?" said Banaski from the television.

"State versus Miranda McGuire."

"Miranda McGuire," the freckled guard echoed.

She stood and smoothed her rumpled jumpsuit. Then she headed to the front of the room.

"Good morning," trilled Banaski in her ornate white Notorious RBG collar.

Step into my parlor, said the spider to the fly.

"State your name for the record."

"Miranda McGuire."

"Very good." She frowned through her reading glasses at something on her desk, flipped through some pages, and looked up. "Let's get you sworn in Ms. McGuire. Raise your right hand please."

Miranda showed her palm to the camera. In the box next to the judge, a vitamin-deficient redhead with plum-colored bags beneath hollow eyes mimicked her movement.

"Do you swear to tell the truth, the whole truth, and nothing but the truth, so help you God?"

"I do."

"Very good," said Banaski. "Now on the screen in front of you is the prosecutor in your case, Mr. Alexander. And you're obviously well acquainted with your attorney, Mr. Tipton."

Her public defender smiled in front of a bookshelf lined with *Statutes Annotated* and *Southern Reporters.*

"We're all here this morning to discuss . . ." She rifled through unseen papers on her desk. "Aha. This. A plea agreement which you recently signed. Are you still interested in pleading to a single count of . . ." She scanned the paper. "Trafficking while armed?"

"I am," she said quietly.

"And is ten years in state prison your understanding of the plea offer?"

"It is."

"Your Honor, if I may," her public defender interjected, "that is ten years *minus* credit for time served and any time off for good behavior she might accrue."

"Naturally," said the judge.

"And I would like it on the record . . ." the prosecutor paused and tasted his mustache with the tip of his tongue, "that the State's offer is in accordance with the minimum mandatory law regarding possession of a firearm in the commission of a felony. The statute calls for ten years."

"Noted, Mr. Alexander." The judge stared into the camera; blowtorch-blue intelligent eyes burned from the wrinkled flesh that pooled around her orbital bones. "Anything else before we proceed, counselors?"

The prosecutor shook his head. "That's all I've got."

"No ma'am," said Tipton.

"Very good." She held up a paper. "I have here the psychological evaluation and determination by Dr. Silverstein that you are, in fact, competent. But for the record, do you understand the gravity of your situation? Are you cognizant of the fact that you are charged with a crime that carries up to life imprisonment?"

She nodded.

"Speak up, please."

"I understand."

The judge searched her face. "And after careful consideration, you feel like pleading guilty is the best course of action."

"No contest," Tipton intervened again. "The agreement is for a no contest plea. Not a guilty plea, Your Honor."

"That's correct." The prosecutor stifled a yawn. "Nolo contendere."

"Semantics," she grumbled. "Ms. McGuire, do you feel that pleading *no contest* in exchange for a ten-year term of imprisonment is the best course of action in your case?"

"Yes, Your Honor."

"Has anyone coerced you into this decision?"

"No, Your Honor."

"Do you understand that by entering this plea, you are forfeiting your right to a jury trial?"

"I understand."

"And you're comfortable with that?"

"I am."

"Have you taken any drugs or alcohol in the last 24 hours?"

"I don't do drugs."

"Are you satisfied with the job that Mr. Tipton has done as your attorney?"

She glanced at the square inhabited by her frat boy public defender. "Yes."

"Very good." The judge removed her glasses. "Now I want you to think hard about the next question because it's of grave importance."

Miranda waited in front of the screen, hands behind her back.

"Does the fact that Covid cases appear to be on the rise at the jail factor into your decision to plead no contest today?"

"Not at all."

"You are not fearful of catching the coronavirus?"

I would love to catch the coronavirus.

"No, I'm not."

"Very good." She shifted some papers around and nodded to someone off camera. "Ms. McGuire, as to the charge of trafficking heroin in excess of 28 grams while in possession of a firearm, how do you plea?"

"No contest."

Time stalled. She could almost feel the molecules in the room grinding to a state of inactivity, falling all around her like snowflakes.

"I'm going to accept your plea as knowingly and willingly made. I hereby adjudicate you guilty as charged and sentence you to a term of 120 months in the Florida Department of Corrections with credit for time served plus any court costs, fines, and fees. Best of luck to you Ms. McGuire." She whacked her gavel on the bench. "Next."

The sound did not translate well to the screen. It felt anticlimactic. She was sent on her way not with a thunderous crash but with a dismissive token gesture. *Tick.*

There was a surrealistic element to the entire experience—the judge's thin blue lips, the prosecutor's salt and pepper mustache, Tipton's telegenic teeth. It was as if she were watching a bad Lifetime movie about some other woman's unraveling.

The tall, freckled deputy touched her shoulder. "You can go now."

She turned away from the screen and walked back up the aisle, past Nebraska, past the scattered faces of the women and men in the back, to the waiting guards by the door, and into the next decade of her life.

ACKNOWLEDGEMENTS

When I began this journey in 2019 I thought I was going to just crack my knuckles, grab my pen, and let the magic happen. After all, it was a story about a young woman trapped in the criminal justice system. Right in my wheelhouse. I knew the system, grew up in the system. And aside from a few obvious anatomical differences, women are really no different than men, right? Ha. Like most endeavors where I've charged in arrogantly, I quickly realized I was in over my head.

I'm grateful to the mothers and daughters who bailed me out with insider info. Ginger Wolford, Hailey McGuire (no relation), Renee Greene Kelly, Faith Kelly, Shannon Rose, Florala Reese, Amber Rhodes, Ashton Roland, Hannah Peters, Megan Collins, Amy Elliott, Sheena Law, Dara Stokes, Brittney Knapp, Marlo Knapp, and April Tate.

A thunderous shout-out to the real Marcia, a first-ballot hall-of-fame midwife who walked me through the entire 40 weeks of pregnancy and taught me words like colostrum, Pitocin, and effacement. If Miranda's labor experience is at all realistic, it's because I have friends like Marcia Ensminger. All errors and inconsistencies are mine.

I also want to acknowledge the lady who transcribes and transforms these messy pages into legible paragraphs and chapters. Deciphering the slop is second nature to her. She's been reading my work since kindergarten. Ten years ago we were sitting in a prison visitation park on the Florida panhandle when I asked her a pivotal question. "If I wrote a book, would you type it?" Five novels, a couple hurricanes, and one global pandemic later, we're still going strong. I love you Ms. Doris. You're a national treasure.

Special thanks to my good friend and editor Kelly Conrad. A straight up voice in a crooked world. Who knows what America will look like by the time this goes to print. I'm fortunate to have intelligent people like you in my life to help make sense of it all. Facts.

To my incarcerated sisters, I wasn't bullshitting in the dedication—I wrote this for you. (If the last four are any indication, you're the only ones who'll be reading it anyway.) Cancel culture will say that I have no right to tell this story . . . your story. They'll say that straight white males should stick to straight white male subject matter. But my race is prisoner. My gender is prisoner. So, too, is my tax bracket, my religion, and my political affiliation. My mission from the gate has been to humanize us. To show that we are more than mugshots and rap sheets. Though society may say otherwise, we are not defined by the worst instances in our lives. I hope you see yourselves in Miranda, the way that I see myself in you.

Finally I want to thank the incomparable Shonda Kerry. The smartest girl I know. More than a research assistant, more than a partner, more than a best friend. It goes without saying that your fingerprints are all over this one. We are waveform.

Turn the page for a preview of

The Weight of Entanglement

The next Miranda McGuire novel
by Malcolm Ivey

Available Fall 2021
from Astral Pipeline Books

>ij=

PREVIEW

The seven-hour van ride had taken its toll. Her legs buckled from cramps that rivaled opiate withdrawals. Sweat trickled down her stiff back as she stood in line, naked except for her mask.

The woman in front of her was violently scratching her backside. Islands of blood encrusted bumps and purple welts littered the landscape of her hefty body. The woman behind her was whimpering.

"Shut the fuck up," drawled a corn-fed guard in mirrored shades and a faded FDC cap. She lifted a black Covid bandana to spit chew in a milk carton, "and for gawd sakes quit scratching your fat ass. You're worse than a damn dawg. You got chiggers or something?"

The line shuffled forward. Someone up front kept coughing. She wondered if any of the women around her had the virus. Thoughts of toxic droplets and aerosols made her think of her dad again. His memory had been a constant companion since the county van had pulled onto the I-10 on-ramp. Especially over the stretch of interstate between Pensacola and Crestview. Everywhere she looked there were ghosts—ghosts of a father and daughter—wandering down the rows of pines, waiting out the rain beneath the underpass, scrambling up the embankment with Coke cans full of creek water to pour into the radiator of the overheated truck.

She hoped he was still alive.

Another loud cough, another step forward. She glanced back at the bench where she was ordered to leave her property so that she could be strip searched. Some of the women had mesh bags full of letters, cosmetics, canteen. All she brought was a single manilla envelope containing a birth certificate.

Cameron flashed in her memory. More than just his image, she could smell the crown of his head, feel the softness of his cheek, hear the innocence of his gurgling. He would be nine when she returned to Pensacola. Some other woman would potty train him, teach him to say *Mama*, cook his food, clean his wounds, comfort him when he had nightmares.

Nine years. Nine more trips around the sun. Did planet Earth even have the stamina? Between the melting ice caps, disappearing rain forests, hurricanes, tornadoes, wildfires, pandemics, and violent clashes across the globe, it all felt so combustible.

"Y'all two," a skinny black guard with a gold tooth hooked her finger at Miranda and the woman in front of her, "step in here."

The room was no bigger than a walk-in closet. There was a mural painted on the wall of the FDC logo: a circle encompassing a map of the state. *Florida Department of Corrections Est. 1868.* Right below it was a mission statement in drippy, spray-paint stenciled letters. "Inspiring success by transforming one life at a time."

A second guard who could have been Gold Tooth's sister saw her reading the credo and smirked. "Don't believe it, Red. The only transforming you gonna do in here is from straight to gay." She smacked her flashlight against her gloved palm. "Unless you already gay."

Miranda shivered. The woman next to her scratched her butt.

"All right y'all, quick and painless," said Gold Tooth. "Take off your masks, set them on that bench behind you. Now hold out your hands. Wiggle your fingers. Good. Open your mouths. Wider, come on. Lemme see under them tongues."

Miranda squeezed her eyes shut as the second guard shined the flashlight in her mouth.

"All right, lift your titties up. Both of y'all, let's go."

Her face burned with humiliation. Flashlight noticed her discomfort and smiled.

"Good. Bend at the waist. Run your fingers through your hair. Keep doing it till I say stop."

"That ain't gonna get it, Red," said Flashlight. "Shake that shit out like fat girl over here. You hiding something in there?"

She frantically clawed at her hair, raking down from the scalp, not only to prove she had nothing to hide but to show she could follow instructions. Ten months in Grayskull had taught her that guards liked making examples. She could feel the spotlight narrowing around her and did everything she could to resist it.

"Stop. Stand up and turn around. Palms on the wall," Gold Tooth mechanically instructed. "Lift your left foot. Let me see the bottom—"

"Your other left, fat ass!"

"—okay, right foot. Good," said Gold Tooth. "Now listen carefully. You're gonna bend at the waist again. Touch your head to that bench right there. I want you to reach back with your left hand and grab a handful of ass. Same thing with your right. Separate and cough. Let's go."

Miranda was mortified, traumatized. This was nothing like a county pat search.

"Now reach down to your vagina. Same thing, separate and cough."

"Ahem. Ahem."

"That ain't gonna get it Red."

The bench was cold against her forehead. She opened her eyes and looked back between her legs. The flashlight was inches from her genitalia, illuminating her most private places.

"Fat Ass, you can go. Make sure you tell the nurse about all that itching. Red, I'ma need you to cough louder."

"Ahem. Ahem."

"Louder, damn it. If you hiding something in your pocketbook, I will find it."

"I'm not—"

"Shut up and cough!"

"Ahem!"

"Quit trying to be all prim and polite and belt that shit! I wanna see those vaginal walls shake. You're not getting up until it happens."

"Ahem. Ahem. AHEM!"

The flashlight clicked off. "Get your ass outta here."

She stumbled through the doorway covering herself, half blind with fear and outrage, feeling violated on every level.

"And hush up all that damn crying too," said Flashlight. "What'd you think this was *Orange is the New Black?* This ain't Danbury, Piper. This is the Florida Department of Corrections. You better act like you know."

She found a spot in the corner. An orderly in starched blues handed her a worn set of underwear. She had never been so grateful for second-hand granny panties in her life.

Another woman was coughing in the shakedown room. Another victim.

And you thought it was corona, her inner narrator scoffed. *Dizzy bitch.*

The world was against her. Hard faces surrounded her. Across the room, Flashlight was conferring with a tomboyish Latina inmate who had lips tattooed on her neck. They kept cutting their eyes at her. Probably assessing her new girl abusability. Even the voice in her head was piling on. She backed deeper into the corner, closed her eyes, and wrapped her arms around herself.

Suddenly she was back on Blue Six. Back in her cell. Amity sat cross-legged beside her bunk, polishing her nails with card glitter and floor wax, babbling away.

Have you ever heard of havening? What you have to do is hug yourself, like this, and rub your arms up and down, up and down. I know it looks dumb but if you do it, and breathe slow through your nose, it'll trick your brain into releasing oxycontin which makes you feel better . . ."

"Oxy*toc*in," she murmured, gently rubbing her shoulders and arms.

The room gradually faded, overlapping voices and sounds diminished. The trauma of the shakedown room subsided as she embraced herself and breathed deeply; embraced herself as she would Cameron or Amity or some other precious child.

She understood what was happening on a molecular level. She was coaxing the pituitary gland into secreting a hormone that flooded the mind with a sense of well-being. The same hormone that was released during childbirth and activated fully during what Marcia would call *The Golden Hour*, when mother and child were snuggling for the first time. Amity nailed it: she was hacking into her brain, but that did not render the experience artificial or any less soothing. For Miranda, oxytocin was more than a feel-good hormone in the pituitary gland, more than a chemical in the brain; it represented an experience forever tied to the only memory she had of her baby.

She drew air through her nostrils, breathing deep and slow. Her heart rate plummeted as she transitioned out of the fight or flight sympathetic nervous system and accessed the more tranquil parasympathetic subdivision. Serotonin levels rose. Endorphins plugged into receptors. She kept hugging herself, kept havening. And bit by bit, the old Miranda returned. Maybe for the first time since Cameron was ripped from her arms.

She saw herself on the hospital bed moments after he came wailing into the world. Sweaty strands of hair were plastered against her flushed face, eyes bright with wonder and love as he was placed on her chest—a little red bundle, covered in amniotic fluid, quivering with life. The umbilical cord had yet to be clamped and cut. They were still connected, still one.

The hovering nurses and beeping monitors melted out of the picture. Only a circle remained with mother and child in its center. It was as if she were looking back in time through a telescope. The circle accelerated out into the darkness, shrinking into a solitary point of light, spinning in space.

Then one became two.

Her thoughts turned from molecular biology to the quantum world of superposition and shared-state photons. She recalled something her quirky eleventh grade science teacher, Mr. Fudge, said in a rant about Albert Einstein, Niels Bohr, and their longstanding beef over nonlocality. "*Think Tupac and Biggie, kids. Only much nerdier.*" It was a debate that raged on for years and one that split the physics world like the atom. Decades later, when technology made testing available, a posthumous winner was finally declared. And in a shocking twist it was not Einstein. Bohr's hypothesis that two previously entangled particles could instantaneously interact, even if they were at opposite ends of the universe, had been tested repeatedly and repeatedly upheld.

She always wondered if the same was true for the macro world. Now she had her answer. Pensacola was hundreds of miles northwest of the cage where she sat breathing, acclimating, havening. Hundreds of miles . . .

And yet.

She could still feel the tug of her infant son, gentle but insistent, calling her home.

"Oye pelirroja." A silky voice breathed into her ear. "Como te llamas?"

She opened her eyes. Red lipstick tattoo.

"What's your name?" The Latina orderly clarified in heavily accented English.

Red, her inner narrator declared, *Snowbunny Red.*

She shook off the annoying voice in her head and attempted her best new-girl-at-school smile. "Miranda McGuire . . . Nice to meet you."

Made in the USA
Middletown, DE
14 February 2021

33581225R00172